M000094316

Waking the Dreamer

K. Aten

Silver Dragon Books
by Regal Crest

Copyright © 2018 by K. Aten

All rights reserved. No part of this publication may be reproduced, transmitted in any form or by any means, electronic or mechanical, including photocopy, recording, or any information storage and retrieval system, without permission in writing from the publisher. The characters, incidents and dialogue herein are fictional and any resemblance to actual events or persons, living or dead, is purely coincidental.

ISBN 978-1-61929-382-3

First Edition 2018

9 8 7 6 5 4 3 2 1

Cover design by AcornGraphics

Published by:

Regal Crest Enterprises

Find us on the World Wide Web at
http://www.regalcrest.biz

Published in the United States of America

Acknowledgments

I owe a huge amount of love and thanks to the wonderful people at Regal Crest that deal with me regularly, Cathy and Patty. And even more love to my editor, Mary. I'd also like to thank Kari because this was the first novel she seriously liked and she doesn't care for most genres I write. It gave me hope that it would be well received by more than just the science fiction and dystopian fans. And finally I'd like to thank Ted for being my sounding board and for encouraging me when I have lightning bolts of inspiration, which is exactly what happened in this novel.

Dedication

This book is for the dreamers in all of us. It's for those that want to see a better future. *Waking the Dreamer* reflects human fear but it's truly dedicated to human perseverance and ingenuity. Let's hope we don't find ourselves at the brink of destruction before stumbling upon the spark of progress.

Chapter One

Dreamer Zero

ON MY TWENTIETH birthday I dreamed of a man who would die in a war that started with me. He was a psychologist by the name of Jonathan Cisco, and although he did not know it at the time, he saved my life. In the dream, he was in his office late at night. All the lights were off and the only illumination came from the comp screen on his desk. When he spoke, his voice was quiet but clear.

"Computer open email, keyword Dreamwalker. Read last received. Authorization: Cisco738497Jonathan."

A loud digitalized voice replied and Dr. Cisco quickly adjusted the volume down. "Authorization confirmed, welcome Jonathan. October eighth, two thousand eighty-eight, Sender is Doctor Olivia Morgan." The computer paused momentarily to access the body of the encrypted email, then continued. "Starting email. Jonathan, as you probably know by now, the Electorate and Council have finally passed that damned amendment. Though I'm sure it was more in line with what the General wanted. Not only is it now illegal to be an unregistered Dream Walker in the United States, it is also a felony to so much as speak to an unregistered Dream Walker. A close friend inside the administration has warned me that all is not as innocent as the people have been led to believe. He said that General Rennet himself has created a special government agency dedicated to Dream Walker investigation and that all non-government controlled research will be shut down with the files confiscated. I seriously fear for the safety of our patients if that happens. I have taken the necessary precautions by destroying all my hard and soft copy patient files and I recommend that you do the same. Our careers and maybe even lives depend on it. It is sad to think that the last ten years of my life have been reduced to so much static and ash but we do what we must to survive. My only hope is that a few of those children will make it through and that the government will relax their witch hunt. I am especially worried for your Dreamer Zero. I wonder how long before they come for her. Being the first Dream Walker discovered, she has the most experience with the project. I know you're an amazing scientist,

Jon, but you're not a geneticist and I truly believe that there may be secrets locked within her DNA that we have not discovered yet. I wish we had more time but it's too little too late I suppose. As for me, James, and our daughter Lette, I think we will head northwest to Edmonton. The university there offered both of us good positions and I think it would be healthy to put some distance between our family and this program. The air is better there, at any rate. Good luck, my friend. In the current political climate, we will surely need it. With regards, Olivia." The computer paused again then added, "End email."

In the dream I move closer to peer at him and I was shocked to see how old he truly looked. Worn and weary, he scrubbed his face with both hands before leaning back in his chair and closing his eyes. The man had been so many things to me while I was growing up—teacher, taskmaster, and friend. He was worried. Without opening his eyes, he spoke again. "Delete all messages containing keyword, Dreamwalker. Authorization: Cisco738497Jonathan."

The computer responded "Confirm delete please."

The doctor added "Delete confirmed. Empty cache and all temporary folders." He suddenly sat forward again and addressed the screen, watching intently. "Computer, open patient file Thiel, Julia."

"Please specify."

"Playback video file 06142073." The video that started playing was of me at age five. I was obviously scared with my red-rimmed eyes and tear-streaked face. In an instant my own memory became superimposed over the dream.

"What did you dream about last night, Julia?" The doc looked young in the video. My recall wasn't so distinct to pick out the smooth skin around his eyes and mouth or the lack of gray hair at his temples. At the time I didn't know why I was in the room with the doctor. I only knew bedtime fears. My parents were only aware that my nightmares had been getting steadily worse. We lived in corporate housing in a questionable part of the city at the time—they were engineers working for BioMed and only earned blue wage. And there weren't many good parts of the city left for the people in the middle.

As long as I could remember, suits and breathers were needed just to go outside. When Robert and Anna Thiel would ask me about my dreams, they learned a great many things that neither adult nor child should know. My dreams were about situations and people I would never have been aware of or witness to normally, and they had no idea where I would see such things. Finally, unable to help me sleep and keep the nightmares at bay, they brought me to Dr. Cisco. He was a psychologist who ran the Bay Point Research center and had a reputation for helping children with night terrors. While he didn't cure me, he was able to discover something that would eventually change the political and societal landscape as we all knew it. Diving back into my memories I could see that little lost girl in my mind's eye. I didn't answer the first time because I was still incredibly frightened. He had been questioning me right after one of my "nightmares" and I struggled through the memories. He asked again in the video and the child me finally looked up.

"It was bad men, Doc." Right from the beginning he had instructed me to call him Doc. I think he was trying to form a bond with me, to get me to open up about my fears and dreams.

"What did the bad men do, Julia?"

In the dream I watched the older man stare at the little girl on the computer screen. He seemed just as affected the second time around as he was when he witnessed my original response. The little girl on the screen, in the dream, immediately reacted to the question. Her eyes filled with tears and her bottom lip started to quiver. My bottom lip. "The bad men hurt someone real terrible. I was floating down a hallway and I saw them. They grabbed a lady and hit her then tore her clothes. Then they took turns bouncing against her and making her cry. She didn't move again when they left." She looked like she was going to stop talking then, but I knew better because it was my memory, it was me. "She didn't move again when they left, Doc. She didn't even cry no more."

Jonathan, the younger from the video, reached out and held my hand across the table. "You don't have to worry about those men, Julia. It was just a dream, okay? We're going to figure out why you're having these dreams and help you out. But I want you to remember one thing, all right?"

I waited on him, in my dream and in my past. "What do I 'member, Doc?"

"None of those bad men in your dreams can ever hurt you. Never. Do you understand?"

"So I shouldn't be afraid of anyone?"

He shook his head. "You should always be afraid if you're scared, but I want you to know that the bad people in your dreams can't hurt you." He was trying to reassure me, but he didn't know either.

I nodded in the dream as I watched myself nod on the screen.

"Okay, Doc." I wish he had been right. But not only could the people in my dreams hurt me, so too could the ones in my waking life. Dr. Jonathan Cisco saved my life because he trained me to use my gift for fifteen years, although many eventually called it a curse. I guess opinion was dependent on which side of the lab table you were on. He also got me out of the program before it was too late. Before the government started knocking on doors and asking all the Dream Walkers to register at the nearest BEN station. He helped me find a new identity before agents came around to collect everyone with a serial number that had become more important than their name. I dreamed of the night he destroyed my files and the files of all my fellow Walkers. I also dreamed of another night almost exactly a year later. The second and final dream of him was of the night the agents came to knock on his door. I watched as the man who had become like a second father to me was killed along with his entire family, by soldiers in black. That was when the government gave up asking politely, the very same night the world turned to chaos for all Dream Walkers. But Julia Thiel had been gone a year by then.

We fugitive Dream Walkers call it the "night of silent dreams," although sometimes we just referred to it as "the silence." The chaos wasn't from that alone because it took a lot more than government imposed martial law to break the world. It required crumbling infrastructure, cities underwater, acidic oceans, decreased food sources, drought, super hurricanes, massive weather fluctuations, and reversed air and ocean currents. The world scoffed at the scientists one hundred years ago. They made predictions about the effects of global warming, and then they made more predictions. I read the history books on the net, just like everyone else.

The world was actually on the cusp of great change until one political leader tipped it all back into the dark-age. Figuratively, of course. It took just one powerful man to back out of climate initiatives, to roll back renewable energy programs, to eliminate the Environmental Protection Agency, and increase funding and subsidies to the fossil fuel industry. It was a far reaching ideological shift and the world paid for it. Being the "greatest country on Earth" meant that we led the other nations by example, poor though it was. The major countries in the eastern world increased consumption, the United States increased consumption, and the poor tunneled further into poverty. A new war started when it became apparent that oil was suddenly popular again. The Middle East, always a hot bed of dissention and conflict, became ground zero for the battle between the east and the west. Oil prices went up along with emissions. It's been fifty years since Mother Earth has seen any northern polar ice and more than that since the last polar bear sighting. With famine, plague, and summer temperatures maxing out at sixty-five degrees Celsius in some places, those same regions of conflict became uninhabitable by the end of the 21st century. And humanity was left to harvest the fields we seeded with our own ignorance. According to my comp, Earth's population was last estimated at a little over a billion, a mere fifteen percent of the estimate at the beginning of the century.

It was a lot to take in, especially for kids in school. I was never completely sure what the real truths were about where we came from. I just knew that in my country, the further we slipped into disaster the more people scrambled for answers. I remembered my parents talking about their history classes, a mere generation before my own. Their history was quite different. My parents learned all about the founding of our nation, the struggles between races and the industrial revolution. By the time it was my turn to learn, the physical schools were all gone. They had been slowly disappearing for years until eventually everything we learned was through the net. The government had more control that way. If you had a console you were expected to take virtual classes. The difference though went beyond the logistics of how I learned compared to how my parents learned. By the time I was old enough to study the things that mattered, our founding history had been scrubbed from the system. Not just the history of our country, but the history of the world. It was like everything before the mid twentieth century never existed. We had some old books, real books made with paper and ink, passed down from my mom's family to her. It was rare to find texts not caught up in the massive government burn initiative. That was how I found out about the differences. Our lack of history was sad and it would surely guarantee the repeat of past mistakes. But how did those things stack up against a planet that was slowly spiraling into flaming oblivion or half the world becoming extinct because of human ignorance and hubris?

Too many natural disasters happened in too short a period of time and the United States economy collapsed. There was no more money to save people once earthquakes and tsunamis hit the west coast. Japan suffered a major quake at the summer of 2020 which triggered another nuclear meltdown and tsunami that was felt along the northwest coast of North America. Washington and Oregon declared states of emergency when their port cities were hit by a fifty foot wall of water. Just a year later the Great Western Quake hit us and the California/Mexico coastline was all but lost. Millions died. Power grids were devastated in the southwest as upstream dams failed in a chain reaction, which eventually led to the destruction of the Hoover Dam. By the year 2057, decades of storms had ravaged the Gulf of Mexico and the east coast and what was left of the population revolted. With the collapse of the American government we fell under martial law. General Rennet took control of the military and the governing system was forever altered with the creation of the Electorate and Council. They made the laws but the ultimate control was held by Rennet. According to my parents, the first thing he did was strip the populace of their defenses. Projectile and explosive weapons were banned completely and the penalty for being caught with weapons, parts, or even ammunition was execution or indefinite servitude. It was a harsh world and the consequences for disorder were swift and extreme. We were controlled by the military and a few savvy political leaders and they held power with an iron fist.

Overall the spirit of life hadn't changed much in the past fifty years. Despite all the damage that our human minds wrought on the world, we also came up with some great advancements too. The damage to the planet was done but we had finally slowed and stopped the environmental decay by dropping fossil fuels altogether. Though I suppose it would have been impossible to continue when the planet all but ran out of easily reachable oil. Solar became the most common energy source, as was wind and heat induction. We had an abundance of heat and sun, especially in certain regions of the world. Advancements were made with power conveyance and conductivity, transportation, and hydroponic food production. No matter how bad it got, society still had to function. Businesses still ran, goods were produced, and money changed hands, although the currency had moved back to the digital gold standard.

The human condition remained as it had always been since perhaps the beginning of time. People had always and would always find themselves in a struggle to survive. But the landscape itself had definitely changed. The superpowers melted into completely new creations, like wax in molds. Russia, once a wasteland of cold, inhospitable climate became a mecca for people from Asia and the Middle East. Canada was the same for the peoples of North America and eventually General Rennet took control of the entire continent, or at least the habitable part north of the thirty-sixth parallel. Europe was ravaged as coastal countries were lost completely and the rest were destroyed by drought. Central America was also a victim of drought, coastal flooding, and hurricanes. And South America had become a wasteland with roaming primitive bands trying to stay alive south of what used to be the Amazon rainforest. With humanity shattered and scattered, the world saw a rise of the corporations. They had more money than the dysfunctional governments and were the drivers of innovation. I worked for the largest company in North America, in the new U.S. Capitol of Chicago. In most places people were either driven to live underground or find cities that were still intact and had ready access to fresh water. Shipping routes on the Great Lakes could easily bring food and supplies down from Canada. The windy city had become the safest major city environmentally although maybe not politically.

But even as governments toppled across the globe, corporate espionage was still a very real thing. My job was that of a secure courier, traversing the city and surrounding region to convey sensitive information to the various research and development facilities we had around the capital. Most electric power was local to your building or person because grids and lines had failed long ago and were deemed not a priority to replace by the government. My company was responsible for the power that nearly all people had today. Thirty-five years ago, in 2064, Vanguard created a cheaply produced solar paint and thirty-one years ago they created micro batteries, capable of storing days' worth of power in the palm of your hand. The buildings left standing were coated with the stuff so that each place became its own power source. Sunlight was all too plentiful and so as long as you had a place to put the power, there was no problem with source. Vehicles, if you dared to drive them outside, featured the coating and ran completely on electricity. Most didn't use personal vehicles though since it was so hazardous to go outside without a solar powered enviro-suit. They took public transport trains, tubes, and sealed buses. The white wage earners who were the heads of the corporations and governments had private cars. Standard fossil-fueled vehicles had been prohibited long ago.

It was high summer in Chicago but night had fallen so my suit didn't have to work so hard to keep me cool. The breather in my helmet was working at full capacity though because the air had turned to a toxic soup a week ago when the heat started reaching fifty-five degrees C each day. That was hot even for the capital. I liked night better anyway. It was easier to make my way through the rutted streets when there weren't as many people watching from windows. As a secure tech courier I was entrusted with top secret documents, sometimes even technology. Hard lines could be tapped and wireless transmissions could be hacked for the right price. And tech was the biggest business that the world had left. Everything that remained, power, food, transportation, information, even the air we breathed, owed itself to technology. Vanguard could and did sometimes hire an armored transport to take their prototypes from one place to the next. The problem with something so visible is that you couldn't trust that government agents wouldn't seize the tech for themselves. Private courier teams were small, personal, and stealthy.

The thought of working as part of a team never set well with me and I had convinced Vanguard early on in my employment to let me be a solo courier. It helped that I was the best they had. I had two different digital chips stored beneath my skin. One was located on the inside of my left forearm and was camouflaged by a black geometric tattoo. The other was under my right breast. The data that went on the chip, be it information, digital currency, or blueprints, was all encrypted and could be stripped from the chip by a reader programmed with the decryption code. Our company's codes changed every twenty-four hours to prevent major security breaches, which meant my window for delivery was fairly small if I ran into trouble. I could wipe the chip myself if I were caught or stopped in some way but I carried a lot of pride in the fact that I'd never missed a delivery. That was one of the reasons I had two chips. The other was a backup that no one knew about, not even my employer. The backup chip was special, different from the one Vanguard gave me. I could copy data from my main chip to the one under my breast by simply touching the two embedded chips together. The information would be transferred via wireless communication. And when I got to my safe destination, I could do the same and the data would flow to the empty chip again. The tech was created by a hacker friend of mine, Souza. He was a genius but more than a little rogue with his mindset. But if you needed tech or gear that wasn't legal, mainstream, or well known yet, he probably had it.

On the occasions that I was required to carry a physical prototype, the container had a self-destruct feature that would cause it to heat until melting if it got out of range of my Vanguard chip. I didn't carry the prototypes often, but when I did I was extra careful with my surroundings. That was why I didn't leave the Daley compound until after sundown. I had a proto-tube in the panier of my bike. Daley was our main facility downtown and I had to get the sample a couple miles north, to the Lincoln Park group. There were only a few bridges left that crossed the sluggishly flowing river system. I had to cut west past the crumbling opera house, then go up a number of streets and cross again. I didn't have my standard headlamps on. When doing transport at night I typically only used the night vision in my helmet. That would be paired with thermal imaging and a heads up display of my city map. There were other things off to the side of my HUD screen, battery charge for both the suit and the bike, outside temperature, air quality, perimeter alert, and my own heart rate. It also had one more thing that was essential to who I am. There was an alarm I could set for when I went walking.

Because there were few remaining bridges out of the loop I had to go south down to Roosevelt. Both north side bridges closed at curfew each night and all deliveries were routed to the west. It was near midnight as I made my way through the city, picking up speed and dodging the debris that never seemed to go away. I slowed abruptly when thermo-imaging picked up fires two blocks ahead and around the corner of a building. While things had gotten better, the world had definitely paid a price for its greed and arrogance. The first people who were affected by the disasters and global warming were the poor, the degenerates, and homeless. Now, because of high temperature and acidic air, there were no more homeless. Of course there weren't really any emergency services either. Police, fire, and medical were all cut back because of safety and lower population. Drones took over most fire duty, with a chemical spray that could quickly stifle almost any fire. The spray was of course a Vanguard innovation, although the fire drones were made by Boeing-Lockheed. Ambulance drones were staffed by two-man paramedic teams. They were also made by Boeing-Lockheed and piloted remotely. There actually weren't any police left. The entire security of the nation had been coopted by one massive government force. The Binary Enforcement Network agents, or "BENs," were responsible for two things, Law and Order.

I could personally attest that those two words left a lot open to interpretation. If the government needed someone caught and brought in, those soldiers dressed in heavy black armored suits were called. If they needed a riot quelled, or criminal executed, also black BENs. It was the degenerates, or de-gens, that warranted their attention more than anyone else. That left

enormous city space to cover and black BENs couldn't be
everywhere, nor would I want them to be. It was black BENs who
killed the doc and his family. It was black BENs that would take
me in if they ever discovered I was the Walker known as Julia
Thiel. That was why I had buried the identity of Julia Thiel long
ago. Jules Page was a simple tech courier and nothing more.

Because the fires were so close, I slowed and found a set of
steps that led down into a sub-street level doorway. There was
just enough room for me to back my bike down the stairs and sit
upright on the seat. It was dark and out of the way of prying eyes,
therefore perfect for what I needed to do. I cut the power and set
my suit to cool so I wouldn't be caught on anyone else's thermal
scan, then I set my helmet alarm and closed my eyes. After close
to twenty-five years I had learned a few things about my gift.
Things that would either get me killed, bred, or dissected on a
table in some government laboratory. It was common knowledge
that Dream Walkers needed to be asleep for their conscious mind
to leave their bodies. At the very least they had to be in the
deepest of meditative trances. But everybody was wrong. By
simply clearing my mind and lowering my heart rate I could
leave my body at will. I could and did frequently scout ahead on
my missions. It was an advantage I had over other couriers. It
was only one of the reasons I was so good.

As I was going under I could hear and feel heavy transports
coming from another direction. I suspected that the black BENs
were coming to quell whatever disruption was between me and
the west bridge. The distinctive high pitch whine of the fire drone
sirens also came through my audio feed. I wasn't too worried
since someone would literally have to stumble down the steps to
discover me. The only issue would be if the BENs had a Dream
Walker in one of their transports because Walkers could see each
other if they were both walking at the same time. As far as I
knew, any Walkers taken by the government were brainwashed
to serve willingly. If they couldn't be brainwashed then they were
either bred, studied, or bolted. I wasn't sure what would be the
worst of my options should I ever be captured, which was why
I'd eat a bolt before that ever happened.

The Walkers that were successfully 'washed would be
sedated and sent out in transports with large groups of BENs to
scour the city for more like themselves, more like me. The doc
had lied to me all those years ago about not being afraid of the
people in your dreams. Sedated black Walkers could not only see
you, but they could turn you in via the neuro-transmitters they

wore. The transmitters would communicate with the HUDs in the BENs helmets, even providing a map of the illegal Walker's location. So people in your dreams could hurt you in a way. But the black Walkers didn't know that I could hurt them back. I'd been seen often enough over the years by those traitorous brothers and sisters, but I'd never been turned in. Every one of them died by my hand. Walkers weren't just good spies that could bypass the most stringent security feature to spy on foreign dignitaries, company scientists, or other government officials. One of the many things I knew that the government didn't was that we could leave our bodies and kill people in their dreams, both Walkers and the sightless. That was something that could never get out or it would mean either death or a lifetime of servitude dealing death to others. I only killed as a last resort, as self-defense.

I floated up slowly from my hiding place and watched as the last transport turned the corner two blocks up. It was dark and I didn't have the advantage of a heads up display as I did in my body but I was effectively invisible and untouchable in my Walker form. My corporeal self remained safe and protected with the bike. I only made it a block when a figure rounded the corner ahead of me, desperately sprinting in my direction. As the runner got closer I could hear the breather and it was loud even over the noise happening blocks away. The figure's head scanned back and forth, probably looking for a hiding place from the black BENs. Knowing exactly where he would go, I did a rapid return to my body. I received a mild headache by snapping in so fast but I had to get back in time to be prepared for him. The stairwell was the only hiding space nearby. As soon as I dropped into my body I brought my systems up and jumped off the bike. Then I pulled my stun batons from each thigh and awaited his arrival. I had to take him out quickly because it was only a matter of time before the BENs came after him. Even though I was on a legit mission by my employer, anyone seen near a point of unrest would be rounded up and interrogated. I could not afford that. I would never survive.

I could hear the man's approaching footsteps, surprisingly light, then the figure appeared at the top of the stairs. My HUD scan gave me an instantaneous readout of one and three quarters meter height and estimated weight of sixty-three and a half kilograms. Only a couple centimeters taller than me and surprisingly small for someone in one of the local anarchy gangs, but who was I to judge? With one last desperate look back the way he came, he bolted down the dark stairs straight toward me. I knew then that he didn't have any tech in his helmet, just a breather. Crouched low in front of my bike, I held the batons ready. He didn't see me until he got to the bottom of the stairs and by then it was too late. I brought the batons up and planted one against his thigh at the same time I put the other on his ribs. The jolt was enough to drop him instantly. HUD said he was still alive but before I could investigate more the sound of transports grew louder as they rumbled toward me. I had to think quickly to disguise the man's heat signature so that I myself didn't get caught. I grabbed a thermal blanket out of my bike panier and threw myself over the man on the ground, unrolling and drawing the blanket over both of us. The rumbling grew louder and my heart started to pound with the fear of being caught. Shutting my eyes in the dark of our cover, I slowly brought my vitals back in optimal value. Thankfully, the transport didn't even slow down, and it continued on until it rounded another corner, back the way it came.

With a sigh of relief I activated my headlamp and looked down at the man I had been lying on, the man I had stunned. Shock rippled through me as dark lashes opened to reveal one of the only pairs of blue eyes I had ever seen. It was not a man that had been running from the black BENs, it was a woman. Her eyes widened and I knew she was about to panic. I couldn't allow that to happen until I was sure all the BENs were gone from the area. With my helmet volume on low, I spoke to her. "Stay still until I know we're safe. Do not move or I will kill you myself, understand?" Her head nodded almost imperceptibly but the tension below me seemed to relax. I shut off my headlamp and immediately grew aware of the position of our bodies. Despite the situation and the suits we wore, it was surprisingly intimate. As I lay atop her, the woman's legs had fallen open allowing our hips to press seamlessly together. I had been in less intimate positions with actual lovers, if only in my dreams. It felt surreal pressed against a stranger. A woman who, while not necessarily a foe, was certainly no friend of mine. We waited five more minutes but I wanted to be certain we were clear. I was confident that within the pitch black confines of the thermal blanket, the woman would never know if I went walking. The sightless were called that for a reason. I just wanted a quick visual before I compromised our hiding place. Turning on the light again I looked down into her fearful eyes. "Relax, let's give it a few more minutes just to be sure. Okay?" She nodded again. "All right, be

very quiet though and do not move, understand?" Another nod
and I shut my light off. Slipping out was easy enough, I just left
my body there on top of the woman and beneath the blanket. I
rose up and sped down the street to the corner where the riot had
occurred. There was nothing left there but bodies, which I knew
the drones would come to dispose of soon enough.

I had nearly made it back to where I started when a figure
standing at the top of the stairwell brought me to a halt. It was a
woman wearing a thin synthetic jumpsuit, much like my own.
Her hair was cropped short around the back and sides but longer
on top. One lock fell distractingly into her eyes. I wasn't sure
what led her to this place but she had the look of someone who
didn't spend a lot of time in a helmet. My own was shaved close
to my scalp and nearly black to her brown. It was easier to have
short hair in a world where so much time was spent in a helmet.
The woman stood there looking at me and while she was a
stranger I knew exactly who she was. I knew because I had just
seen her face minutes before. Her body was lying below mine in
the stairwell. I had found another Walker, another fugitive like
me.

Chapter Two

Saving a BEN

I GLANCED AROUND one more time and when I spoke my voice was low and harsh. "Go back now or I swear I will kill you as you stand there!"

She cocked her head, voice well-modulated and curious. "You can't kill me, you're walking."

I took a menacing step forward with serious intent written all over my face. "I can and I will." She gave a little shake of her head, defiant. In the blink of an eye I was in front of her and I grabbed her by the neck. I noticed right away how soft her skin felt beneath my hand. Walkers were real to each other in their dream state. It was something I had discovered long ago. Not only could we feel pleasure, but we could also feel pain. And if we received enough pain in our walking state, it would force our real bodies into cardiac arrest or worse. The thing that most didn't know is that we could do the same with a sightless person who was just dreaming. In REM their minds were susceptible to manipulation by Walkers. The myth that if you died in your dream you died in real life had been around for centuries. And it really was a myth, unless you were killed by a Walker.

The woman's strange light eyes widened when I appeared so fast in front of her and her breathing rate increased as she watched me warily. She didn't move though so I used my thumb to caress the skin just above her larynx then started adding pressure. The stranger's teeth seemed very white and straight when her lips parted. "This is a friendly warning, just one. If I have to tell you again you'll be just another body left on the street for the trashers, go!" Before she could answer I shoved her harshly away from me, throwing a bit of extra energy into it that sent her into the wall ten feet from where our dream bodies were standing.

Reality was a strange thing. Despite being able to leave our bodies at will, despite not being able to physically interact with the sightless during their waking hours, our environment still ruled if you were an untrained Walker. If we could see it, it became real to us. So if you saw a wall, you couldn't just go through it without the correct mental outlook. The same went for

any other physical object. It took time and training to get over
that particular mental block and I had mastered it by the time I
was a teenager. By hitting the wall I learned something
important. The woman must have been a new Walker. I wanted to
investigate, to question her but I had no time. I still had a job to
do.

The woman seemed slightly dazed as she pulled herself off
the ground. Her words were rougher and fear was a newly added
component. "I'm sorry." I didn't answer. I just took another step
closer and she fled down the stairwell. I thought it best to get
back myself. It was never wise to piss off someone who had
access to your body while you weren't there. I closed my eyes and
just like that I was slipping back inside. My body felt heavy and I
was immediately reminded of the intimacy of our position. It had
been years since I'd been so physically close to another person,
one who wasn't trying to attack me. It was dark under the blanket
but I could feel the press of her through my suit, the way her
chest moved up and down with each breath. I sighed in my
helmet and pushed myself up to my feet. Real people weren't
safe. The only interaction I had with real people was in the course
of my job. Everything else I saved for my dreams.

While she pulled herself upright I quickly rolled up the
thermal blanket and stuffed it back into its pouch, then into the
panier on the side of the bike. It was time for me to go if I wanted
to make the delivery and get back before the sun broke over the
horizon. I swung my leg over the saddle and hit the switch to
power up. I looked up at the stranger as she stood there with her
helmet breather struggling loudly in the night. I knew she
wouldn't be able to see me since I had no lights on, but I could see
her just fine with my night vision. The woman's solar suit looked
ill-fitting. I couldn't tell what the body below it looked like but I
noticed the broad shoulders right away. The suit pulled tight
there, and along her biceps and thighs. The de-gen was
abnormally strong for someone scraping by at the bottom. "Good
luck out there de-gen, and try a little harder to stay away from
the BENs. You're not always going to have someone come along
to save your ass."

I started forward toward the stairs but she jumped in front of
my bike with her hand outstretched. "Wait!"

Irritation bubbled upward at her actions. "Wait for what? I
don't have time for street trash. Go back with the other de-gens or
I'll make good on my promise!"

She didn't move. "I'm not a de-gen. I—I'm a BEN."

Fear crawled up my spine and I quickly checked my proximity scanners to make sure it wasn't a trap. There was nothing nearby. "Explain yourself!" My helmet moved slowly as my head took in her poor gear. "You're not very tough for a BEN." She couldn't see me checking her out in the near blackness but I was certainly a witness to her anger.

"I've been a BEN for a decade now. They took me right out of secondary for my training! I was caught off guard but I won't make that mistake with you again."

The speaker in my helmet always made my voice sound strange, harsher than normal. "You're right, you won't because if you're lucky this is the last time you'll see me. Move now."

Stubbornly, the only move she made was to straddle my front tire and put her hands on the handlebars. "Please! I need your help." A small part of my brain thought the pose seemed kind of erotic. But I ignored that part, just like always.

I paused for a second to study her. I couldn't see as much with night vision on as I could with the lamp so I gave in to curiosity and lit her up. I had plenty of power in my suit and bike, so it wasn't like I would run out. My heart gave a curious thump of pity at the terrified look on her face. "How is it that you're a BEN and a Walker?" A thought occurred to me, and a small bit of terror flitted through my thoughts. "How were you able to walk without sleeping?"

The woman looked away for a second, then addressed me again. "I realized I was a Walker a few years ago and I was terrified of getting caught. I kept experimenting, trying to slip free from my body before sleep. Eventually I was able to discover the right way to do it. I just assumed that was the way walking was done. It's not like the sightless enforcers got training in such things. You mean others can't do what we can do?"

I looked at her curiously and with more than a little alarm. She had clearly picked up that I myself was more advanced than the average black Walker. I cursed internally for giving away such damaging information. "No, they can't. You should be brainwashed in a transport somewhere."

She nodded slowly in the pale wash of the helm light and I listened as her breather labored on. "That's why I'm running. From the beginning, I've always kept my walking a secret. About twenty-four hours ago..." The stranger looked away toward the wall of the stairwell and paused her words. After a few seconds she met my eyes again. "My lover figured out what I was doing at night and turned me in. We had only been together for six months. The only consolation was that she warned me about what she had done. I had just enough time to get out of the compound before they came after me. I hid in a delivery drone and escaped into the city at its first stop. I ditched the black suit immediately and stole another from a man who had died in the building around the corner. It was just dumb luck for me that de-gens decided to riot where I was hiding. I had to run. I couldn't be caught by them."

I thought about what would happen if she were caught, the brainwashing and reconditioning they'd put her through before sedating her into a nap each day. I couldn't imagine the life of a black Walker being much of a life at all. I peeked into a transport once after killing their Walker and it was something I'd never be able to forget. Nutrients and waste entering and left his body via tubes, his breathing was controlled by a machine more intrusive than any breather could be. I shivered at the plight of the woman in front of me and felt pity, but her situation was not my own. I shook my head slowly at her. "I'd help you if I could but being an unregistered Dream Walker, I'm a fugitive too, and I have a job to do."

"Please! I'm begging you for my life here!"

I looked back at her coldly, imagining her body wrapped in the black suit of a BEN. My mind was cast back ten years to the death of my friend and mentor. Logically I knew it was impossible that she was one of the blacks that killed the doc and his family, just as I knew she wasn't responsible for my own family. But the stain of her training colored what I saw nonetheless. "And how many have begged you for their life, BEN? How many men, women, and children lay on the ground at your feet with arms upraised, begging you to spare the bolt?" I didn't want to speak with her any more. I wanted to go.

"None!" I paused to listen. "I was an inside guard, personally assigned to the general's cadre. Please—" She raised her hand again, imploringly. "I can't do this on my own, I don't know anything about the low districts. They'll find me and kill me or worse."

As I sat there staring at her, watching the terror crawl across her face, I had an urge to take my baton and bring it across the side of her helmet. I wanted to take my boot and shove her lifeless body from the front of my bike and continue on through the night. The only thing I needed to do was complete my duty and nothing more. But none of those things happened. Instead I stood frozen as my thoughts raced with each filtered breath.

My resolve to stay uninvolved crumbled and I thought ahead to what she would need and what I would have to do for her. I wondered if a trade could be worked out somehow. Favors were just as valuable as gold in the city. My mind tested the motivations for my creeping consideration to help. Was it because she had an attractive face with a finely arching brow line and deeply colored lips, even in the washed out helm light? Or because when I looked at her I felt a measure of pity for her situation? Maybe it was due to the fact that I hated the black BENs so much that any way I could stifle them was enough to bring me joy. After immeasurable seconds ticked by I settled on the reason. I saw myself in her. Someone gave me the help I needed once, to make a fresh start and a good life. If I could do the same for her perhaps the debt of my conscience could be repaid. "Fine. I'll help but we need to do something about that suit." I switched to thermal scan and could see numerous breaches in the liner and in the helmet. The breather could fail at any time and if I had to guess I'd say it wasn't doing a lot of filtering in its current state. The delivery would just have to wait for a few hours. I checked the time on the HUD then I quickly brought up the map to Souza and scooted forward on my seat. "Get on, I know someone who can help."

She stood frozen, watching me with momentary disbelief. "Thank you!" Then she quickly came around the bike and scrambled on behind me.

I turned my helmet to look back at her. "My bike has a gyro but it's not calibrated for two people so hang on tight and lean the way I lean. If you tip us I'll leave you in the street!" Then I switched off the helmet lamp and gunned it up the stairs.

SOUZA LIVED IN a warehouse west of the old downtown loop. I had to cross the river to his side anyway, so it wasn't like I was going out of my way. We passed numerous grower buildings on the way. With the decline in population, the government bought out many high-rises and turned them into food factories. Floor after floor of nutrient algae and meat farms. The algae could be turned into a variety of plant product and all meat was lab grown from a primary feedstock of glucose and amino acids. Shortly after the turn of the century, the country realized that traditional animal stock was not a sustainable crop. As the summer temperatures soared and weather became more erratic, the beef industry sustained devastating losses. My parents told me that it was a great boon that at the same time the environment began jeopardizing food sources, science had found a way to grow meat from the stem cells of cows, fish, chicken, and pigs. By the middle of the twenty-first century lab grown meat had become the norm. You could still find some real livestock in the northern climates of North America and Russia, but only the top one percent of the population could afford natural meat.

Milk was also made in a similar way. Scientists discovered how to convert the amino acid sequence of all six milk proteins into a DNA sequence and integrated that into yeast cells. Once milk protein production began then water was added. I learned all about it because before my parents went to work for BioMed, they were engineers at NutriTech. But that was before I was born. Not everyone ate lab grown meat though. Many subsisted on the lower priced cricket meat and cricket flower. It was an inexpensive protein source that kept many of the de-gens alive. I was lucky enough in life that I never had to live off the stuff. Even though my parents were only blue wage earners and in the bottom half of society, being engineers they always had good perks. That meant rations of higher quality food and upper-end health care. I was in that percentage of the population that got the disease and radiation inoculations when I was a baby. Basically it was gene therapy that made us withstand the environment a little better. Being outside daily as a courier, I was definitely grateful for the treatments.

Despite the fact that we were in the manufacturing district, there wasn't a lot of traffic. It was not due to the late hour but more because most shipping out of the city was done in the sealed trains below ground. While the filtered train cars were people movers during the day, at night when curfew set in they became the shippers for goods and material throughout the city and beyond. A percentage of the food was shipped to government market centers in the capital and to the main BEN headquarters, and the rest was sent to ports and over-ground trains for export purposes. Souza's building looked much like the other low rent warehouses. It was smaller and only five stories high. After checking my perimeter scanners one more time I pulled into an alley that looked like a dead end. It was dark but I could still see the brick wall at the end of the short corridor. With no word of warning to my passenger, I activated my beacon and accelerated toward the intimidating surface.

The woman's grip tightened painfully. She was very strong. "What are you doing? You'll get us killed!"

"Trust me." The digitalized voice of my helmet hit her ears just as the wall slid open in front of us. I slowed to a stop inside a long and narrow room and waited for confirmation. It was a safety feature that Souza had put into place to avoid detection by the black BENs. People coming into his facility had to go through a bio-scan. Any visitors had to be properly vetted or they were killed instantly in the containment room and their bodies would be discarded in the nearby river. I waited for the green light to come on then unclasped and removed my helmet. I turned back to look at my passenger. "Take off your helmet and look toward the plate on the wall." After a moment's hesitation, she followed my lead and it was a good thing she did. I could see in the light of the room that her lips were blue, signaling a lack of oxygen. It was a wonder that she was still conscious with the rate that her filter had been failing. Perhaps it was due to the rigorous training that Binary Enforcement Network agents went through. Soldiers were a breed outside the rest from what I'd noticed over the years. I was scanned first and a digitalized voice came over the speakers.

"Page, Jules. Secure Tech Courier, Vanguard. Confirmation for entry, level eight access."

"What..."

The woman started to speak and I quickly quieted her. "Look at the plate or you'll be killed where you sit."

"Morgan, Nikolette. Captain, Binary Enforcement Network. Access denied."

The light at the end turned red as a low level alarmed sounded all around us. I was surprised by how high ranking the woman was with the black BENs but I didn't have time to ponder the new information. Access denied meant that I had about sixty seconds before gun turrets opened and she would be executed. I raised my voice to be heard over the cacophony. "Protocol Orange, authorization JP8. Please confirm."

The alarm abruptly cut off, as did the flashing red lights. "Protocol override confirmed. Morgan, Nikolette, please remain still."

The woman started to speak again but was abruptly cut off when the security system fired a nano-driven tracking device into the side of her neck. She gave a light gasp and slapped the injection spot. "What the hell?"

I looked back at her. "Relax, it's just a nano-tracker. I know it doesn't feel good because I had the same done to me years ago. He does it to everyone. It's insurance. If you want Souza's help then you play by his rules. He's tough, but he won't sell you out or cheat you like others in the dark market."

The woman, Nikolette, looked at me curiously. "Dark market?"

I nodded grimly. "The place you go when you want to disappear. It's the only way for Walkers to hide." The door opened ahead of us and I propped my helmet in front of me on the bike. "You can leave yours off, we won't be going far. At this point it's probably doing more harm than good." She followed my advice and I pulled forward into the first parking bay. Despite the fact that it was after midnight, we were met by none other than Souza himself. He stood near one of the security doors that led farther into the building. Two other men flanked him with bolt rifles aimed at each of us.

"Give me one reason why I shouldn't kill you for bringing her here. You've broken my first directive, Jules."

I glanced at his two guards, men I recognized but didn't know well. Despite his question I had my own rules, which made answering his inquiry a little difficult. "I don't know if I have a good reason for breaking your directive. But I will tell you this, she's like me and has suddenly found herself in need of assistance." ·

Souza was lean and dark. His skin nearly matched his black hair but his eyes held all the intelligence of a top tier predator. He cocked his head at me. "Like you?"

I met his gaze unflinchingly. "You know what I refer to. I won't say it aloud in front of your goons."

He nodded and made a hand gesture and the goons in question lowered their weapons. "By all means then, mi casa es su casa." He turned to look at Nikolette. "Because Ms. Page is sponsoring you to my patronage, I will give you a room to freshen up where Jules can go over my directives." Without another word he turned back toward the door.

"Wait!" He paused but didn't turn around in response to my plea. "I need a secure line to contact Vanguard and let them know I'll be delayed. I have twenty-four hours to deliver my sample but the facility was expecting me tonight."

He didn't acknowledge my request at first but just before leaving our presence he called back over his shoulder to me. "Two-G, Jules. You'll find your secure line and you can both stay there until morning."

I let out a sigh of relief as we were left alone with the bike. I motioned for her to get off and I followed. I left my helmet where it was and quickly retrieved the prototype tube from my panier. I wouldn't do any good to leave it there. The minute I was out of radius it would slag out and take my bike with it. Watching me closely, she left her helmet on the bike as well. "Do you trust him?"

"I trust him with my life." I led us to a different door than the one he had just gone through.

Her voice floated quietly in the dimmed garage space. "But you seem so uncertain, so wary."

I leaned forward to look into the optical scanner next to the door. When it clicked I turned the handle and pulled it open, holding it for her to enter. "Like Souza, I have my own set of directives. The first one is to never speak aloud of who or what I am. The second is to trust no one completely."

I watched her to make sure she understood and instead of fear I saw only sadness in her eyes. "It sounds lonely."

She was awfully idealistic for a BEN. "Better lonely than dead. Come on." I didn't want to be stuck in a room all night with her but Souza gave me no choice. We were only allotted one room and I was not going to push his professional courtesy for the sake of comfort. In the past I'd found that his suggestions were not really suggestions at all.

When we got to the second floor room I was glad to see that it had two beds and a shower facility. It also featured a fridge and microwave. I looked inside and saw pre-packaged meals. I waved toward the facilities. "I'm sure you're more than ready to get out of your dead man's suit. Feel free to clean up while I make a call." I stopped as I thought of something. "You're going to need a new name. What did you go by as a BEN?"

Her face darkened but she still answered my question. "Captain or Captain Morgan. My friends called me Lett."

"Since they were not with you I'm guessing all your friends were loyal and understanding. Tell me, were they the first to come after you when you were reported?"

Her face darkened further as the anger finally came out. "You know nothing of me or my friends!"

I looked at that angry face and remained impassive. I cared not for her life, loves, or betrayal. "I will call you Niko."

"Who are you to say what my name will be?"

My smile was grim as I shook my head back and forth. "I am no one, and truthfully you can choose whatever name you want when Souza makes you a new identity. But as for me, the woman who rescued you, I will forever call you Niko. Also, it is good to retain a little of who you used to be, if only to preserve your sense of self."

"Is that what you did?" When I didn't answer, she turned and stalked into the bathroom then shut and locked the door. I was pleased to note that she didn't trust me either.

Chapter Three

The Identity of Us

IT DIDN'T TAKE long to check in with my employer. Their main concern was for the safety of the sample. I assured them that security wasn't compromised and that I would make the delivery in the morning. I ate while Niko was in the shower and was pleased to find that the pre-packed meals had beef and actual vegetables, not cricket and algae paste. Perhaps prepacks were below the good captain's station but I'd had worse for longer. I made a good living now but I was still grateful that Souza put us someplace with food available. I hadn't eaten in fifteen hours because of my check-in and prep schedule with Vanguard, and it would have been a long night with a rumbling belly. My original delivery plan would have seen me home already.

When Niko came back into the room I took a second to observe the woman whom I had saved. She only wore a standard white synth-suit, pretty close to what I myself wore beneath my outerwear. Based on her shape and muscle tone I could tell she wasn't just a captain in name. She was in prime condition. The strength was obvious in her arms and legs. She was trim and muscular, but not at all skinny. My deduction was that she ate well and trained well. She was a little over my height but a heavier build than I was. Freshly washed, her medium brown hair fell damply over her forehead. I watched as a missed drop of water slowly made its way down the soft skin of her neck. A subtle shift of her stance caught my attention and I was drawn up to Niko's gaze. Those strange blue eyes peered at me with wariness and more than a little exhaustion. Shaking myself mentally, I cleaned up my meal debris and waved toward the fridge. "Help yourself to the food. It's decent for prepack." I got a nod in response and I did my best to ignore the obvious relief on her face. I assumed that if she'd been on the run for over twenty-four hours that she hadn't eaten in a while. Not that I cared, she seemed well enough. I grabbed the proto-tube and made my way into the lav facility.

The shower felt amazing after spending so long in my suit. The tube came into the stall with me because I never took chances when making a delivery. It would not leave my presence until it was placed into the hands of Vanguard's receivers at Lincoln Park. After cleaning my skin, hair, and teeth I stood beneath the dryer and stared at myself in the mirror. My body was long and lean with muscle definition but not the bulk of a soldier like Niko. There were plenty of scars to be found but those were older than my current identity. I had full combat training but my job wasn't to fight. It was to make my deliveries. Self-defense knowledge was a must though. Between the roaming bands of degenerates, Vanguard's competitors, and the black BENs, being a secure courier wasn't the safest of jobs but the perks were hard to beat. I was paid very well. I had top-level medical care as well as access to Vanguard technology to both enhance my personal function and aid in my capability as a courier. My suit was top of the line, as was the tech in my helmet. I had cochlear implants that allowed me to enhance my hearing at will. I could also make sat calls and connect them to my wrist comp. The reason I didn't use the satellite communicator often was because like most other things, it wasn't completely secure. I could be tracked via the signal, and my communications could be hacked. But it was nice to have in emergencies. Most of the time I just kept it switched off. The last enhancement I got from them was an adrenaline booster that was installed in my suit. I had only used that one once because it was risky tech. But when speed and reaction time meant the difference between life and death, you took the risk.

I decided to leave off my outerwear since I trusted in Souza's security. Sleep would be more comfortably done in the lightweight synth-suit. I put my wrist comp back on and picked up the tube and my clothing and made my way toward the main room. When I opened the door to exit the facility, I stopped in surprise. Niko had stripped from her synth-suit and was in the middle of a plyometric workout. She was doing decline pushups with her hands on the floor and her feet up on the seat of a chair. I raised my eyebrows while she quietly counted out reps but I didn't say anything. Watching her was fascinating. I remained frozen as the muscles of her back and arms rippled with movement. Her plain white undergarments did nothing to detract from the shear athleticism on display. When she reached forty, she moved into a handstand then flipped from the handstand backward to her feet again. Her face was flushed and I grew warm as our eyes met. I didn't know what to say to her. This woman, a soldier and a criminal Walker like me, held challenge in her strange light colored eyes. Though we shared a major commonality, our lives were very different. Realizing that I had been staring, I moved quickly across the room and silently claimed the bed closest to the door.

"Do you have a problem with me?" Her voice took me by surprise, as did her aggressive tone.

I shrugged as I folded down the coverlet on the bed. "I have no problem with you. You wouldn't be here if I did. You would have been left for the BENs with the rest of the street trash and de-gens."

I thought my words would be the end of it but she pressed on. "Your eyes say different."

Setting the tube down on the stand next to the bed, I turned to face her. It was disconcerting the way she remained in her undergarments. I ran a hand across the dark stubble on my scalp while I tried to pull my thoughts together. She was a distraction and I had to remain clear. "I wasn't aware that my eyes had a voice. Tell me, what do they say?"

Niko continued to stare but her stance relaxed slightly. No longer aggressive, she morphed into a creature of curiosity. "I wouldn't say they speak words, more like emotion. You come across as harsh and calculating, but your eyes tell secrets I think your lips would never speak."

My heart raced but the rest of me didn't react. "You're pretty insightful for a BEN, even a high-ranking prodigy such as yourself."

"How did you know I was a prodigy?"

I shrugged at her basic question. She was testing me. "You told me you were pulled into the BEN program at the age of fifteen, which meant you had to have completed all your advanced education. You must have breezed through your training because you've been a soldier for ten years. You accelerated quickly through the ranks because you are—were the highest ranking soldier in charge of General Rennet's security. Only a prodigy would move so far, so fast. As for your assumptions about me, well we all have secrets, especially Walkers." Her eyes didn't leave mine and she took a step forward. I backed up but I didn't know why.

She shook her head. "Not just secrets. You're angry, which I understand. I've caused you delay and time is precious for a courier. You're also afraid, and I get that too. I'm a BE—I was a BEN, and people are afraid of BENs. BENs are the government boogeymen." She took another step closer and I tensed. Still, the words continued to flow from those dark lips. "But there is something more. It is in the way you look at me with eyes nearly black. I know that look because I've seen it many times. I would hazard that we are alike in more ways than one."

I swallowed her words, feeling them as they moved down the inside of my body. They made me shiver. With difficulty I moved my eyes and cast them about the room, searching for something neutral. I knew exactly what she referred to, but that was personal information and she didn't need confirmation of her suspicion. "Every human on this planet carries the potential for thousands of similarities between them and another." She took another step toward me, putting us at less than a body length apart in the room. My gaze roamed one last time over the expanse of her flesh before I could wrench them back to safety. "I suggest you catch some REM while you can. Souza will roust us early."

Tension sang through my body as her lips curled into a smirk. "I suppose that's as good a suggestion as any." Niko stared for a few seconds longer then nodded her head. "Thank you for saving my life. I owe you a debt."

I relaxed with her admission. "Yes, you do." Without waiting for another comment from her I crawled into the bed and turned on my wrist comp sensor. If anyone touched or moved the proto-tube I would know.

She shut down the light and I heard her crawl into the other bed. Her voice drifted to me in the darkness. "Who are you?"

I thought about simply not answering but in the end my mouth betrayed me. "Page, Jules. Secure Tech Courier, Vanguard." The information would do her no good. She'd already heard it. But it would frustrate her while she transitioned into sleep. She sighed but didn't say another word. After deep breathing for a handful of minutes, I slipped into the dreaming world. Unlike other nights I resisted the urge to hone my craft in the first hour of sleep. I would not walk while Niko was in the room because I knew with certainty that she would be waiting for me. Instead I built a wall in my head to keep her out of my dreams. Trust was as rare as clean air and more fleeting than safety. And for most of my life it was not easily given.

MY COMP WOKE me before Niko and for that I was grateful. I knew from observation that soldiers were trained early risers but I assumed the exhaustion of her escape had finally caught up with her. After taking care of my morning functions, I dressed and did a warm-up then some simple exercises to get my blood flowing. I wasn't hungry but I forced myself to eat anyway, knowing I'd have a delivery to make in a few hours and one never knew when they would need the extra energy. She woke as I was starting to eat. Niko's eyes were closed as she sat up and stretched. There were wrinkles on her face from the pillow and her hair looked more tousled than it was the night before. I pulled my gaze back to my food before she could catch me watching. I knew what my fascination was. I had just never experienced it before in the waking world.

"What time is it?"

I glanced down at my wrist comp. "A little after seven hundred."

She stood and made a face at me and I continued to eat. "Did you even sleep?"

Swallowing another bite of food, I shrugged. "Enough for now. I'll catch up after the job."

"Why do you work alone? I thought it was standard practice for couriers to work in pairs?" So many questions.

I finally stopped eating and met her eyes, feeling more than a little annoyed. "People slow me down. I prefer to be by myself."

A look of disbelief crossed her face. "And Vanguard just lets you?"

Appetite gone, I stood and threw my mostly finished meal container into the composter. "I make all my deliveries, and they don't question me." I hoped that hearing my tone she would get the point. She didn't.

Before I could even grasp that she had moved, Niko was in my personal space. She stood much too close and when I drew in my next breath I caught the scent of her. Both musky and sweet, it intrigued me. So this was what being real was like. "What are you doing?" I shoved my left palm toward the center of her chest to push her back. She grabbed my wrist and used it to pull me closer. Faces nearly touching, I trembled with the first stirrings of fear and more. I had no weapon on me. Knowing Souza's preferences I had left my batons with the bike. Niko was still in her undergarments but she was also heavier and stronger than me and probably better trained in combat. Our breathing picked up and I could feel the moist warm air from her mouth caress my cheek with each exhale.

"You watch me. I see you staring at me with hunger, admit it."

I tried to wrench backward away from her strong grip, away from her knowing smile and soft lips. "You know nothing. Now let me go or I swear the next time you walk you are a dead woman!"

Niko didn't respond to my threat, instead her lips curved into that infuriating smile. I had developed a dislike for that smirk in an incredibly short amount of time. But I still couldn't take my eyes off its slight crookedness or the way one eyebrow raised whenever it made an appearance. She started to move closer, meaning to kiss me I think, when the door opened abruptly. Souza had arrived. I took advantage of Niko's surprise by grabbing her wrist with my free right hand and bending it backward. As soon as the pain distracted her I locked my foot behind the knee closest to me and pushed her upper body off balance, riding her down to the floor. I was sure my weight on top when we landed felt less than pleasant. I purposely shoved off of her when I stood again and just stared down into those disconcerting eyes. Then waiting a few seconds to be sure I had Niko's full attention, I gave her the only warning she would ever get. "If you so much as touch me against my will again, I will kill you. Or worse yet, I will turn you over to the BENs myself!" With those words I grabbed the tube from the table next to us and brushed by Souza on my way out the door.

My rage fueled me for about ten steps until he called my name. "Jules, I don't want your stray dog here past twelve hundred hours!"

I turned back to look at him, resignation hardening my face. "I need to make my delivery. I give my word that I'll return by then. If I don't make it back I'm probably dead."

He laughed loud and long and shook his head at me. "So just another day then?"

I shrugged. "Just another." With that I left. I knew the way back to my bike and I didn't need anything from him to complete my delivery. Whether I wanted to or not, I'd be back.

My bike was exactly where I left it. I placed the proto-tube into the panier on the right side of the bike and took out the batons. Each one attached via strong magnets sewn into the suit at my thighs. Then I put on my helmet and threw Niko's on a nearby bench. The city was still quiet in the early hour. I verified with my HUD sensors that were no vehicles on the street outside the alley before exiting. It would do Souza no good to advertise excessive traffic in the neighborhood. On my way north I passed the occasional courier riding bikes much like mine. The buses were starting to run for the morning commute but I knew the majority of people moving would be taking place below the street and high above the city on the maglev trains. The sealed cars were by far the most popular, with filtered tunnels connecting many businesses and platforms. Blue wage earners still wore an enviro suit as part of their day kit. You never knew if a train or bus were going to fail and leave you stranded in sweltering heat with no good air to breathe. One thing that did catch my attention was the greater quantity of black BEN transports on the streets. I had a feeling that they were looking for Niko and I wondered why so much effort was being expended for one defected soldier.

The BENs had a roadblock set up on each side of the last bridge I needed to cross. Lucky for me I was nothing more than a courier and had all my paperwork in order. They didn't say what they were looking for as they searched the paniers of my bike. They could have been robots for all the emotion they showed as they roughed up a few blue wage commuters. With blacked-out face shields their gazes were unknown which made them seem not particularly human. Of course, my shield was the same way. Dressed in all black as I was, I probably appeared very BEN-like myself. But coloring aside, that was where our outfit similarities ended. BEN suits had hydraulic function to aid all physical movement. They were armored and held a variety of lethal and non-lethal weaponry as well as restraint devices. Each BEN carried a handheld bolt gun as well as a bolt rifle. Gunpowder had gone out of favor around the middle of the century when re-invented gas-driven projectiles became cheaper, deadlier, and more accurate. A commotion off to my left caught my attention just as I was cleared to cross the bridge. I paused. A de-gen was lying prone on the ground, face mask turned toward me. He was screaming at the BEN who held a bolt pistol aimed at his head.

"I swear, I don't know where she went! She showed up where we were squatting, and Joza attacked her. She killed him and stole his suit. We scattered and I don't know what happened to her. The BENs came and chased us off. Why don't you ask them where she went?" It was obvious they were talking about the night before, when the BENs came in to quell the de-gen riot.

As if in slow motion, I saw the helmet of the BEN with the bolt gun turn toward another with a commanding officer insignia on his suit. They didn't speak aloud. I assumed their communication was helmet to helmet, but the BEN with the gun turned back and put a bolt through the de-gen's head. The screaming stopped, as did all other activity around us. I couldn't help staring at the lurid mess of red on the concrete. The BEN that had checked my paperwork turned back to me, perhaps wondering what my interest was. I simply shook my head as if in scorn and spoke aloud. "Fucking de-gens!" Before he could change his mind I mounted my bike and sped across. The entire incident left me with more questions than was healthy. I stayed away from people as a rule and never involved myself in the tragedy that went on around me if I could help it.

The rest of my trip was uneventful. When I arrived at the Lincoln Park facility I had to go through a bio-scan, an optical scan, and have my ID chip read before they'd let me in. It was standard procedure even though they'd known me for years. Two familiar figures met me as I rode into the south bay entrance. Dr. Elizabeth Rook and Dr. Daniel Bosche were watching with curiosity as I pulled to a stop and hopped off the bike. I took off my helmet and gloves then retrieved the proto-tube and walked it over to them. However, I didn't just hand it off. They had to meet security on my end as well. Dr. Bosche was the first to speak. His voice was lower than most men I'd known, but he had more sense of humor than any scientist should rightly have. "It's so nice seeing you in the daylight, Jules. To what do we owe for the pleasure of not being roused from slumber in the middle of the night?"

They frequently grumbled when they were the receivers of my delivery because I preferred to work in the middle of the night. There were reasons I was the best courier Vanguard had, and it wasn't just because of my tech. One of the disadvantages of working solo was that I had to take more care with my personal safety so I frequently traveled when there were less people about. Dr. Bosche was a good enough sort but I never allowed our interactions to stray from other than professional. He always tried to cajole and draw me out and despite my best efforts I had grown fond of the man. Perhaps he reminded me a little of my father, or maybe I was just lonely. Either way, despite my continued aloof demeanor, it had become a game between us. "I was delayed. With a window like twenty-four hours, you should never fear failure when I'm making a delivery."

"He is only teasing you, Jules. We are well aware that you are the most reliable courier Vanguard has, which is why we put up with your strange quirks and penchant for darkness."

I inclined my head slightly toward Dr. Rook. "Shall we begin?" They both nodded and I pushed a button on the end of the tube then held it out horizontally in front of me. A yellow light started flashing the second I pushed the button. I had a hand on each end with my right index finger resting on the sensor located on that end.

"Page, Jules. Security confirmed."

Dr. Rook reached out to touch the side sensor closest to my left hand. "Rook, Elizabeth. Security Confirmed." Last was Dr. Bosche. He started to reach out, then pulled his hand back and grinned. "Gotcha!"

Dr. Rook sighed and turned to look at him. Her voice held exasperated warning and I suspected that his humor wore on her as the days went by. "Dan..."

He shrugged. "Just kidding." He touched the third sensor without any more delay.

"Bosche, Daniel. Security confirmed. Delivery successful."

Two things happened simultaneously. The blinking yellow light switched to green, meaning it could be successfully handed off without slagging out when I walked out of range. My wrist comp vibrated indicating that funds had been transferred into my company account. It was a good day that got you paid. "Are you walking in with us?"

Dr. Rook's voice startled me and I realized what she was asking. I usually came in to eat after a delivery but my schedule had been thrown off by the events of the previous night. I shook my head. "Not today, I've already eaten." I paused and they stared at me before I realized that further social norms were expected. "Thank you, though." Dr. Rook shrugged at me and Dr. Bosche simply grinned affably then they walked away with the proto-tube. My job was done. With my delivery complete I wanted nothing more than to go home and sleep for a good twelve. I had two rest days due. Unfortunately I also had an obligation to return to Souza's and retrieve my "stray dog" as he put it.

I hadn't thought through what to do once I had brought her back to his place for kitting out. Perhaps I assumed that he would get her set up and my rescue would end there. After seeing the increased BEN presence throughout the city, I feared my plans were going to change. I wasn't sure why they weren't checking visual ID on the couriers at the checkpoint. Perhaps they assumed that the security standards we had to meet for employment guaranteed against infiltration. After all, any company that had contracts with the government had to get advanced security approval for all its employees. But the government had always underestimated the power of the dark market. After all, they had yet to find me and last I knew I was the highest priority on their wanted list. That thought sparked an idea in my head. I just had to run it by Niko and Souza. And of course Vanguard.

Chapter Four

Taking In A Stray

THE RETURN TRIP was much the same as the one to Lincoln Park. If anything the number of checkpoints increased. They were no longer limited to the river crossings but seemed to be about every six blocks or so all the way down the major streets. I took a different way back to Souza's. Halstead allowed me to go south all the way to Roosevelt, and it let me see the state of two more non-curfew river crossings. The heightened security was sure to affect my deliveries until things cooled off. Souza, his guards, and Niko were all in the main garage when I got back. She was kitted out in a black solar suit very similar to my own. They were arguing as I pulled to a stop and both guards looked tense.

"Why can't I have a bolt gun?" Niko glanced at the guards then turned back to Souza. "And don't tell me that you can't get them, either!"

Souza's face darkened with anger. "I can get whatever I like, but what I choose to sell to you is entirely dependent on my goodwill. Your lack of actual cred and shitty attitude has it quickly running out."

I pulled off my helmet and gloves and interrupted them before things could escalate. "What's going on here?"

The dark market dealer pointed at Niko. "She wants a bolt gun but your friend is stupid if she thinks I'll give one to her, of all people."

"First of all, she's not my friend. I know her exactly as well as you do, probably less. Second—" I turned to Niko to address her specifically. "If you go out there with a bolt gun right now you'll be killed or captured. I promise you." I sighed and rubbed the back of my stubbly head. "Patrols have quadrupled over their normal numbers. Whoever you are, or were, has them on high alert. They are questioning anyone without official business papers."

"I can get by them!"

Niko's stance was determined, aggressive even, and I admired the figure she cut in the enviro-suit. She looked predatory. "Maybe you can but definitely not during the day. And if you leave here with a bolt gun then my help ends now.

You will be on your own to pay back Souza for your kit. Do you understand?"

The look in those blue eyes moved from anger to one of resignation. Perhaps the reality of her situation had finally settled in. She nodded once, just a short motion, but telling with its admission. "I understand." She turned to Souza and gave him a chin tilt. "I apologize for being discourteous in the face of your goodwill."

He stared at her for an uncomfortable amount of time, making me think he would continue to hold his grudge. In the end Souza gave her a return nod. "You are forgiven. I understand how it can be to find your life suddenly turned upside down overnight. I also know that sometimes an enemy can become a friend when circumstances change. I trust Jules with my life, and I trust her judgement of you."

I started laughing, startling all four people in the garage with me. "Of course the nano-tech in the side of her neck helps too."

Niko reached up to rub the spot, probably wondering what more the nano-tracker could do besides track, and Souza just wore a knowing smile. He enjoyed her discomfort for a few seconds longer then turned back to me. "I assume you have a plan?"

"Maybe. I'll need to use your secure line again." I waved at her suit and helmet. "Are you finished with her or is there more still?"

He looked at me curiously. "What more are you thinking? If you go much beyond that, things get expensive. I was going to loan at ten percent on the payback, but not for more than a suit and helmet. That's too much cred to collect from someone wanted by the BENs."

I considered the cost of my total kit and shrugged. "I'll cover it." He looked skeptical and I threw him a withering look. "Don't act like you haven't hacked all my accounts seven ways to Sunday. You know I'm good for it."

Souza glanced at Niko who watched us curiously. "Oh I know you're good for it. I'm just surprised you're taking the risk. You're not exactly known for your, hmm, humanitarian side, Jules."

With one last glance at the stranger between us, I shrugged. "Everyone needs a hobby."

"Do I even have a say in this?" We both turned to Niko at the same time.

"Would it help if I listed all the facts?" She nodded. "As of right now you owe Souza for your suit and breather helmet. You have no way to pay him back. You are a wanted fugitive who has apparently caused the entire hive of BENs to explode overnight. I'm going to assume you have no cred since all your accounts were most likely frozen when you ran, right?" She reluctantly nodded again. "They are doing a visual check, on top of IDs and papers, for anyone not working in a government validated position."

"Wait! You have validation?" I think she was surprised that a Walker could hide in plain sight like I was clearly doing. I suspected a lot about Walkers would surprise her.

I smiled. "Of course I do. I'm a secure tech courier for Vanguard, who has multiple government contracts all over the North American continent. Everyone working for Vanguard has to be vetted for high level security clearance."

Souza took over. "That is where I come in. I don't just deal with goods, but also services. I can hack the network and they'll never know. My code will alter your old identity in the system, everything from fingerprints to retinal scan. It will replace the biological data and image for Nikolette Morgan with data that has been changed slightly so that you new identity won't be pulled up with facial or other recognition. It will add a new ident into the public and private databases, one that is vetted for government work. I will provide sufficient references to anyone looking and assign you a cred account that is more than five years old." He smirked at her. "I am the best at what I do."

"Holy shit!" Niko looked a little shocked at the extent and depth of what he was capable of. She paused and I could tell her thoughts were racing with all the new information. "If you're such a good hacker, why can't you just siphon some cred to me from a corporate account somewhere?"

Souza shook his head and made a face at such a suggestion. "I'm good because I'm not stupid. If you steal money from a cred account, people and companies notice and they start investigating. I'm a hacker, but the companies also hire hackers to trace stolen cred. It's big business. However, I'm not stealing anything when I change the bio signature information for Nikolette Morgan. No data will be missing or added to your old ident, just altered. I will add a new identity with your current bio signatures and image to the networks, both BEN and private. You just need to pick a name that you'll respond to, and think of a backstory. Maybe you've moved into the area from Detroit. I hear the rioting has been getting bad there of late."

I nodded at his words. I'd seen the news reports on the comp before I left for this last delivery. "One of the major weapons facilities was bombed out a few days ago, and in response the government shut down the bridge crossing from Michigan to the state of Ontario. Ontario imports a lot of blue wage workers so people aren't getting paid and they're taking it out on every BEN agent they see."

"It's not the BENs fault that the government closed the border crossing..."

Anger filled me instantly and I rounded on Niko. "Never stand in front of me and defend the actions of BENs when it comes to the safety of the people. They are hired thugs who murder families in their sleep! The government has plenty of enemies but it's not usually the blues that would do something as extreme as bombing."

She stepped back, holding both hands up in front of her with palms facing me. "I'm sorry. It appears I am wearing on your goodwill as well."

I blew out a breath and stepped even farther from her. A part of me wondered if she provoked me on purpose with her constant prodding and pro BEN rhetoric. When I was calm enough to meet her eyes again I resumed what I was saying. "We got sidetracked. Anyway, my idea is to recommend you to Vanguard as a courier if you would be interested in such a thing. It would allow you to travel freely once you are separated from your old ident in the network. They'll scan your paperwork and never go through the effort of requesting the clearing of your face shield. You'll be fully vetted and above reproach. Even if they do start verifying facial recognition, you won't match the altered image in their system."

Niko cocked her head in thought then suddenly gave me that annoying smirk. "Will I be working with you?"

I shook my head. "No, I already told you that I work alone. If accepted, you'll be put into a mentoring program with a senior courier and after that moved to a two-person team."

"How long?"

I knew what she was asking. "It varies based on each trainee's level of skill. It can take anywhere from six months to a year. But for you..." I paused, sizing her up and reconciling what I had observed with what she had told me. "You're already well above most courier requirements. I think it would just be a matter of learning routes, facilities, and company protocol. Once you pass your tests and sign the contract, you'll receive a courier chip and be paired up when you begin training."

Souza glanced at his wrist com and it made me realize the day was wasting away. If she chose to go my route he would need time to set everything up in the networks. "One last question, would I be able to work by myself like you do?"

I shook my head. "No. They will not allow it." Niko gave me a look of disbelief and I elaborated. "Besides the fact that I've been with them for a decade, I was the one and only special allowance they made. Doc — a friend set up the job for me and that was his stipulation. They've always honored it and in return I've never given them a reason to question that decision." My patience had run out just as Souza's had. "Make your decision. I'm tired of wearing this suit!"

Souza looked over at me and grinned. "You on downtime now, Jules?" I nodded.

"I think a courier position sounds like my best bet and I want to thank you both for all that you've done for me, for all that you are doing." She turned to me with a hesitant look. "Are you sure you can get me in?"

I knew Souza's skill as well as the weight of my own word where my employer was concerned. "Yes. Now let's get this finished up. Souza, I can take her to pick out a machine while you get started on the program, if you like?"

He nodded. "That will save the most time, yes. Just bring me the chip cards for whatever kit you take. I'll scan them and give you a cred tally when you're done." He pulled a bioscanner from his belt pouch. It was a box with an optical reader and a print scanner. "I'll need samples from you to get started." He held the box out to Niko and she readily complied. When she was finished he also pulled out a knife and snipped a small bit of hair.

"What was that for?"

He scowled as he dropped the sample into a sealed bag. "DNA. I'm not sure what they have on you but I want to be prepared and I'm nothing if not thorough."

After that he turned and left with his guards, and I didn't want to waste any more time either. I led the way back to another garage and she followed quietly behind, waiting while I unlocked and pulled open the large rolling door. Her voice was jarring with no one else around. "He must place a lot of trust in you. You seem to have access to everything."

I shrugged but otherwise ignored her question. As we walked through I started asking questions about her skill set. "Can you drive a bike?"

I heard her stop walking so I stopped too and turned to look back at her. Disbelief and cockiness warred for control of her face. "I can drive or fly anything!"

I shrugged. "I had to ask." We stopped near a row of machines, all sleek and covered in black solar paint like my own. I waved at the dozen bikes lined up along the wall. "They're all about the same cred cost. Each one is just a little bit different. Pick one that suits you but make sure it has securable paniers."

There were only four bikes with storage so it made her decision a lot easier. She sat on each one, getting the feel of both seat and balance. All bikes were equipped with standard gyros to help keep them upright. When she got off the last one she walked back to the second one she tested. "This one."

I walked behind the bike and grabbed the card off the rack hanging on the wall. "All right, let's talk non-lethal weapons. I'm assuming you can use most as well?"

She nodded. "I like yours with the built in stun capability. Are they solar coated to self-charge or are they powered up by your suit?"

"Charged with my suit. They're held in place by magnets but charge wirelessly while there." I pulled the one off my outer right thigh and tossed it too her. The electromags automatically cut out when they read circuit completion, which is what allowed me to easily remove the weapon. Basically that only meant that if it weren't my own hand grabbing the baton, it would be very hard to separate it from the holder. Her eyebrows went up with surprise as she caught it.

"They're solid!"

I shook my head and smiled. "Not solid, but they've got a core to give them nice weight and balance. I can go through a helmet if I have to or break a neck."

She looked at me curiously and I easily read the thoughts that flickered behind those eyes. I knew she wondered if I would make good on my threats from that morning, maybe wondered if I could. "And have you? Taken out any helmets or broken necks?"

I nodded carefully, as if the weight of those I'd killed or injured still hung around my neck. They didn't of course. I held no regrets in life because I didn't care enough to hold onto such things. I didn't hold on to anything. She tossed the baton back to me and I saw clearly that she'd made her choice so I walked over to the third door from the left along a length of closed cabinets. Pressing my index finger to the scanner, the light turned green and I was able to open the door. Souza did hold a lot of trust in me but that was a story that few if any knew. There was a small collection of stun batons in a variety of sizes and shapes. I stepped back and waved her forward. Each pair was in its own cubby with a scan card tucked inside. "When you find what you like just pull them out and give me the card." In less than a minute she had made a selection. I shut the cabinet door again and watched to be sure it locked then turned and pointed at the rectangles sewn into her own suit. "He gave you a suit that's already rigged for them."

She attached a baton to each thigh and grinned at me. "Perhaps he already knew what your suggestions were going to be, despite your secretive nature."

I didn't respond to her dig. Instead I headed for the door. "Get your bike, Nico. We still have to finish your identity set up and I'm tired."

The bike barely made any sound as she started it up and rode through the open door into the main garage. Once she was through I shut and locked the kit storage room. I noticed right away that she had parked her bike right next to mine and left both gloves and helmet on the seat as well. Her boots were loud on the floor as she walked back over to me, echoing in the large garage space. I watched the march of her steps as she drew closer and slowly inched my gaze up her body. The suit hid the lines of the muscles that I knew were just beneath the surface, but it did not hide her curves or the way she moved like a predator stalking its prey. When our gazes met I flushed at the knowing smile on her face. "You were watching me again. While you claim no interest, your eyes certainly have a mind of their own." Niko stopped a safe distance away and I tried my best to ignore those scalding words. In the silence that followed I turned and led the way back into Souza's main facility.

The hack took less time than I remembered it and I wondered if he had perfected the technique over the years. Within the hour Souza had lost his goons and the three of us were back in the garage by our bikes. I put my gloves on and grabbed the helmet off my seat as Niko did the same. She had her new ident set up in the system and the old one altered to make her unrecognizable. It surprised me that she chose to keep the name Niko. She let Souza pick her surname and he settled on something basic like Jones. Niko Jones. I still had to take her to Vanguard to register in the program then we could finally go our separate ways. For whatever reason I was equal parts relieved and anxious at the thought of no longer having her near. The trip to Vanguard provided the first test of Souza's hack. Since it was still hours before curfew, BENs were manning roadblocks on both sides of the Roosevelt Bridge. I briefly wondered if the roadblocks would continue once curfew set in and had a feeling that they would. We slowed together for the soldiers and I immediately pulled out my ident card from a zippered pocket in my suit. Niko did the same with her new one. The BENs were working in pairs for each person crossing, one to check identity cards and the other to aim the bolt rifle. It seemed that they were taking no chances.

"You're clear." My guard waved me through but the other was still looking at his reader. I began to sweat inside my suit and kicked the cooler up a notch. The BEN that was finished with me looked at the long line behind us then turned to the one checking Niko's ident. "What's the hold up?"

The other BEN, a woman by the voice that came through her helmet speaker, pointed at Niko. "She doesn't have a chip or courier papers."

Confident now that it wasn't Souza's hack that was the problem, I spoke up. "She won't have anything yet. She just transferred to Chicago from Detroit. I was contacted by Vanguard to pick her up on my way back in. She's scheduled for testing today in..." I looked down at my wrist comp, then back up at the guards. "Twenty. I don't think they anticipated the need for extra paperwork or they would have just sent someone out from corporate to meet her."

The two BENs went silent for what seemed like forever, but it was only about ninety seconds. Finally the one with Niko waved her through. "Vanguard operator says you check out and they're expecting you, Niko Jones. Welcome to Chicago."

I gave a little salute to both soldiers and led the way across the bridge. The trip after that was anticlimactic and we pulled into the parking garage ten minutes later. Courier parking was better than most others, save white wagers. When she switched off her bike I motioned toward the door. "This is the courier entrance. The first room we go through is sealed with lockers for our helmets, gloves, and weapons. The locks are fingerprint activated so more secure than most."

I took off my right glove and scanned us through the security door. Just as I promised, we entered into a massive locker room. Niko jumped slightly when the digital voice of BERC sounded all around us. "Welcome back Page, Jules. I see you have company, do you need to register a guest?"

My locker was on the far side, next to a support beam. Unsure what she should do, Niko followed me like an orphan. "BERC, my guest is here to enter the courier training program. Her name is Niko Jones." I turned to the guest in question. "Biological Entry Reception Computer, BERC. Can you just go touch the finger pad on this side of the door to verify your identity for our watchdog?" She nodded and complied with my request. When she returned I waved at the vast array of lockers. "Claimed lockers will have a name displayed on the screen." I pointed to my own which clearly displayed 'Page, Jules' above the scan pad. "Green light means it's empty, red signifies kit inside. Just find a locker with a blank screen and an empty indicator."

"What about that one?"

Predictably she pointed at the locker right next to mine. I shrugged. "Suit yourself." The storage lockers were large enough to hold multiple suits, and mine actually had two others as well as a few spare synth-suits. There were two helmet shelves at the top and I placed my current helmet in the empty slot. Niko made no secret of the fact that she was blatantly checking out the kit in my locker. She gave me an incredulous look. "You have a fortune in gear in there!"

I shut my locker and motioned her toward the door opposite the one we originally entered. "It's not so much. Vanguard gives you a kit stipend on top of your regular pay once you go beyond level five. And I don't spend as much as some because I get my kit from Souza and he cuts me a deal."

"What level are you?"

I scanned us through into the facility proper and she fell into step next to me. "I'm a level ten."

She was silent all the way until we got to the elevator at the end of the hallway. "That's what, a level a year for you?"

"Yes."

She kept on. "Is that normal?"

"No." I didn't look at her, just led the way into the elevator and pushed the button for the sixth floor. "Once we get to the training facility they will test you and pending the results you'll be given a contract for signature. If I remember correctly, the program has cycles, with trainee classes starting at the beginning of each month. It's just good luck that you'll only have to wait a few days to get started. The sooner you can legitimize your new job, the better."

The elevator stopped and I led the way off. We hadn't taken

more than a step when she asked her first serious question. "What are the tests like?"

"IQ and personality tests done on the comp, physical tests done in the training facility itself. Stuff like strength and agility. The reviewer will probably quiz you on your background and training. Just stick with the story and references that Souza gave you."

I scanned us into the courier wing and hoped that her questions were nearly over. I really wanted to get home. "Will they assign lodging after I get my contract?"

Confusion washed through me. "Lodging? No, they'll recommend local hostels until you can qualify for a corporate apartment."

She grabbed my arm as I made to move forward again. I pulled up angrily and spun my head around to warn against touching but stopped at the look on her face. Niko wasn't just being cocky and disregarding my request for personal space. The look in those blue eyes made me think about how much of all her talk and action over the past twelve hours was nothing more than bravado because her eyes told me just how terrified she really was. Niko's fingers were strong and they clutched me desperately just to hold on to something, anything, safe. I wondered all the more who she really was and why she was so important. She leaned near and her voice was an urgent whisper. "I can't go to a hostel! That's the first place BENs will search! And they'll keep tabs on all of them until they find me or are convinced that I've moved from the city."

Suddenly I found myself with a dilemma. I had taken it upon myself to be her rescuer and I could not leave a job half done. I sighed and scrubbed at the back of my head, trying to come up with a solution. In the interim, I motioned her toward the receiving desk. She hesitated and I was prompted to speak. "I'll come up with something but in the meantime you need to sign up and get checked in." She didn't need me for anything that came next but she seemed reluctant to leave my side. I supposed that even the bravest of soldiers grew fearful when so far out of their element. Joana waved at me from behind the desk and I nodded back to her. She set Niko up at a comp station to begin her testing and I ducked into an empty room to make a few calls. The cochlear implants were handy when the calls didn't have to be secure. I tried all three contacts I had for housing and there was nothing available without a rapacious down payment of cred. I was frustrated after spending so much time on the phone. At a loss, I walked farther into the courier facility to find my boss. Karen Yates was a petite woman, nondescript but still pretty with her brown hair and slightly tilted brown eyes. I didn't see her much with the exception of quarterly evaluations and deliveries with special circumstances. Her assistant waved me back into her office when I arrived and Karen greeted me at the door.

"Jules! It's great to see you outside during the daylight hours. Are you here to drop off our new recruit?" I nodded and she smiled. "Good, good, it's always nice when our senior couriers help bring fresh blood into the company. It's very noble of you to help her out after moving here from Detroit. Did you hear about the riots? Horrible! I'm so glad we don't have to deal with that sort of thing in the capital." I waited patiently for her to stop talking. It wasn't that her voice was unpleasant, it was just that there was so much of it. Her words poured out in a never-ending flow unless you stopped her early. Perhaps realizing that I had come to her for a reason her talking ground to a halt. "So what brings you my way, problems in the field?"

I shrugged and tried to maintain an air of nonchalance. "Well the BENs are in a tizzy again and they've set up checkpoints all over the city looking for someone. I don't know who. I try to spend as little time as possible in their company."

"Well, damn. How comprehensive is the net? This could slow down or otherwise hinder our deliveries."

I looked at her curiously. "Is there something hot coming up?"

Her normally expressive face turned into a blank mask. "I'm not at liberty to say."

So they did have something hot coming down the pipe. I didn't say it aloud. Instead I nodded. "I understand. Actually I'm here to see you about Niko. She doesn't have housing in the city yet and I was wondering if you had something on your end you could do."

"Have you tried hostels?"

I made a face. "I asked her about hostels and she said she'd never get any sleep there."

Karen tilted her head at me curiously. "If she's such a good friend, why not just let her stay with you until something comes available?" And just like that, she had me snared in a trap of my own weaving. Damn. She was right though. If Niko, whom I had just vouched my career for, was as great a friend as I mentioned on the recommendation, then I should have no problems letting her stay at my place. She smiled at me. "I know what your pay grade is allotted. You have plenty of space. In the meantime, I'll make a note to keep you informed if something turns up on my end."

"Thank you."

I could tell by the look in her eyes that my time was up. "Is there anything else, Jules? I'm sorry to push you along but I've got a conference call with Goeta-sen in five." I shook my head no and she smiled again. "Well thanks for stopping in and keep up the good work. You're the best we've got now. Let's hope your friend turns out to be something special as well."

I nodded dumbly at her response. "Yes, let's hope." I walked out of her office and back to the comp area where I had left Jules nearly an hour earlier. I was weary of making calls about lodging and really wanted a stint in my own bed. Of course it was looking more and more likely that I'd have a guest in the spare room. Niko would be the first visitor I'd ever had and somehow I didn't think she would be displeased to see my personal and intimate quarters. I sighed and more than a small part of me regretted not taking off the second I saw the suited figure running down the street toward my hiding place. I chastised myself for wishing to change what had already come to pass. Wishes were for fools. I settled in to await the end of her testing. After all, Niko and I were slated to become roommates soon. The thought of her so near to my private sleeping space each night filled me with doubt and longing. I collapsed onto one of the lounge chairs in the corner and shut my eyes to the coming days ahead.

Chapter Five

The Wall of Fear

AS MUCH AS I wanted to rest there were more important things that had to be done. I knew I'd have some time so I thought I'd do a little walking while I waited for Niko. I called out to Joana behind the nearby intake desk. "Joana, I'm running on fumes right now. Gonna try to nap a bit until my friend comes out from testing."

She smiled. "You want one of the empty rooms?"

I shook my head at her. "No, this is fine. The chair is comfortable enough and the little bit of background noise won't bother me." Within seconds I had slowed my breathing enough to slip free. To any passerby it would appear is if I were merely sleeping. I wanted to know what the hot item was and there was only one place I'd find out. Vanguard Daley facility, the one we were in right now, was the company hub for all research and development worldwide. Yasushi Goeta was the director of our facility and if Karen had a meeting with him, it was probably about that hot item. Curiosity was a powerful motivator and I sped back down the hall where my boss's office was located. With minimal effort I shut my eyes and walked straight through the door. She was on a conference call, the screen jumping randomly indicating that the signal was being scrambled on both ends.

"Goeta-sen, when will the first samples be ready?"

"William-sen's team is still running tests on the first five proto-types, but he assured me that we should have measurable results soon."

Karen smiled at the graying man on the screen. He was smartly dressed in a dark suit with a blue tie and I was surprised to see that he wore glasses. Corrective surgery was cheaply done with a robot, but I'd noticed a resurgent interest in nostalgic devices. "What happens after the first round of testing?"

On the flickering screen I could see him shuffling papers around on his desk until he found the one he was looking for. He read carefully from a spot midway down the page. I assumed he had a hard copy memo because that was the only way to be completely safe. Hacks were everywhere. "After initial round of testing, samples will be taken to the lab. They need to analyze the average output to power ratio, the rate of decay, and estimate the conversion time per square meter. After that they will build more samples and start another round of testing."

"How many rounds until we're satisfied the prototype will work?"

He looked up at her and smiled, or rather, smiled at the camera on his end. "They will perform ten trials. If everything falls into the predicted parameters we will deliver both samples and schematics to all our production facilities. James Carville-sen would like to have a three month stock built up before marketing it to the world. He is afraid others will try to steal the tech and get it to market before us. But he is more afraid the government will shut it down."

My boss's expression turned from curious to wary. "Is anyone else working on something like this?"

Goeta-sen shrugged. "Not that we are aware of, but you know that secrets run deep in this business. Tell me, you have someone in mind for the transport, yes?"

"Yes sir, I'll have my best on it once the samples are ready to go."

I didn't need to hear any more after that. While I didn't know what it was they were working on, I at least had a timeline of sorts. They were still on the first round of tests, with nine more to come. That would mean months, at the very least. I also knew that I would be the one getting the initial delivery. It was a big deal, one of the most serious ones I'd heard of and I wondered if she'd bring in more than one team. It was rare that they would devote production capability of all facilities to one product. I also wanted to know why Goeta-sen thought the government would shut it down. The questions spun within my head as I slipped back though the door and made my way slowly down the hall. I preferred to float above all the people traversing the hallways and corridors of the building. As I was returning to the waiting area I saw Nico head into the bathroom across the way from the comp room. In the blink of an eye I was outside the door, then through it. I never expected to see what was on the other side. Or rather, I didn't expect to be seen. Nico was leaning against the wall with her arms crossed, directly opposite the bathroom door. Her gaze was intently aimed my way and I looked around for a second to make sure there was no one else in the bathroom. Without a word being said she straightened and strode across the small space and stopped right in front of me. My voice was nearly a whisper. "You can see me, can't you?"

She nodded and cocked her head to the side. Moving slowly, perhaps hoping I wouldn't move away, she reached her fingers up toward my lips. I didn't move because I knew I would have no substance to her touch. Her hand passed harmlessly through my face and I shivered. There was no actual physical sensation while interacting with a person who was awake. Walkers were only able to connect with someone who was walking or someone that was in deep REM sleep. "But I can't touch you. You look like you did when I first met you. And how did you just go through the door like that?"

"That's because when we are walking we control what we look like. Your brain has an imprint of 'self' that you can't lose, but you can imagine that 'self' any way. I could pick my enviro-suit, or I could stand before you nude; however, this is how I'm most comfortable. It takes a lot of practice. You shouldn't be able to see me either."

Her look was skeptical. "Really? How do you know all that?"`

I shook my head and knew I should get back to my body. "Because I just know. I need to go back now."

"Please..." I looked at her and waited for the words to continue. "There is so much I don't know, so much I need to learn. And you seem to be the only one who can teach me." I didn't answer her, thinking about her words and what they would mean for my future, for my solitary life. "Please don't abandon me here, Jules. I don't even know where to go after my testing is done. I have no home, no friends, and no creds..." She ran a hand through her hair and I caught the slight tremor of it.

With the shaking of those strong fingers I knew that I was fully invested in her safety. "When you're finished here you can come back to my place and stay in the spare room until they give you corporate housing. But after that you're on your own." Something tickled my awareness and I was overcome with a sense of urgency. "I have to go now, Niko. Besides, if anyone comes through the door right now they'll think you're talking to yourself. Find me when you're finished."

The infuriating smile returned to her lips before I could leave. "You were watching me again."

I didn't answer her, nor did I push through the door gradually. It was only a short distance to my body so I accepted the slight headache and returned to consciousness all at once. A hand on my shoulder had me in motion before I could register who or what was touching me. I launched myself out of the chair and pushed back on the large figure in black then spun around and foot swept him to the floor. I stopped immediately upon seeing the familiar face of a fellow courier. Ryan and I started working at Vanguard at the same time more than a decade ago. After a few years in the field he transferred into the training division and always kept me current on the gossip at headquarters. He held up his hands and grinned at me from the floor. My longtime colleague had straight white teeth and a perpetually youthful look that said he was a man who would age well. "Whoa there, killer! I was just waking you up to say hey and to ask if you wanted to come back and watch your friend go through her final tests."

I blew out my breath and reluctantly held out a hand to pull him to his feet. Since I was responsible for putting him on the floor, courtesy dictated I help him back up. "Sure. Gah, but you're a big-ass man!"

Always one to ignore my preference for personal space, Ryan laughed and clapped me on the back. We walked over to the double doors and he scanned us into the training center. "As a matter of fact, I am an ass man, and your friend that you brought in has a mighty fine one." I ignored his familiar idiocy only because I'd known him so long.

Niko was already inside when we arrived. The training center had different sections. There was a large gym and exercise facility as well as rooms for individual self-defense training and other classes. She was standing with one of the assistant facilitators, Syrah, who was wearing a look of disbelief as she stared at the tablet in her hands. She turned to Ryan as we walked up. "She got a perfect score!"

I met Niko's disconcerting eyes and Ryan whistled and responded to her comment. "Damn, she's the fourth one, and Vanguard has been using this test since 2060!"

Syrah looked at him in surprise. "Three others?" She hadn't worked for the company as long as Ryan and I.

"Yasushi Goeta, our R&D facility director tested perfect back in 2075. William Kinet in 2082, and Jules Page in 2088." The answer slipped out before I could censure myself. I had rules. I didn't volunteer personal information, and I definitely didn't encourage familiarity. Angry that I no longer knew who I was anymore, I closed my mouth to prevent more words from coming out.

"You?" Syrah seemed surprised by my admission, although I found it interesting that Niko did not. I nodded. "Shit, no wonder you're a level ten!"

I shrugged at her and my irritation started to show. "Can we wrap this up? I've been going nearly twenty-four and I'd like to get some solid REM soon so I don't drop."

"What, your nap wasn't enough?"

I glared at Ryan. "No."

After that they ran Niko through her paces, so to speak. They tested her strength and agility on multiple machines, then Ryan put her through a combat test. She passed all with flying colors, but then I knew she would. The last steps were to visit medical for her chip and then sign the contract. She was told to review the corporate rules and policy on their net site, and I assured her that she could use the comp at my place. Ryan shook her hand after we made our way back out into the courier wing lobby. "All right Niko, we'll see you back here in two days where you'll be paired up with a senior courier for the first part of your training. Remember to read through the material on the site because that has routes and protocols you'll need to know."

She nodded. "Thank you, and I will."

As we made our way back to the locker room I could see her discretely rubbing her arm where the courier chip was inserted. I tried to block out the image of her stripped to her waist so they could run a physical and do the insertion. She asked me to stay in the room with her and her eyes never left mine throughout the procedure that slipped the mem chip beneath her skin. I had no choice but to meet them otherwise my gaze would have gone wandering once again. The chip was specially coated to not cause infection or rejection by the body, but it was an irritant until you got used to it. It would also become sore as the local anesthetic wore off. When we reached the locker room we both scanned our lockers and grabbed gear. I slowed before we exited into the garage. "I've got some cream at my place that will help when the chip site starts hurting later."

"Thank you."

I shrugged and put on my helmet. "It's nothing really, just some leftover analgesic cream from a previous injury."

Niko reached out to prevent me from opening the door. Maybe it was because our helmets were on and I couldn't see her face, or maybe it was because she was becoming much too familiar with me, but when she spoke her voice held a measure of vulnerability that I had not yet heard from her. It was strange thinking of someone sounding vulnerable through the speaker of a breather helmet, but that was the only way to describe the wavering quality of her voice. "No, I mean thank you for everything, for my kit, my cred, and my life." She stopped and I thought that would be it but she moved her hand closer to lightly touch the back of my glove. I froze and listened. "I had a good life with the BENs. I had lovers, friends, family, and a career. But none of them were there when I needed it most. You were. A complete stranger has treated me with more honor and more respect than all those that I thought I loved. I can never repay you for that. I can only offer my friendship, for whatever it's worth."

"Friendship is stronger than the stone of any mountain, more powerful than the greatest star, and more valuable than a planet's weight in gold."

Suddenly her face shield cleared from its normal impenetrable blackness and her light colored eyes were shiny with emotion. "Raphael Coronado."

I nodded and pulled the door open. As we mounted our bikes I opened a direct line between us so we could speak helmet to helmet, and so I could push the map to my place. My corporate apartment was in a high-rise on the corner of Wacker and North Lake Shore Drive. I was on the northeast corner of the forty-second floor with a view of the lake on two sides. As soon as we entered I showed her the closet where she could stow her helmet, gloves, and boots. I usually plugged my suit and helmet into the ports there when I didn't spend enough time outside to charge the batteries. I showed her the extra ports and plugs and Niko nodded stoically at the information. I left my helmet charging but immediately stripped from my suit and walked toward the facility. "If you want to tumble your suit, follow me." Souza had only given her one suit. That's all he had that fit her. Her only other clothing was the synth suit she wore beneath, and her undergarments. It wouldn't take long for the suits to be clean and disinfected. Every apartment had their own tumbler, a small machine that used a dry spray and de-ionized air to clear any contaminants from your clothing. Fabrics were also woven with anti-microbial filaments to prevent additional buildup. After loading the machine I spun around to head into the kitchen, running straight into Niko who stood right behind me. She grabbed my shoulders to keep me from falling and I stiffened at her touch. She let go immediately and backed up to give me space. "Why do you hate me so much?"

All the arrogance that she had shown at Souza's warehouse was gone. Fear and uncertainty had taken its place. Niko was about five years younger than me and her life had been irrevocably changed over the course of twenty-four hours. As much as I had lived the past ten years isolated, she had been surrounded by other people. Now we had come together in the middle of where we once were and where we were going. She continued to stare with those strange blue eyes, her pupils wide in the darkened apartment. Something had pulled us together and bound us inextricably, our fates intertwined for good or evil. I hated that my secure life had been changed so thoroughly and so abruptly. I hated being wanted for something I had no control over, and I hated that I wanted things I could not have. But I didn't hate her and I told her as plainly as possible. "I don't."

"When you dare to look me in the eyes at all, it's with scorn. Otherwise you only look when I'm not watching, like you're afraid of me. You shy away from my touch, accidental or otherwise."

I just shook my head at her disarming words. "I don't hate you." I left her there to walk into the kitchen area. There was a built-in eating space with stools not far from the counter next to the main appliances. The cooler held filtered water and I poured myself a tall glass. I had a bottle in my panier but warm water, no matter how refreshing, was not as good as cool. I also had a hydration pack that I could install under my suit but I didn't wear it for the most recent delivery. I had not anticipated that it would take so long. I heard her soft footfalls behind me so I waved toward the cupboard and she grabbed a glass to match my own and set it on the counter. "I have water, juice, and milk." She raised her eyebrows and I clarified. "Not real, it's lab milk of course." I brought up the inventory screen on the front of the cooler. "If you're hungry I have prepacks, some cooked grains in bowls inside, and some dry goods in the cupboards." I turned back to her. "Are you hungry?" She shook her head and I watched as her arms came up to hug herself. Did she receive a lot of hugs in her old life? I wondered what it would be like to be so open with other people. With real people. I filled her empty glass and topped off my own then put the container back in the cooler. "Okay then, I'm going to go try to sleep. I'll write down the password so you can use the comp. It's in the main room. If you'll follow me I'll show you to your room before I head to bed." We each carried our water back through the apartment and I pointed out all the things she would need to know as we made our meandering way back to the spare room.

"What's the password?"

I slowed because I had completely forgotten in just a matter of minutes. I shrugged it off as a lack of proper sleep. "Let me write it down for you—"

"No need. Just tell me and I'll remember." I recited the long string of digits and numbers and she merely nodded and I had no reason to doubt her mnemonic capabilities. I detoured us to show her my room and left my water on the stand next to the bed, then took her next door to the spare room.

The spare room was spartan but had a bed with coverlet, a pillow, dresser, and vid screen. Both rooms were on the same east wall of windows. I had the tint darkened nearly eighty percent along the entire wall to keep the light out. Unless it was an unusually low smog day, there wasn't much to see anyway. The lake had receded a lot in the past fifty years, but the water still sparkled on days the sun shone brightest. "I know it's not much but I've never had company. The furnishings all came standard with the apartment. We can check the web later to order more clothing for you but for now I need some sleep. Will you be all right?" Niko moved to set her glass of water on the bedside table then came back to stand in front of me. She looked lost with her arms folded in front of her. Niko's face held a curious wash of emotions. She looked sad and resigned and I knew why she would feel so, but she also looked puzzled. "What is it?"

She turned her head to look back through the doorway behind me, then met my gaze. "You've never had company?" I shook my head. "Just as a guest in this room, or no one at all has ever been to your home?"

I swallowed fearfully because she had seen too much. I should have known she would. My admission was quiet in the filtered hum of the apartment air. "No one at all."

Niko seemed taken aback and a look very similar to pity crossed her face before she wiped it neutral again. "Why do you isolate yourself? Aren't you lonely?"

I shrugged. "You can't trust other people, only yourself. And I'm not lonely. I see Walkers in my dreams all the time."

"It's not the same!" I stepped back at her sudden and too loud voice. She moved closer again and quieted herself somewhat but continued to speak words I didn't want to hear. "Even though you're the only one I've ever seen while walking, I still know that it's no replacement for real human touch." She raised her hand and slowly ran a single finger down the side of my cheek.

I shivered at the unfamiliar sensation. Goose bumps marched along my arms and my heart raced. "Please don't."

She persisted. "Give me one reason why I should stop." Her

finger traced its way along my jaw and down the side of my neck. The lower she went the more I trembled beneath her touch.

"Because I don't like it."

"That's a lie." Her hot gaze moved from my parted lips down the front of my synth suit and I knew she took in the sight of my hard nipples pressing against the thin material. I was relieved when she finally pulled that roaming digit away from my skin. My relief was short-lived as she moved her hand down to my breast to feel just how hard I had become.

I knew I could not bear the real touch to my person, and I immediately fled to my own room. I shut and locked the door, chest heaving as I leaned back against its reassuring solidity. Eventually my breathing slowed as I began to calm. I was safe. I stripped as I walked over to my bed, crawling in nude and reveling in the feel of my own space. Exhaustion settled over me and sleep came fast. I gave no thought to other defenses. Unnerved as I was I had forgotten to guard against her in my dreams, and she was suddenly there as soon as I hit REM. I would have been fine had I built a wall to keep her out to begin with. But once she was already inside it would have been difficult and painful to force her away. We were in a place of emptiness and she stood right in front of me, as close as we had just been in her room. I shook my head at her. "Please — please just leave."

She moved closer, and I was overwhelmed by those light colored eyes. "But isn't this where you feel safe? Isn't this the only place you want people?" Niko reached out and cupped my cheek and I had no choice but to close my eyes. Her hand was hot against my skin and I felt curiously light. I didn't understand why she was affecting me so. I had touched and interacted with plenty of other Walkers in the dream state. On rare occasions of walking over the years I had met others like myself, others that would only allow personal comfort in the safety of their heads. And that was the only place I would allow myself to feel, to touch or be touched. I had never had an intimate experience in the waking world. And I knew it would be a mistake to have such an experience with someone whose physical body was in such close proximity to my own. A woman whose gaze would greet me each day, whose knowing stare would come back from the dreamscape with all my secrets and fears. My eyes opened as her hand slid around to the back of my neck to draw me near.

"Please — we can't."

"We can."

My eyes widened with the promise of her words and they

were caught in those bright universes of blue. When her lips covered mine I shuddered at the sensation of softness and heat. Her tongue begged for entrance into my mouth and as I let her in I felt colors swirl out of me and spin around us. Her other hand came up to grip the back of my head and I clutched the sides of her waist. Despite all my protests to her in the real world, I found Niko more attractive than anyone else I'd ever met. She pulled my eyes and body any time we shared the same room. It was disconcerting. And in that moment, my brain had already accepted the immense attraction between us. She was in my dream, in my space, and I had control. The touching and the pace were familiar in the depth of my dreams, only the person was new. Niko was dangerous and forbidden but my head didn't care. I drew the darkness down around us as we continued to taste and caress. When we finally came up for air, her eyes were shut and I didn't want that. I had to see her. "Niko."

Her eyes opened and widened slightly. We were in a place of my making. Colors swirled all around the walls and there was a bed of soft coverlets at our feet. "What?"

I covered her lips with my finger because I held the power here. She may have experience in the physical world, but the dream world was mine. "Watch." She watched as I started to rise into the air, slowly. I floated about a foot above the surface we stood on in my dream. "We are in our dream. If you want to go up you simply stop thinking about what is real and what is possible in the waking world. It's much like walking in that way. You stop thinking and you simply do. Will yourself to rise." She closed her eyes then and nothing happened so I floated near and whispered in her ear before floating back again. "Let go, Niko. If you want to be taught then you have to be willing to learn." Suddenly she rose up, and kept going. "Slowly Niko, take it slow." I could see the panic hit when she opened her eyes and she began dropping rapidly back toward me. I jumped up to meet her and wrap her in my embrace. "You have control here, we both have control. Relax."

Those blue eyes looked at me with wonder. It smoothed her features and I felt her body lose tension within the circle of my arms. "Are we really doing this?"

"This is only a dream, and it's our dream." I suddenly let her go and she remained afloat in front of me. "We are both doing this."

In an instant, the look in her eyes changed to one of heat and passion. It promised something that I knew would be a mistake once we returned to reality. I backed up away from her because I knew if she touched me again I would not be able to deny her. When you spend your entire life starving yourself of something, temptation becomes impossible to escape. "Don't." Clearly having a mind that was beyond most, Niko wasn't just a fast learner. She was fast with application as well and before I could react she took me into her arms. Her breath was hot in my dream as she skimmed my ear with her lips. Strong hands clutched at my back, desperately drawing us together. Those warm lips moved from my ear and tasted their way along the skin of my jaw to just below my mouth. She pulled back and we were millimeters from each other, breathing the same air. Then she moved in that last little bit and kissed me before moving back again to give that finger's width of space. The words were pulled from me slow, stretching out with time and meaning. Each instance that sound came from my mouth she would cover it with another tender kiss and my heart would beat even faster. "We...should...not...do...this..." The last kiss was unlike the others and took me deep. We were so close I could feel the beat of her heart against my own chest.

Niko slowly pulled away from my swollen lips. "We should, we are."

Suddenly she was nude within my arms and I reveled in the feel of her bare skin beneath the whorls and pads of my fingers. I thrilled deep inside as I traced the muscles along her arms and shoulders. She was learning much too fast and if I were to let this thing between us happen she would not be in control. I willed my own suit gone and pulled us both down to the mounded coverlets below. She may have been physically stronger in the real world, or even a strong Walker, but she was in my dream now. No matter how fast a learner she could never match a Walker with twenty-five years of experience, especially not in their own head. When we dropped to the nest of my dreams I made sure she was on the bottom and positioned myself above her. "Even as a Walker, you should be careful what you wish for. There will always be someone stronger than you in the dream world, someone with more experience."

Niko looked up at me with eyes shining bright and chest heaving. "And how do you have so much Walking experience when you're not much older than I am?"

I reached down to take both her breasts into my hands, letting the hard nipples caress the skin of my palms. She sucked in a breath and I leaned in to claim her lips with my own. When I pulled back again I gave her the last serious words we would have within the bounds of my sleep. "That knowledge is not yours to hold." With that, I claimed her as I had done with other Walkers before. Our bodies molded to each other, touching and being touched. When she finally brought me to the peak of passion in return, brilliant white light radiated out of my body, blinding both of our dream selves. She was startled, as was I.

"You're beautiful." Her words held awe and reverence even as they caused a thrill of fear to run through me. Such a thing had never happened before. My control was never so poor to allow dream expression without my consent. Fear seized my body and without a thought to the pain that would follow for both of us, I abruptly forced her out. I woke and muffled my own cry even as I heard her cry out from the other room. My head throbbed with the psychic backlash of such an action but I knew it had to be done. Quietly, in the silent hum of the apartment around me, I built my mental wall and slipped back into slumber. My sleep was lonely once again.

Chapter Six

Pushing Boundaries

WHEN I NEXT woke, my head throbbed in time with my heartbeat and I remembered my actions of the night before. I reached into the drawer next to the bed for a pain tab. A sigh of relief slowly released with the next exhale about thirty seconds after I placed the analgesic under my tongue. I thought about Niko in the next room, most likely feeling the same headache and knew I was responsible. I let my fear control me and in turn I hurt us both. I did that, no one else. I felt guilty for her pain when she did nothing wrong. She was an amazing dream lover and it was my own uncharacteristic reaction that caused me to panic. I was the person clutching at my solitude the same way she clutched at any semblance of normalcy after the recent upheaval of her life.

Needing motion and purpose for the day I stood and pulled out clean underclothes and a synth-suit then went to use the facilities. It was early morning. Despite going to bed before sunset the day before, pain and exhaustion had kept us there for nearly twelve hours. The door to the spare room was still closed so I assumed Niko was asleep. Once I was clean I grabbed another pain tab from my drawer and went to stand in front of the spare room door. Before I could knock I was struck by the realization that I didn't know how to comfort someone. It had been years since I'd held a hand or given someone a hug and I'd never really had a friend. In the light of the new day I could clearly see that she had been searching for a connection in my dream. When she thanked me for helping in the locker room at Vanguard, she was telling me more than what was said in mere words. She was admitting to me that of all the people she had in her life, I was the only person she had left. And because of my own fears I'd been pushing her away since the moment we first met.

The door abruptly opened and I came face-to-face with the woman who had literally haunted my dreams. "Oh!" Her eyes weren't as bright as they had been and there were little lines of stress between her brows. Pain was evident in the set of her mouth and the tension she carried across those strong shoulders. Despite the obvious headache, she looked at me curiously. I quickly held up the pain tab and her eyes widened with understanding and more than a little relief. She carefully took it from my fingertips and placed it under her tongue then waited with closed eyes while the suppressor took effect.

"I—" As soon as I started to speak those startling blue eyes opened and stared intently at me. Suddenly unsure, words stumbled from my mouth. "I'm, um, I'm sorry for last night." Niko started to raise her hand toward me and I stepped back out of habit. The hurt look that skittered across her face prompted me to speak more. "My av—aversion to touch has nothing to do with you. It is a habit, I guess. Something I learned when I was much younger. I don't like to be touched by strangers."

Her eyes were distant for a few seconds then they refocused on me. "From what I've seen, you don't like anyone touching you."

I met her penetrating stare with my own, willing her to understand. "Everyone is a stranger." It seemed surreal to admit something so personal aloud to a woman I barely knew while standing in my own home. A home that had never seen anyone but me. Would that mean that Niko was no longer a stranger?

As if she could read my thoughts and heart, she spoke. "I'm not a stranger."

Niko had a look in her eye, one that I'd seen many times over the past day and a half. I took another step back to preserve my personal space. "Aren't you though? I know nothing about you, only that you are a fellow Walker who is being hunted by the black BENs. That you yourself used to be a high ranking BEN. Those are macro details that are easy enough to find out. But I don't know you, Niko."

She smiled but didn't step any closer. "You know my heart."

I shook my head at her sadly. "I know your mind and only that. I don't think anyone's heart can truly be known."

"Not even yours?"

I had to look away from those knowing eyes then. They were too much. "Especially mine." I had tried. I apologized and that was all I was willing to do so early in the morning. The heavy conversations would have to wait until never. "I was just getting ready to heat some grain. I'll make extra if you're hungry." She nodded and I turned and walked back toward the kitchen. Our breakfast was warm by the time she had finished using the facilities. Her hair was slicked back, highlighting the angular lines of her face. My gaze drank her in and I could feel my pulse race ever so slightly. No one had ever caught my attention as thoroughly as this fugitive soldier. I wrenched my eyes away with effort and took in the rest of her. Niko's synth-suit looked a little worn and dingy and I wondered how disgusted she must be continuously wearing something that had been inside the suit of a dead man. "After we eat I'll show you where you can order more clothing. As long as the package is less than a square meter, they'll drop it off in my window box via drone."

"I still don't have any cred."

I smiled at her, trying to be friendly, but the attempt felt stiff and unfamiliar on my face. "I have cred and it doesn't hurt me to help you."

Niko sighed and stood to take care of her empty dishes and I watched her. "I can feel your eyes on me." My face flushed with her words and I hastily looked back at my porridge. I quickly finished the last bite and stood to clean up but she remained in my way. "Why did you save me, Jules?" She held so many questions inside her and I lamented the loss of my silence. I didn't want to put answers to her words. Responses of information only led to more questions, only peeled back the layers of my psyche for all to see. I didn't want to be so exposed to her. She was too smart, too analytical to not put the pieces together. She took the dishes from my hand and quickly racked them in the cleaner then turned back to me. Her eyes were curious and curiously sad. "Please?"

"I saved you because I could." I turned abruptly and went back into the main living space. In just a few steps I was seated at the comp and had brought up a general merch site I used often. "You can pick out what you need here and just order it. The charges will automatically go to my cred account. Don't worry about the cost, just fill out your kit." Niko had walked up much too close to where I sat. I could not stand without bringing our personal spaces together, without touching the front of her body to mine. I shivered at the thought. "Please step back."

She stubbornly refused. "I want to talk with you and you keep avoiding me."

Anger at her demands rose within me. "I've given you my aid and given you my hospitality, I don't owe you my words. Step back, Niko. Don't make me regret helping you."

I watched as her weight shifted slightly, planting her feet. She expected me to simply push through her. I remained wary as her arms came up to trap me, one hand on the back of my chair and one on the comp table. "Why did you help me?"

Not wanting further confrontation, I gave in just a little. "Because someone helped me once and I thought maybe it was time to pay it forward."

Her eyes took on that unfocused "thinking" look she had. When they returned back to me I could see she had more answers than I intended to give. "A decade ago, that's when you started at Vanguard. Someone helped you hide then, didn't they?" She was much too smart. "Ten years...is that how long you've known you were a Walker?"

"No. Now please move, I've answered your questions."

Niko persisted. She always persisted. "You're much too skilled. How long have you known?"

My heart beat faster and faster the longer she stayed in such close proximity. I could smell the faint odor of her suit, one that obscenely mixed with the clean scent of her shower. I was afraid to speak more but she gave me no choice. "Move, Niko."

"How long, Jules? How do you know so much about us?"

"I won't ask you again!" I closed my eyes to her proximity, hoping she would be gone when they opened again.

In a move born of a soldier's reflexes, I felt her pluck me up out of the chair and spin me around within the circle of her arms. Before I could register what she was doing she had me pinned in an arm lock. I could feel every part of her pressing into my back. Not expecting the abrupt action, my eyes flew open and I started to panic. "How long have you known?" I struggled but she held me tight. I wasn't in pain but the fear clawed at me. She was too strong and I was trapped. In my own head I was strapped to a table like so many times before. "How long, Jules, how long have you known? Tell me and I'll let you go."

The words echoed in my head, repeated themselves over and over through the space of my panic. Finally I could take no more and the words flew out of my mouth, forever exposing me. "Twenty-five years!" I babbled, nearly incoherent, just wanting her to let me go. "Since I was five, t—twenty-f—five years! Please!" Suddenly her arms released me and I fell to the floor with legs unable to support me in my crazed state. I scrambled backward until my back hit the wall next to my desk. When I hazarded a glance upward her face was white with shock.

"Fuck. Jules—Julia. You're Dreamer Zero."

Blinding terror struck me then and I clawed at the desk drawer to my right. When my hand emerged I pointed the bolt gun at her. Just like that, the familiarity of self-preservation kicked in and washed away the panic. With one hand holding the gun steady on the center of her chest, I used the other to balance myself as I rose from the floor. "You should never have pushed me. I'm sorry, Niko, but no one can ever know what you've just learned." Things had changed between us so fast. I could see the confusion and fear in Niko's eyes.

Her hands went up in an instant as her eyes desperately cast round the room then locked on me. "I'm sorry but I swear I won't tell. I won't ever fucking tell! I'm wanted too, remember?"

Once I was standing I steadied my aim with both hands. "No one is wanted more than I am." I could feel the cold calmness wash through me and knew I would pull the trigger. My mind raced ahead to what I would have to do with the body. I'd probably call Souza. If he couldn't help with something then he always knew who could.

"Please, Jules! Consider the patrols on the street right now. They probably want me just as much! I've done a lot of thinking since I ran from the compound and I realized some pretty hard truths. Please, let me explain!"

I paused because something told me that her words perhaps had some truth to them. Why else would BENs be scouring the city for a lone Walker? It couldn't have just been her rank within the Network. I thought about what I needed to know and how I could guarantee my own safety until I got the answers I wanted. Keeping the gun aimed in her direction with my left hand, I reached into the top desk drawer next to me and pulled out two sets of plastic binders. I knew that people could break them if trained in the trick of it and that meant they weren't the most secure solution, but they would have to do. I still had my bolt pistol, just in case. "Put one set on your feet and the other on your wrists. Use your teeth to pull the wrist tab to tighten them."

Looking wary still, she sat on the floor and did what I asked. "What now? Will you kill me?"

I checked her restraints then backed away to sit on my desk chair. "I don't know." I honestly didn't. I put a lot of time, cred, and effort into saving the woman's life. It seemed wrong somehow to be the one to end it. Or maybe that was the only right way for her to go.

"Julia, please!"

Something twisted inside me with her words, with that name. "My name is Jules. You'd do well to remember it for the time you have left on this godforsaken ball of rock! Do you understand?" She nodded. "Now, what I do with you will depend solely on the answers you give. Who are you?"

Frustration colored her features. "You already know who I am, I haven't lied to you. I've never lied to you! Souza's own system knows better than anyone."

I ignored the way fear made her eyes widen and washed the color from her cheeks. "Why are the BENs so hot to get their hands on you?"

"I didn't know!" I raised the gun and she rushed to explain. "I said I didn't know, not that I don't know now. At least, I think I've got it figured out."

I waved the gun for her to continue. "Go on."

She blew out a breath and turned her eyes up to the ceiling then brought her chin down and met my gaze unflinchingly. "I think it has to do with my mother."

Curiosity pulled my finger from the trigger. You never put your finger on the trigger unless you're prepared to shoot. Or be shot. "And who is your mother?"

"Dr. Olivia Morgan, the government's chief geneticist. She works directly for the General."

Had she rushed me at that very moment I would not have been able to shoot. I would have done nothing but sit there dumbfounded as I was. That name brought back a lifetime of memory, decades of loss. I remembered needles and tests. I flashed to a man and woman, one holding me down on the floor as I shook and thrashed about, and the other trying to staunch the blood flow from my head and mouth. I was taken back to the night I walked through Doc's evening, when he first learned with certainty of the government's betrayal and thus the destruction of his life's work. It all came back to me in a rush. "Edmonton. Lette. You were supposed to go to Edmonton."

"What?" The sharp retort brought me back to the present. I didn't answer so she pressed me again. "How did you know that?"

"I saw it in a dream." My eyes grew unfocused again as I remembered the night that the cold and impersonal computer voice read Dr. Olivia Morgan's email to Dr. Jonathan Cisco. Dr. Morgan had such hope that her, her husband James, and their daughter Lette would be able to move up to Edmonton.

"You were walking?"

I nodded my head. "Yes. Where is James Morgan, your father? You didn't mention him and he was also a geneticist, working with your mother."

Something tugged deep inside at the sorrow that shone in Niko's eyes. "He's dead. Before we came to live in the government facility my parent's lab had a break-in and my father was killed. Binary Enforcement Agents came to our door and informed us that he had died and that the intruder got away. After a long talk with the agent in charge my mother said we were moving to the compound inside the city because it was safer." My mind raced through the details of what I already knew and what she had told me. Pieces fell into place and suddenly the answer was there. I looked up at her and felt deep pity. Her words startled me despite the fact that I was staring straight at her lips. "I can see it in your eyes. It's a look that says you know something and you're afraid to say what it is. But you don't have to. I've already figured it out. My mother lied to me for over a decade. Everyone lied to me. They killed my father and have been using me to keep my mother on their project all this time."

"Niko." Her name slipped out as a whisper. I tried to soothe the pain that washed from her in waves but the path was so unfamiliar to me. "You don't know that they killed your father. You don't know that they haven't lied to you both all this time."

I was not practiced with untruths of such a nature and her face showed clearly that she didn't believe me any more than I believed myself. "Where are your parents, Jules?"

It was one question too many. Dark memory spun me down a rabbit hole in my mind. Everything faded when the images of my past seized me within their grip. The bolt gun, Niko, my apartment, they all disappeared into the darkness.

A little over a decade ago there was a night my parents and I were supposed to go see a presentation being given by one of the leading researchers on tech innovation. I begged off at the last minute, having already tired of human interaction by the tender age of twenty. The presentation hall was about a mile away from the dream clinic where I asked to be dropped off, and my parents opted to take a drone shuttle from there. They were going to pick me up on their way back home. I followed the safest way I knew how, stretching the boundary limits between my Dream Walker and my corporeal self. For me it was an ideal situation though. I got to see the presentation without having to be near so many other people, so many strangers. Afterward, I walked out into the darkness with them and listened contentedly as they spoke about the newest advancements in their field. And at that moment in time I thought they had no idea I was there. But my parents knew me, perhaps better than I knew myself. Soldiers came out of the shadows before they could get into the waiting shuttle. While they didn't wear the trademark armor of today's BENs, there was something about the way they all moved together that said it was a well-planned operation. One spoke and his voice crashed like thunder into the night.

"Where is your daughter, Julia Thiel?"

My dad stepped forward, placing his body slightly in front of my mother's. "Why do you want to know?"

The man in black raised the bolt rifle and aimed it straight at my father's head. "Where is Julia Thiel?"

It was then that I saw my mother look around and her gaze almost seemed to slow as it passed over me. Her voice was a whisper but clearer to me than all the rest. "Julia, no—" The muffled sound of a bolt gun being fired filled me with dread and I watched with rising horror as my father's head snapped back. It was too fast to see the progression of the bolt, only the shattered hole that appeared in the faceplate of his helmet and the spray of blood and gore out the back. My mother's scream pierced the air around me. "Robert!" She threw herself to the ground next to his body and cradled the broken helmet in her shaking hands.

"Where is Julia Thiel?"

I wanted to yell at her, to tell her to go and save herself but there was no time and she would never have heard me. There was no chance. She looked up and there was also no mistaking the fact that she looked straight at me. Perhaps it was the connection we shared as mother and daughter that allowed her to know where I was but I'd never been able to figure it out. In that moment of sorrow and clarity she screamed at me, confusing the soldiers around her. "Julia, run!"

I wasn't home and I knew I'd never go home again. My body was back at Dr. Cisco's lab and when my mother screamed I didn't just retreat into myself at a safe pace. That was the first time I had ever snapped back in and to this day the longest distance. Luckily I was wearing the headset that doc had made for me. I told him I was going to attempt to stretch my distance so he had me put the gear on to monitor my progress. When I snapped into my body all my vitals redlined for a second, enough to sound alarms in the room where he was recording data into his tablet. He found me shaking and pale, blood rushing out both nostrils and babbling incoherently. Once he got the full story out of me he immediately went into action, clearly having prepared for such an eventuality. He sent me into hiding and worked out the details of my new life. The official story was that my parents died in a freak shuttle crash and neither of us were ever able to prove it was government soldiers that killed them.

My parents' life insurance money went to him when I was presumed dead, something they had set up years before. Through a series of subsidiary and out-gov systems, the money eventually came to me. But the government desperately wanted me and a year later they killed my last remaining friend when he refused to give up my location. Both he and his family died as pawns in a game that was bigger than all of us. I was the first, I was Dreamer Zero. Pain seeped into my awareness as the memories seeped out. My scalp was burning and the stinging pinpoints registered with my returning consciousness.

"Julia. Julia!" Reality came back in a rush with Niko's voice. I was sitting on the floor with my back against the wall and the hands on my cheeks snapped my eyes open wide. "Look at me, hey, are you okay? I'm so sorry, I didn't know."

I didn't even tremble at her touch, still shaken by the memory of my parents' deaths. Confusion filled me and spilled over into words disjointed and quiet. "How—what did—"

Tender fingers came up to trace a line on my scalp and I shivered. "I don't know. You just disappeared when I asked you a question. It was like you were—walking or something but your eyes were wide open. Then you screamed and I've never heard or felt anything like that before." She looked at me intently with something close to fascinated horror. "I felt you screaming." Those fingers continued to gently stroke me, moving from the self-inflicted wounds of my bleeding scalp down to my neck and face. It was almost as if she were reassuring herself that I was all right.

"I was only walking through my memories, nothing more." My voice was a horse whisper and my fingers hurt where I had been digging into my head, willing the despairing memories away. I had dropped the gun the minute I went under but I knew I wouldn't need it any more. I shut my eyes and leaned into her embrace as a decade's worth of tears cascaded through my dark lashes. I wept for all the people in the world that I had lost, and I wept for the one person I had found. Niko and I were the same with our betrayals. We were the same.

Chapter Seven

Searching For What Is Real

I WASN'T SURE how long we sat there but eventually the tears dried, leaving my eyes feeling hot and gritty. Niko held me quietly and didn't try to engage me. She was definitely learning. But sitting within the safety of her arms, letting her comfort me in a way that had not been done in nearly two decades—maybe I was learning too. I sat up slightly, pulling away from her embrace and she leaned back to look at me. Her eyes were full of concern, full of questions and so much more. What else had she seen? Habit made me scrub my hand across my stubbly scalp, forgetting about my self-inflicted wounds. Wincing, I gingerly touched one of the more painful digs.

"I'm sorry." I didn't say anything to acknowledge the apology for her actions. I merely tried to assess the situation and get my bearings. She continued to speak though, making ripples in the silence we had built after my breakdown. "I can't imagine what it must have been like as a young girl, seeing the things you would have seen as a Walker out in the night, witnessing the horrors of the adult world as so young a child."

I nodded. "Yes." She was indeed too smart.

"And to become the focus of intense study so young. I read about you. My parents spoke often about the Dream Walker project while we ate dinner. They spoke about you specifically. I remember thinking at the time how strange it was that to them you were nothing more than a discovery, an experiment."

"To most of the scientists I was a lab rat and that was it. For fifteen years the scientists tested me and analyzed every bit of fluid they could sample. The put me though DNA tests, psych evaluations, physical evaluations, stress tests, and pain tolerance tests—"

Niko stiffened beside me and her voice was rough with anger and horror when she spoke. "You were a child!"

I shrugged because I truly couldn't remember ever being a child. "I was Dreamer Zero. I heard doc talking to someone from the Council once. They seemed to think I held the key to creating more Walkers. They thought that if they could isolate the gene for my ability then they could turn it on and off. They could create the perfect spies." Niko sighed next to me and when I glanced to my left her eyes were closed. I could see that my words triggered knowledge of some sort. I wasn't sure how I knew, but I did. "What is it?"

Niko rubbed the bridge of her nose as if she were getting another headache. "It's more than that. I didn't get to speak with my mother much. She was always busy, always had excuses why we couldn't meet. Even now I don't know if that was her choice, or theirs. But I kept up with her work and know that they thought the Dream Walker project had a lot more potential than creating spies. Some scientists thought that if a person could project their consciousness outside their body, that maybe they'd be able to project it inside someone else's. They postulated that if they could figure out how the ability worked, that people who were dying or infirm could simply transfer their consciousness into a coma patient or someone who was clinically brain dead but in perfect health."

I shook my head because the scientists were wrong. "That's not possible. We aren't just casting our conscious out into the world when we walk, we are permanently and irrevocably tied to our physical self. You cannot remove one without killing both."

"I kind of figured that. But that's not all. You know I was head of the private cadre in charge of General Rennet's security, right?" I nodded. "He's getting old, Jules. He took control of the military forces more than forty years ago and he fears losing his power every single day. We heard rumors that some of our Walkers had been killed in the field. That their bodies would spontaneously redline in the transports and the BENs could find no cause for it. Sometimes the black Walkers would report another Walker nearby and when they did they always died. It was a rare occurrence but it happened often enough that my mother thought there was a connection. Rennet became obsessed that someone was targeting his Walkers and convinced that it was someone of great power. The general hypothesis was that only someone who had been a Walker for a very long time would have so much control or have developed their abilities so much. The General thought that the Walker responsible for the other's deaths would be the one who held the key to consciousness transfer. It was my own mother who told him she thought the insurgent they were searching for must have been Dreamer Zero. She turned his obsession to you, Julia Thiel."

I sighed, surprised and at the same time not. "She said as much in an email to Dr. Cisco years ago. Even as she was prepared to take her family to safety, she was convinced my DNA held further secrets locked inside."

"It's unconscionable!"

I looked into those sad blue eyes, feeling the wall between us begin to crumble. "Its history, and I am no longer Julia Thiel."

Anxiety blossomed on her handsome face. "But you're still Dreamer Zero! And now they'll search for both of us with a fervor I've not seen in my decade of serving in the Network. I'm endangering you simply by being here!"

Just as she had been thinking about her life and circumstance since escaping the BEN compound, I had been thinking of my own since meeting Niko. My revelation came on swift as a summer storm, leaving me scoured in its wake. Niko's earlier words pried me open and as much as I wanted to think that Julia Thiel was dead, the little girl came tumbling out of the crack in my shell. Julia was still inside me and she needed more than the isolated life I had built for myself. When I looked into those heartbroken blue eyes I saw a way to connect. And for the very first time in my adult life I didn't feel alone. Turning so I was on my knees, I straddled her legs and placed both my hands on her shoulders. I think I startled her with my touch as much as the rapid motion. "No!" Her eyes widened at my loud exclamation so I quieted my next words. "You have not endangered me." I swallowed the emotion that welled up, vowing to get the words out that she needed to hear. "I — I think you're saving me."

"Julia..." Her voice slipped out and trailed off in fearful wonder, with confusion. The look she offered me was a balm for the years of pain I'd endured. What was it about her that touched me when all others had failed? Who was she to wake me in such a way? The reality was that in an impossibly short amount of time I craved her connection. I brought both trembling hands up to cradle her jaw, tenderly tracing her lower lip with my thumbs. Niko froze and stared straight into my eyes even as her lips parted beneath my touch. The softness, the way she seemed to breathe air just for me, it was too much. Before I could be guided away by fear I leaned down and caressed her lips with my own. I had never touched another human in the waking world in such a way. I traced her lips with my tongue before moving to beg entrance. As we twined together, inhaling and exhaling the same life, I could feel my body begin to warm. My respiration rate increased as she brought her hands up to my back and pulled me closer. This thing between us was out of my control and so very different from walking.

A noise sounded, low and intense, and it took heart-stopping seconds to realize it came from me. I deepened the kiss and Niko willingly followed my lead. My hands moved up to thread through her short hair, reveling in the softness as the strands caressed the skin between my fingers. I paused and started to pull away in awe at the allure of something so human, but Niko wouldn't let me. She moved her hands up to the back of my head and pulled our mouths together once again. Sudden pain on my scalp caused me to cry out into her lips at the same time I twisted away from her strong hands.

"Shit! I'm sorry Jules, are you all right?" The initial pain fled fast but I kept my forehead resting on her shoulder anyway as I caught my breath. Her voice sounded again quietly near my ear. "Are you okay?"

I whispered back to her. "Yes."

"Julia, are you in pain?"

Her question prompted me to sit up, suddenly aware of our strange and intimate position. "I'm fine. It's just that I—I've never done this before."

There was no mistaking the confusion in her eyes, even if her words had not given it away. "I don't understand."

I motioned my hand back and forth between us then moved my index finger up to trace her full lips and pulled back. "This. This thing between us. I've never done this before." She cocked her head at me, trying to analyze my words and I felt triumph at deciphering one of her familiar looks. Rather than let her mind race to find my answer, I went on. "You mentioned that in your old life you had friends and lovers. I've never had either of those things." I looked straight into those precious blue eyes. "This connection, our intimacy, it's all new to me."

Niko shifted at my words. I made to move from her lap but she gently reassured me with hands on my hips. "Is that what you want, to be lovers? Or do you want friendship?"

Entire worlds seemed to open up with her questions and I thought about what I craved most. I could not decide. "Can't I have both?" She sighed and the warm air of her breath brushed past my neck, making me shiver. "Did I say something wrong?"

Her eyes were sad when she looked at me and I felt my heart sink. "Julia, Jules, until an hour ago you'd not only been threatening me for touching you, but you actually pulled a gun on me. Those aren't actions of someone who wants to be friends *or* lovers."

She didn't understand and I put my hand on her shoulder. I

wanted to feel the solid muscle beneath, to be reassured that she was real. Most of all I needed that simple connection. I wanted that heat that I could feel though her synth-suit. "I didn't know."

Niko shook her head at me and a lock of her too-long hair fell into her eyes. "What didn't you know, Julia?"

"My entire life I've associated intimacy with pain and fear. People wanted things from me, they took the things they wanted. And if they didn't cause me pain then they abandoned me in one way or another. So I ran away from more than just who I was. I ran from everything and everyone. You said it yourself, I've been isolated for the past decade."

"And what didn't you know?"

I leaned down carefully and placed the lightest of kisses on her lips then pulled back again. Her eyes fluttered open and I saw clearly a reflection of how I felt. "I didn't know how to connect. As strange as it may be, you've taught me the power of connection. I don't understand this thing between us, or why we of all people met when we did, but I still feel it. Tell me I'm not alone, that you're as drawn to me as I am to you."

She nodded, still wary. "I am. But what does it mean to you?"

I pushed that lock of hair back to display the smooth skin of her forehead and remove all obstructions between me and those eyes. "It means that you and you alone woke the dreamer. You've brought me to life."

Time passed by slowly while I waited for her to think about what I had said. Her eyes slipped closed and minutes ticked by. Finally Niko opened them and tapped me on the thigh. "I'd like to get off the floor now." I scrambled off her lap and after a seconds hesitation, I held my hand out to help her up. When I pulled her upright she bestowed on me a real smile, not one of smirking arrogance. "Thank you." She stretched her arms high above her head, trying to work the kinks out of her muscles and joints, and my eyes greedily followed the movement of each limb. When she finished Niko faced me straight on with arms relaxed at her sides. "And how do I know that you won't change your mind again, that you won't panic and run when faced with the next thing you don't understand or have experience with?"

"I won't!"

Before I could register that she had moved, her right hand snaked out and caught me off guard. With her superior strength and training she drew me in quickly and caught me in the same arm lock that she had earlier. I trembled at her touch but managed to stay calm. "Are you afraid, Julia?"

I whispered to her in the circle of those strong arms. "Yes."

Her grip tightened and I shivered. "Afraid that I'll hurt you? Expose you?" She paused and her voice went lower, more menacing. "Turn you in to the BENs?"

"I'm afraid that you'll leave." Suddenly those arms relaxed and the embrace changed to one of comfort.

"Why don't we start as friends first? I think we have much to learn from one another, much to teach. True intimacy starts slow like trickling water in a stream."

I smiled when Niko recited a quote for me at the end. "Sophia Kent." I turned within her arms and pulled her into a kiss, rejoicing at the solidity and warmth of her. But it wasn't the exploration of earlier, it was a most tender expression of friendship, a kiss of thanks. Niko was safe and I couldn't remember a time when I felt completely at ease with someone. I knew I would still have moments of fear and doubt, but something large and permanent had changed inside of me. When Niko pushed me and forced me to crack open, she exposed that little girl and let her out. But at the same time a little of Niko also made her way inside. She had earned my trust like no one before ever had. I pulled away from her lips and she sighed. "Julia, Jules—"

I interrupted with a smile. "I like that."

Niko cocked her head at me. "The kiss?"

"No, Julia. But only from you, and only here where we are safe. Can I be Julia for you?"

She gave me a sweet smile in return. "I'd like that."

Shaking myself from the unfamiliar lethargy of happiness, I pulled away and went back over to the comp table. I pulled out the chair and gestured to it. "Why don't you have a seat and order some clothes and other personal items you'll need. I've got some things to take care of so I won't be available for at least an hour." The new information I had just learned from Niko had my mind rushing for answers once again. I wanted to go out and do a little investigating for myself, maybe see if I could find one of the rare black Walkers that the Network put on patrol.

"Are you going out?" I froze, caught between the truth and more of my self-preservation. If I told her I was not going out then she would know I was going to walk. And it would only be a matter of time before she figured out all I had done, what I was capable of. I shook my head no. Niko cocked her head while she processed the scant information I'd just given. I waited, wondering if she were going over our conversations in her head, if she were analyzing my tense stance and the closed look upon my face. "You're going to find other Walkers?"

I started to sweat because I couldn't lie to her and for the first time in my life I cared what someone thought of me. "Yes."

Her features darkened. The change of expression would have been nearly imperceptible but I had been watching closely for her reaction. "For connection?"

My eyes widened at her words and tone. I had expected a conclusion, maybe censure if she knew what I was up to but I had not expected — what? Was she jealous? I shook my head again. "Not that kind of Walker."

I found it fascinating the way her thoughts so obviously reversed course and built themselves into some new configuration. Surprise lit her face and I knew that she had at last reached the correct conclusion. "Your threats to me when we first met, they weren't empty. The rumors are true, aren't they? Are you the one who has been killing the black Walkers?"

Meeting those clear blue eyes was harder than I anticipated. Up until a few days ago those BENS, maybe even some of the black Walkers, were her comrades in arms and her friends. "When I've had to, yes. I will not be taken in again, Niko."

She looked confused and curious, but not judgmental. "But how? I know we can feel things when we are walking, pleasure and pain, but how does that translate to our physical body?"

I sighed, caught between her curious nature and my own. I wanted to check on the BEN patrols and see if I could get into the head of one of their Walkers. I wanted information and one way or another I was going to get it. Things had gotten more personal since meeting Niko. I raised my hand to scrub my scalp and stopped just in time. In the end, I knew what I would have to do. "Why don't you take care of your ordering while I put some newskin over these scrapes? When I come back we can begin."

"Begin?"

I nodded and gave her a smile that felt strange on my face. "Yes. Me teaching and you learning." Less than ten minutes later I led her into my bedroom and she gave me a rakish look. I didn't respond to her playful smirk, merely waved her to lie down on my bed. Once she had stretched out into a comfortable position, I did the same in the space next to her. As we lay side by side I was struck by the realization that she was the first ever in my bed, save for me. I suddenly remembered that look from moments before and the thrill of it caught up to me. I was forced to tamp down my rising excitement. We had work to do. "You already know how to slip free before you're fully asleep, which is more than most Walkers can accomplish. The first thing I need to do is establish the limits of your ability. We will start with the smaller stuff and eventually take a walk to see what kind of distance you can go."

"Okay."

I set the alarm on my wrist comp for an hour and closed my eyes. Decades of practice allowed me to slow my breathing and lower my heart rate enough to slip free. I only had to wait about sixty seconds for Niko to appear next to the bed. "Before we actually begin your limits test I want to show you how to alter your Walker projection. Watch." It seemed surreal that we should both be standing there while our bodies lay on the bed with such serene faces. I shut my eyes and concentrated on changing my shape, or at least my clothing. When I opened them again I was wearing my black solar suit. With a little more focus the familiar feel of my helmet encased my head. I raised the faceplate completely and watched her wide-eyed reaction. "Can you do it?"

Niko looked apprehensive. "I don't know how to do it."

"Start by closing your eyes." She followed my direction and I continued her instruction. "Now think about your suit and how it felt on you. The way it wrapped around your limbs, how it felt to move inside." Nothing happened after a minute. "It's all in the way it feels and your memory of what is familiar. Feel the suit around your body, Niko." I almost stepped back at what appeared before me. In an instant Niko stood in front of me in full BEN armor. My heart began to race and I knew I had to get my reaction under control or I'd threaten our walk. "Is that what you meant to do?"

She raised her faceplate and suddenly looked less dangerous in the ominous black armor. "I'm sorry, you said think of the suit that was most familiar."

I waved off her apology. "It's okay, now try to change that suit for the black one you got from Souza." Much faster she made the switch in her appearance and I was pleased at her quickness. "Very good! Next you need to work on your reaction to real world objects. Follow me." I let my helmet disappear again and turned and deliberately walked through the door into the living room. I waited for her to follow and when she didn't show I returned to where she stood inside the bedroom door. "Go back to your most comfortable form." She looked at me curiously then complied and reappeared to me in her synth-suit. I pointed at the door that was slightly behind me. "That door doesn't exist, nothing exists in this plane but Walkers and what we make real. Now try again."

She approached the door but every time she reached out her hand simply caressed the solid surface and her progress stopped. She looked back at me in frustration. "I can't do it. I could never get out of my room in the compound either unless I were sleeping in a place with the door open. I didn't even know it was possible. It wasn't like they trained us on what powers Walkers would have. It wasn't intel relevant to our division."

I stood looking at her, trying to come up with another way through the problem. I'd never instructed anyone before so it was a new issue for me. Everything I'd learned was self-taught. I wasn't just the first Dream Walker discovered. I was the only Dream Walker for seven years until another was found with the power. I went over to Niko, an idea formulating with each step. "Embrace me and close your eyes." She complied and I slowly raised us off the floor to hover a foot above the hard surface. "Open them again." I was struck immediately by how very blue they were, at how her look softened as she watched me and held me in her arms. Soon enough though Niko noticed something strange in her peripheral vision and those same eyes widened in surprise. "You see? The room is a ghost to us, just as we are a ghost to the room. Now watch me, watch my eyes." I turned us so she could not see the door then slowly floated us both toward it. Before she could even protest or ask questions, we were through.

"Oh!"

"Did you feel anything?"

Niko gave me her thinking look as I set us down and let her go. "No." I thought she would have more questions but instead she looked at the couch and slowly moved her hand toward it. After her hand passed safely though the dream world construct she turned to me with delight. "It worked!"

I just nodded, pleased at her progress. "Now try the door again." She went over and easily passed through then came back out. "Good! That's an excellent start."

"Start? What more is there to know about moving as a Walker?"

Familiar habit had me rub my hand across my head, although no longer painfully since the newskin application. Even perception of injuries carried into the dream world and those were much harder to imagine away from your Walker projection. Pain was too real, too tied to your psyche. "You're very cocky, aren't you?" She shrugged and gave me that infuriating grin. "You've only just started to understand the dynamics of our dreamscape. There is a huge difference between the world we walk in and the real world. And right now your body doesn't know the difference unless you concentrate. But what if you don't have time to focus your thoughts?"

"Show me what you mean."

I nodded and waved her toward me. Once she was near enough I quickly foot swept her to the ground. She wasn't expecting it and she landed hard with a *wuff*. I reached down a hand to help her up. "You shouldn't have landed at all. The floor is not real and neither is your Walker body. This is like a dream. Get it yet?" She shook her head. "Okay, try to do the same to me. But I'm ready for you so it won't be as easy." The fact was that Niko was better trained physically and a lot stronger, so it would probably be easy if I didn't pull my internal power. I found out the hard way when I tried to circle behind her and put her in a headlock. She easily flipped me over her shoulder and I flew in an arc toward the floor then disappeared into the apartment below mine. Luckily I'd seen a lot in my decades of dreaming and nothing surprised me anymore. I ignored the two couples in the space below mine and slowly floated back upward in a different spot. Then I watched as she frantically cast her eyes back and forth, looking for me. "Remember—" She spun around, startled by the sound of my voice. "The floor is not real, we are not real. Now let's try again and I'll show you another way you can react."

I was pretty sure Niko didn't like being a beginner at anything. She gritted her teeth when she answered me. "Fine."

We started circling again and when she reached for me I performed the same move on her that I had at Souza's warehouse. Clearly having done that move on her was enough because she quickly adjusted her footing and avoided the sweep then flipped me back over her hip. As my body flew toward the floor I focused and in an instant appeared behind her. Not knowing where I had disappeared to, I surprised her with a kick to the back of her knees. She dropped painfully to the floor. Though to be fair, it wouldn't have been painful at all had she learned the first lesson. "Did that feel good?"

Niko spun her head around to look at me and her face raged with pain and frustration. "Fuck you, Jules!"

"Remember your first lesson! The floor doesn't exist therefore neither does the pain. Think, Niko!"

The Walker closed her eyes and drew in a deep breath before

floating gracefully to her feet. When she leveled her gaze on me again all anger had washed away. "How did you do that? And can we pass through other Walkers the way we pass though objects?"

I shook my head. "No, Walkers have a — an energy. And our energy cannot occupy the same place at the same time as another energy. However, real world things, bodies and non-dreaming people, they don't have energy on this plane. It's confusing and simple at the same time. Just know that Walkers are only real to each other. My energy can hurt you, but the real world cannot. And if something hurts our energy, disrupts our consciousness enough, we can die."

A thoughtful look crossed her face. "So only Walkers can hurt us?"

Her thought process was obvious to me but I had to point out all possibilities, even the minor ones. "If you do something in the dream world that you believe will kill you then it probably will. You have the power to do yourself harm, never forget that."

"So how do I learn? How do I get better at understanding what is real and what is not?"

I smiled at her, and it was a smile born of the purest pleasure I'd ever known. "You fly." With that statement, I floated into the air and flew toward and through the door of my apartment. Seconds later Niko joined me in the hall and watched as I flew back and forth along the length of the forty-second floor. "You need to train your mind to do the impossible." I stopped a few feet away from her, floating in the air, and held my hand out. "Join me?"

Her grin left no doubt about her willingness to try. Niko slowly floated upward and then toward me. As our hands met a familiar shiver raced through my body. Her touch was as unsettling as it was arousing. I shook off my thoughts because we had only just scratched the surface in her training. We flew back and forth for a while, joyous in so dark a time in our lives. Sooner than I'd hoped, I felt a buzz through my consciousness and knew it was time to stop. Our frolicking ground to a halt when I held up my hand to her.

"What is it?"

"It's time to go back." Not wanting to risk a headache, even a small one, I slowly made my way back inside the apartment and into my bedroom. I was pleased and delighted to see Niko follow me without hesitation through each new barrier. I settled into my body and reached over to turn off the vibrating alarm on my wrist com. When I looked back at my friend her eyes were shiny with emotion. Concerned, I immediately turned onto my right side to face her and reached out to caress her arm. "What is it? What's wrong?"

She turned to her side as well and shook her head against the pillow. "Nothing."

I moved my fingers up to catch the lone tear that fell onto her cheek, rubbing the liquid back and forth between my index finger and thumb. Meeting those mesmerizing eyes again I had to ask. "Then why do you cry?"

"Because that was the most amazing experience of my life. You are amazing."

I flushed at the unfamiliar intimacy between us as much as the compliment. "I don't know how to respond to you."

My eyes fluttered closed as Niko moved her fingertips to lightly trace my left brow. "What happened here?" She was referring to the scar that ran through the arch of dark hair.

I kept my eyes shut but had to work at keeping my heart open. "When I was eight, two scientists were running a series of tests on me that sent me into a seizure. When they tried to strap me down earlier I flew into a panic attack so they decided to leave off the safety harness for the last round of tests. When I began seizing I fell from the table and struck my head on the way to the floor. I needed stitches in my tongue and above my eye." Her stroking motion abruptly stilled and I felt her trembling from my place next to her on the bed. When I opened my eyes again I was struck by the pain in her gaze, by the fury. No one had ever been furious for me before and I wasn't sure if anyone had ever shared that level of pain.

Niko's voice was strained and quiet. "How could they let someone do that to you? Why weren't your parents or your doctor there?"

I swallowed, suddenly realizing my next words were more relevant than either of us would want. "Because they didn't know what the tests were. They were assured I would be completely safe. The scientists were both well respected geneticists in their field — friends of the doc."

Niko paled and my heart lurched at the stricken look on her face. "My parents." I nodded and found myself wrapped in a strong embrace. I trembled with it, not because of fear but rather with relief. I no longer had to face the darkness alone. I didn't have to remember alone. She was there. Niko would save me.

Chapter Eight

The Awakening

NIKO CONTINUED TO rub my back as we clung together, and I brought my left hand around to rest between her shoulder blades. Once I had calmed a bit I let my fingers wander upward to caress the short-clipped hair above the nape of her neck. Niko shuddered against me and I felt her breathing accelerate as light puffs fell against the top of my head. Still amazed at the feel of her hair against my fingertips, intrigued by the way we fit together, I was unable to still those curiously questing digits. I was lying slightly lower on the bed and my head rested on her shoulder. The more my hand stimulated her scalp, the more Niko clung to me. "Julia..." Her word was quiet and I shut my eyes to hear someone say my true name with such reverence. She shivered and her hand stilled against my back. "Please, Julia — we were supposed to learn as friends first."

I finally dared to look at her and Niko's face was a study of strained pleasure. "I'm sorry. I've never been so drawn before, so..." I struggled to find the word that fit how I craved her nearness, her very touch against my skin.

"I'm not sure if this is the best time. We should wait until things are steadier. Calmer."

I protested, sensing that she wanted to be honorable, knowing she would worry about my vulnerability and penchant for rejection. "We didn't wait last night. We've already been here."

Niko brought her free hand between us and unfastened the Velcro of her suit, along the length of her breastbone. While she was still covered for decency, it left a tantalizing view of her flesh. "Give me your hand." I was reluctant to stop the stroking but I obeyed. As I placed my left hand into her right, she moved it between us and lay my palm against the center of her bare chest. "Can you feel my heartbeat?" I could feel exactly that, the echoing thump that carried through my skin and into the neediest parts of my brain. I swallowed the building nervousness and heat then nodded. Something about the set of her face made me pay particular attention to her next words. "We haven't been here before and I don't want to ruin the future for us by rushing."

I smiled and let my fingers slowly explore the soft skin beneath. "Of what worth is the moon tomorrow when the sun could die today?"

Niko sucked in a breath. "P. J. Banto, The Prophesy of Light."

The smile on my face came unbidden at the simple thought that she knew too. "Niko—" I kept my voice soft, not wanting to pull us from the moment I could feel building between the past and future. "I've waited my whole life."

She sighed. "I suppose you have."

My body would not wait any longer, nor would the tentative thing that was my heart. Just like in my dreams, I pushed Niko onto her back and moved above her. I think she sensed my need for control at the beginning and let me have my pace. Her lips were so very soft, as was the skin behind her ears and down her neck. When my teeth found that little bit of flesh just above her collarbone she moaned and arched into me. My hands gripped her strong shoulders even as my mouth moved up to hers once again. She held me against her, fingers tightening and loosening in time with our breathing. I moved and feeling the thrill of friction, moved again. But it wasn't enough and I sought more from her. Moving my hands to the opening of her suit I grabbed and pulled with all my strength. I lifted slightly and soft Velcro gave way all the way past her navel. I whimpered when I saw there were still more barriers beneath. Leaning down, I covered her mouth and she drew me in, twisting and twining her tongue with mine, stealing my breath away with each soft sigh. My hands gave in to their need and caressed the skin under her suit.

"Wait."

I pulled away from that beautiful mouth and looked down at her curiously, perhaps a little dismayed at thinking I'd done something wrong. "Niko?"

She pushed me to sit upright and I complied, wondering if she wished to stop. But she did not stop. I watched as she sat up to reach me, strong abdominal muscles contracting and changing shape with effort. Those capable hands opened the Velcro of my suit as far as it would go then she pushed it over my shoulders and down my arms. I aided her efforts and within seconds I was stripped to the waist, save my halter. Those eyes, those beautiful blue windows to her soul pleaded with me then and I removed the last barrier. "Thank you."

I reached up to pull her suit apart more, willing her to see that I had needs too. She quickly gave in to my wish and we both sat upright half nude and panting in the room that had always before been for just one. At last my impatience broke and I had to know what it was like. Nothing could have prepared me for the feelings that coursed through me as I pushed her down. I slid our flesh together, breasts dragging their sensitive points across each other's skin. I began to shake, trembling as my tongue tasted the hollow of her throat. She scratched blunt nails across my back when I hit a sensitive spot and I shuddered above her, nearly undone.

Niko stopped the motion of her hands. "Are you okay?"

I paused my mouth to answer. "Yes. It's just—it's not the same."

"Hey." I raised myself up to acknowledge her query. "This is real, Julia. We are real."

She must have seen something shift in my eyes because I quickly found myself rolled to the bottom as her body covered mine. I had no time to protest or ponder the changed position because her hips settled gently between my thighs and I moaned at the pressure against my sensitized corporeal self. She stole my voice with kisses that got deeper each time she surged into me. I responded to the rising passion by digging my fingers into the powerful shoulders above, feeling the muscles that had gone hard as stone with effort. Niko held herself up even as she sought purchase below, and she drove me insane with want for her. I inserted a word between kisses and she froze, trembling. "Wait…" She looked down at me curiously and I tried to explain with swollen lips and heaving breath. "I need to feel all of you, I want to know what your reality is like." She rolled to the side and quickly stripped the suit the rest of the way off her body. I was caught, mesmerized by the sight of something I'd already seen before. But the differences were there and intense, like looking at an image on the vid screen and standing in front of the real thing. She was so very real.

"You're watching me again."

I flushed at her expectant look and quickly removed my own garments. "Can I touch you?" I think I surprised her with the request as much as I surprised myself. Niko nodded and lay down on the bed next to me and I shivered at the hot look she sent in my direction. I moved to straddle her legs, much like I had in the living room, then proceeded to map the skin below my fingertips. Her breasts were smaller, even more so than my own, and so very sensitive. Her back arched as I pinched and tugged at her nipples and reveled at the response. Eventually I covered each with my mouth and alternated between them with a sucking caress. She cried out suddenly and held my head to her. Her breath came in heaving pants and I knew that my mouth to her breasts alone had gotten her close. Those strong hands that had been holding my head desperately grasped at the coverlets of the bed when I moved lower. Every square millimeter of skin was a new world to explore, and I used all the tools I had at my disposal. Hands, teeth, lips, and tongue all joined in the effort to make her into a mewling, squirming reality within my grasp. Her legs naturally parted when I reached a certain point and I felt wetness slick against my skin. "Julia, please!" Even that was different than in my dreams. Lower and lower still, I tasted and touched while she trembled. The powerful legs that helped make her one of the best soldiers had conquered me with their embrace. I slid one finger inside easily and quickly followed with a second. The mewling beast in my bed returned and she pleaded again. "More." A third had her tensing around my thrusting digits even as the silky smooth skin tightened beneath my tongue.

I whispered in awe of her response. "You're so hard, and at the same time so very soft."

Her hand came up to weakly paw at my shoulder as she thrust upward to meet my moving fingers. "Please don't stop, I'm so close—" Niko's voice became a long low moan as I redoubled my efforts. Her substance and certainty were my only goals as I moved her toward that pinnacle. When she finally released she gave a great cry and arched her entire body off the bed below me. I continued to lap at her skin and that hardened bundle of nerves while she pulsed and shuddered around me. After a beautiful amount of time falling, she collapsed to the bed once again and I stilled all motion. Her pulse throbbed around my fingers and against the heated skin of my lips. She sighed and occasionally twitched and shook at regular intervals and I smiled. I had tasted her reality and in return received the gift of her world.

"Julia." I looked up with Niko's whisper and trembled at the fire in her eyes. She lifted a hand from the coverlets and held it out to me. My path to compliance was slow and her eyes followed every move as I crawled up her body, kiss by kiss. Impatience eventually won out and she used her strong arms to pull me he rest of the way up then gently eased me onto my back next to her. Niko leaned over me with a sublime smile and spoke in a hush. The filtered air kicked on and I strained to hear her. All while she spoke she traced the planes of my face and curves of my body. Her right hand followed a meandering path that had my temperature rising despite the chilling air. Wonder prefaced her words. "I have never known anyone like you, never been drawn to someone in such a deep and abiding way—" Her left arm was under my neck, supporting me as she cupped my breast in the palm of her free hand. I barely filled the diameter of her grasp but my nipple became turgid with the manipulation of those knowing fingers. I couldn't remember a time I'd ever been as hard as I was under Niko's touch. Her hand moved from one to the other and I gasped as a soliloquy of words fell from her lips to the breathing room around us. "—nothing more than a stranger whose gruff beauty folded me into a future I never imagined. You were my shield, my protector and savior, even as you make words claiming that I am the one who saves you…"

Her hand wandered lower and her mouth came close enough to whisper and fade those words into the skin of my neck. As Niko's hand slowly made its way down my abdomen to the damp curls below I tensed. She paused while I got used to her touch, her fingers just barely within the embrace of my folds. My head screamed and begged for her to go further, insisting she had touched me before, but my heart shook in denial that anyone had ever touched me in such a way. In the end it was my body that won the standoff as I moved my own hand up to press her firmly against me. "Please." My voice was low with need and my breath had changed to desperate hot panting. As her fingers began to move again so too did those lips. They nipped and caressed my neck, worked along my jaw and eventually bestowed their treasure deep within my mouth. Her tongue entered me as those fingers stroked me fully and I moaned into her. In a too short amount of time I found myself trembling on the precipice of our reality. Again, my brain, body, and heart all reacted differently to Niko's caress. I opened my eyes to her at the same time she just happened to gaze down at my face.

"Julia—what is it?"

Breath seized in my throat as all three parts of my being joined together as one. My exhale came out as a sobbing plea. "So close. Please don't stop, Niko. I need you to save me!"

A thought, or perhaps emotion, shifted in those blue eyes above me and the very next time she moved her caress downward along my path of wetness, she continued on just a little further. I froze as two fingers slipped all the way in. A whimper escaped as one, then both fingers curled up inside me and she waited for me to get used to the strange feeling of fullness. My body slowly relaxed and Niko must have sensed it too because she began those slow movements once again. Fingers slid in and out as the heel of her hand pressed against me with a jaw-clenching rhythm. I raced along the path of my desire and moments later I closed my eyes as pressure began to build. Nothing had ever been like it, nothing would ever be as real as her and me in that moment. When the pressure broke, a red wave of light flashed in the space behind my eyelids. My body jerked and convulsed against hers hard, and she sealed her lips to mine to swallow the guttural scream that exploded from deep inside. In that span of precious minutes there was nothing inside me but Niko. I felt her fingers deep within but at the same time I felt her everywhere else. I had not just opened my body to her pleasure, but I had also opened my mind and a single thought tumbled inside.

Julia

It was a word that whispered without words and I whispered back the same way. *I am.* What I pushed out was a thought, sure and steady, in response to hers. I didn't know how or why, but I suspected that we had connected on a much deeper level when I let down my guard completely, when I let her inside. Much the way she could see me while I was walking in her day world, our energies were synched in some way, one Walker to another.

When at last all motion stopped, with fingers still inside me, Niko lifted her head from my shoulder and gazed at me with equal parts fear and awe. "What have I done?"

I smiled and shuddered when that talented hand pulled away from my heat. When she met my eyes again I tried to reassure her. "That is an answer you already possess from our conversation earlier. You woke the dreamer."

Niko cocked her head at me. "What does that mean?"

A shiver rushed through me at the look of anticipation in those blue eyes. "I've let you in." She made to move but I clutched at her, feeling a neediness that I never had before. "Where are you going?"

She smiled and stroked my brow, perhaps sensing that I was not used to being so vulnerable or exposed. "Nowhere. I'm just going to grab the extra coverlet we kicked onto the floor." Niko crawled down the bed, giving me a view of all those things I wanted to explore further. But the events leading to my broken self-discovery had sapped my energy. She returned quickly and drew the cover up over our naked and flushed bodies. When we were sufficiently entwined again I traced a finger along the skin of her bicep. "We have a lot to talk about."

She nodded. "We have a lot to think about."

I looked up at her and watched as those eyes softened into a familiar look. "Do we have to do it right now?"

Niko smiled at me, and it was slow and languid, full of sleepy lassitude that promised all productivity was probably gone for the time being. "No." She paused and brought a hand up to trace the outer edge of my ear. "No walls?"

"What good is a wall around my heart when you are already inside?"

Niko sucked in a breath at my quote and her eyes grew shiny with emotion. I could see her thoughts racing, trying to remember the author. After a few minutes she gave in. "I don't know that one. Who said it?"

I drew her down into one last kiss before sleep then whispered the answer as we pulled apart. "Me."

Chapter Nine

Learning to See

I ROUSED A few hours later from an unexpectedly sound sleep. I had never slept next to someone before and I found Niko's presence comforting. I sat up carefully so as not to disturb her. Even in rest she had worry lines between her brows and dark smudges under her eyes. I suspected that her mother's lies and possible betrayal weighed on her more that the fact that she was a fugitive. A loud growling rumble came from my stomach and I realized that I had not eaten nearly enough since taking on my last delivery. I had also been walking more than normal, which always made me ravenous. As much as I wanted to reach out and touch the soft skin of Niko's lips, I knew we had more pressing needs. Instead of waking her, I decided to make an evening meal for both of us. I grabbed my discarded synth-suit from the floor and slipped quietly from the room. When I got into the kitchen I tried to focus on the food I had available rather than the deeper thoughts and discoveries of a few hours before. Everything seemed so much like a waking dream, it was surreal. It didn't take long to put together a passable meal of lab chicken, hydroponic vegetables, and seasoned grains. I turned to go wake Niko and found her standing in the transition area between the living room and kitchen. "I was..." My voice trailed off as I became aware of what I was seeing.

"You can see me too!"

I nodded, still a little shocked. I had never seen a Walker as my waking self and I honestly didn't know it was possible until Niko had seen me. It wasn't like there were so many Walkers around that I would have had the chance. I didn't know if it had to do with the fact that Niko and I had opened to each other or if all Walkers were able to see others as such. I thought back to that moment in the bathroom at Vanguard, before Niko and I had intimately connected in any way. My mind moved to another track. Perhaps it had to do with the power of the Walkers involved. What if only really strong Walkers could see each other, waking or dreaming? I wanted to know Niko's thoughts on the phenomenon. "What—" She interrupted me before I could finish my sentence. But it took me a few seconds to realize how.

What are you thinking so hard about? With her first word my eyes jumped to her lips and I was startled to realize that they weren't moving. Connecting mind-to-mind wasn't my imagination or a fluke earlier. *Apparently not.* She smiled as her voice came through clearly, and I smiled back.

I took my own shot at our new and amazing ability. *Can you hear me?*

Niko gave me that familiar smirk. *Of course I can.*

Then you should come eat. Dinner is ready. She made a face and her image simply disappeared. She was definitely learning.

While our brief conversation was fascinating and full of interesting potential, it was also a little alarming after spending so many years isolated. Questions bombarded me and I froze as I was scooping food into a dish. Did I have to always share my thoughts? Could she read me no matter what? I was so insulated in the concept of mental privacy that I didn't even hear Niko as she walked up behind me. I jumped when her arms came around my waist then stiffened instinctually. Something about the way that she froze in response and started to pull away told me that I had hurt her feelings. Rather than let her escape, I grabbed Niko's hands and pulled them tight to me again, holding her in place. "I'm sorry. I told you before, it really is habit." When I turned to look over my shoulder at her, I was given a sad smile.

She nodded at me. "I'm sorry too. I guess I'm just used to being around people, used to a level of comradery that you just don't really experience when you're not part of a team. Unlike you, I've never had reason to keep people at arm's distance."

I could see in her eyes that she needed to understand me. She craved that basic human connection that I had gotten used to denying myself. But I didn't have to deny it anymore. "You've changed me. You continue to change me, but a lifetime of ingrained solitude doesn't wash away overnight. Be patient?"

"Patience is not found in the great mountain as it waits for the water to wash it away. Nor is it in the rains, willing the mountain to wear down. True patience is with the sun, warm and quiescent until the storm passes."

"Mia Thomas." Niko always knew the best thing to say. Before either of us could speak again my stomach gave another rumble and I patted her hand before pulling out of the embrace. Dinner was nutritious and filling though I could tell she wasn't any more invested in the meal than I was. There was too much on our minds, too many things to discuss. As I neared the end of my food I noticed she still wore the old dingy synth-suit and berated myself internally for not fetching her package from the window box. I never gave her the security code for it so she was forced to wear clothing that was better off in the recycler.

Niko put her hand on mine as it rested on the table. *It's fine.* I jumped with surprise and jerked my hand away and when she didn't move or say any more in my head, I put my hand back. Her face though was one of chagrin. "I'm sorry, it's just so new and exciting. I forget that you've fought your entire life to keep people out of your head. And—I guess I just like sharing it with you. I like the way you feel inside when you touch me as a Walker. It seems likely that the Walker energy is what's connecting us now. It just—that's how it feels to me. Does that make sense?"

I thought about her words and analyzed the way things felt inside my own head, both when speaking mind-to-mind and when walking. She was right, they had the same flavor. I took a little more time to fold the ideas over in my mind, adding pieces here and there from my past exploration of power and what I'd learned just since meeting Niko. She waited while I thought though the things I knew to be truths. "What if—" I paused because the idea was still only half formed. My thoughts raced as another idea came to me. I quickly focused my mind on building a wall, the same way I would build a wall in my dream state to keep Walkers out. Then I turned my gaze back to curious blue eyes. "Can you read me now?"

She cocked her head and a look of concentration took over her face. Finally she shook her head. "No, not even a little. What did you do?"

"I visualized the same wall I use when I want to keep Walkers out of my dreams."

Niko had clearly never learned or thought of the concept, but then I wasn't surprised. "Show me."

I waved my hand at the dishes on the table. "Let's clean this up first then I can tell you the things I suspect, what I've learned since this new development in our ability." When everything was put away I brought one of the chairs over next to the comp and she joined me in front of the large screen. "Okay, throughout history humans have always found a way to communicate, yes?" She nodded. "Before genetic mods and basic surgery there were people who were born blind or deaf. We had languages created for both. For instance, if you were to write words that we read today, a blind person would never see to understand. And if you were to speak to someone who was deaf, they would not hear you. So each is a method of communication that the other person would not be able use or even be aware of in some ways. However some things can be learned over time."

"That makes sense." Niko's eyes were bright as I tried to put thoughts into words.

"Now there have been other ways to communicate in the past that could never be learned by people that had a handicap. For instance, some people were born unable to see certain colors." I did a quick search on the net and brought up a strange image made entirely of different colored circles. "Can you see that?"

She nodded. "Yes, it is the number fifty-seven."

"Correct." I did another search and brought up another image, the same but in gray scale. It just looked like gray circles. "Can you see the number now?"

She looked at me as if I'd gone crazy. "Of course not!"

I waved toward the vid screen. "That is what a color blind person would have seen. They could never learn to see it. Color blindness was a genetic abnormality that had a treatment discovered fifty years ago. Just as a deaf person would not be able to hear us speak."

"Julia, what are you trying to say?"

I sighed and rubbed my hand across my scalp. "I'm saying that humans have always been thought to communicate with each other along the five basic senses, but I think there are more than the traditional five that science has always assumed. The norm might be five, but there are outliers that are born with more or less. Less being blindness or lack of hearing, more being—" I paused before saying the word aloud. "—telepathy."

Her face registered shock. "But that's nothing more than science fiction!"

"Niko, think about it! What is a Dream Walker if not a mental projection of ourselves into another plane? What if that plane is not some magical 'Dream Plane' like everyone has thought for the last few decades? What if it is something bigger, something greater than any of us imagined?"

She scowled. "And why wouldn't the government have figured out any of this by now?"

"Because they shut everything down years ago! From what I've seen, government research can be a very narrow minded approach, mostly with only one or two goals. They kill or imprison Walkers so you start to lose ones with the most experience, and no one will want to cooperate beyond the basics of their jobs. We are rare and often too afraid to have contact in the dream world, let alone in the real world." She looked skeptical and I grew frustrated. "Put your head into it, Niko! Think about what or who your Walker self is and how it works. It's nothing more than a psychic projection outside your body. You can enter people's dreams because that is when their subconscious takes over and their mind is open to intrusion. During waking hours their guard is up."

"Yesss..." The word was drawn out and trailed off even as her eyes remained unfocused. I knew that the genius intellect would figure it out soon so I waited. I'd had years to gather all the pieces, but she was the person who brought the last one to my hand. Finally she looked up and the excitement that radiated from her was palpable. "The rest of the world is color blind!"

That was it, she got it! "Exactly. We have simply been born with one more sense than the majority of people. As for the other Walkers, what good is it being born with sight if you've never learned to read? The government scientists would be no help at all. It would be like someone blind from birth teaching you the letters of the alphabet. They would have no clue how to see the letters let alone know what they were called or how to string them together."

Niko shook her head in incredulity. "So the past couple decades, the dreaded Dream Walkers have been nothing more than telepaths?"

I nodded. "I think so, yes."

"Well shit." I smiled at her because the very idea was mind blowing, a game changer. But it would also make the government even more afraid if they knew we were not strictly limited to dreams.

She interrupted my dark thoughts. "So what do we do now?"

I stood and moved away from the main comp chair, waving her toward the seat. "You still have to review rules and protocol on Vanguard's net site. I'll retrieve your order so you can change into something a little fresher."

"But—"

I held up my hand to still her protests. In many ways she was a lot younger than I felt. "We still have a job to do and you only have one more day to review all the courier data before you start training. Our jobs keep us legal and out of the hands of the BENs, and that allows us to live on the outside and learn more about what we can do. If you get this done tonight, we still have one full day before we have to return to work."

"Julia, this new intel is more important! We should be

exploring every potential application of our power."

I dropped my wall and found myself flooded by — irritation, impatience, and — more. I wobbled a bit and held up my hand. "Hey, easy." I put the wall back up so I could focus. She needed to learn control and I wasn't sure how to teach her or even if I could teach her. "How is your memory?"

She paused and looked at me curiously. "Perfect, why?"

"I promise it won't take you very long to read through then you're done. The rest I can teach you when you start training."

A cocky smirk slowly spread across her beautiful lips, infuriating and attractive all at the same time. "You'll teach me? Since when?"

I shrugged. "As soon as we return to Vanguard and I tell Ryan that I'm going to be your trainer."

"Just like that, huh?"

I gave her my own look. "I'm a level ten and I've never taken a trainee before. He will find it hilarious. Not only that but I outrank him." I walked over to the window box, wondering if we would have to order more gear for her. "What did you have delivered?"

Niko stood but rather than move to the main comp chair she joined me as I punched in the code and opened the sealed door. "I got three synth-suits and a backup solar suit with helmet, boots and gloves. Also ten sets of undergarments and a wrist comp." I raised my eyebrow at her and she just shrugged. "You told me anything. It's not like I ordered a private transport or anything." I hefted the bundle out and set it on the table nearby that was placed for just such a purpose. I turned to shut the door as she opened the bundle and started separating items.

"You should sync your wrist comp to both helmets before we report back to Vanguard. Would you like me to put your extra kit in the closet for now?" She nodded but her face was hesitant, like she wanted to ask me something but was afraid. "What's wrong?"

Niko glanced from the clothing to me then she shook her head. "It's nothing."

She began gathering her things together and I grasped her forearm to stop her movement. When she looked at me I tried to get through to her. "Truth without friendship is a harsh reality, friendship without truth is no reality at all."

"Leo Durand, The Fifth Day of Silence." She sighed and her words came out in hesitant spurts. "When I complete my courier training — and I'm issued corporate housing — will you still ask me to leave?"

I sucked in a breath at her words. Truthfully her question felt like a punch to my solar plexus. Could she truly still think I'd want her to leave after she had touched me so deeply? How could two people with the ability to read minds be so confused about the other person? In a moment of clarity I realized that the silence between us was my own fault. I abruptly dropped the wall I had erected, that I had put up to keep all others out. I didn't need to keep Niko away from my head or my heart. I trusted her above all others. *I will never ask you to leave!*

"Oh!"

Drawn to her skin and wanting to ease the worry I saw etched onto her face, I reached up to smooth those brow lines with my thumb. Niko's eyes fluttered shut as my hand moved down to caress her cheek. I leaned in to the opposite side of where my hand rested. Our cheeks brushed together, the barest stroke of skin against skin that made me break out in goose bumps. When my mouth drew close to her ear I let those same words and more fall from my lips. "Niko, I will never ask you to leave. You're part of me now. We are connected on some deep and deliberate level and your absence would carve a hole into who I have suddenly become."

Her kit and clothes were forgotten as she brought her own hands up and drew me to her mouth. The kiss was as fierce a connection as I'd ever felt and I shivered at her response in my head. *You fill the parts of me I never knew were empty.* I knew then that we needed to be better, I needed to be better. There were too many things to understand and explain and I had to learn to communicate not just on her level, but on the new one that we'd discovered. They would eventually come for us. Ten years was a long time to hide from the Network and my luck would surely run out. We needed be ready for them, or we would die.

HOURS LATER FOUND us lying side by side on the bed again. It wasn't for rest, or anything more pleasurable. Niko had completed her Vanguard data review and the online comp test. With that out of the way, it freed us up to start the real training. I was surprised to find that I could slip free of my body a lot faster than normal. It seemed significantly easier than any time before. Niko appeared almost right after I did and she wore a shocked look as well. "It's never been that fast before!"

I pondered the change and hypothesized the reason. "I think it's because we've been speaking mind-to-mind for the past few hours. I wonder if that has only strengthened our mental muscles more, and we'll now find it easier to do the things we've always associated with being a Walker." We started speaking mind-to-mind right after the incident with the delivered kit, hoping to get a better understanding for each other's feel in our heads. Before she could overthink it I pointed at the closed bedroom door. "Quick, run through it now."

And she didn't think at all. She just ran straight through the door that I had been pointing at — and into the couch that sat in the living room. I knew because I heard the *thump* as she hit. Niko appeared a few seconds later with a red face. She rubbed the back of her neck in frustration. "I thought I had it!"

I knew better than to laugh at her. "It just takes practice." She scowled and it was so cute I had to turn away so she wouldn't see me smile. The big strong soldier really didn't like failing at anything. I managed to clear all mirth from my face before I looked back at her from over my shoulder. "Let's try a different way. Attack me from behind."

Niko gave me a skeptical look. "You can't flip me if I'm expecting it. I've got at least ten kilograms of muscle on you."

I shrugged. "If you say so." That cocky look returned to her handsome face and I knew I had her sufficiently baited. She came at me from behind, trusting in her physical strength and superiority. Tapping into my internal power, I grabbed her arm and twisted then flipped her perfectly over my shoulder. But while she was surprised by my move, she did exactly what she needed to, disappearing through the floor into the apartment below.

Niko floated up seconds later with a disgusted look on her face. "Do you know what they do down there?" She pointed at the floor below her feet.

I nodded. "I've seen worse."

She shuddered. "Depravity is everywhere."

"Gibbons." Niko smiled at my response. I addressed her again, back on task. "Now, what lesson did you just learn?"

Those blue eyes looked back at me but were lost in thought as she pondered the answer. "Physical strength means nothing in a mental world."

"Good. Now on to the next lesson. Where do you get the mental strength?"

Her answer was immediate. "From within."

She was fast, she was smart, and Niko seemed to excel at whatever task was placed in front of her. "Let's teach you how to build a wall to protect yourself from other Walkers..."

WE TRAINED FOR HOURS after that. It was near twenty-four hundred when we finally decided to stop for the night. When we finished training in the dream world, or rather, psychic plane as we had been surmising, we slipped back into our bodies. I wasn't surprised to find myself tired and with a slight headache. I had experienced mental exhaustion many times as a Walker. Niko stirred in her own body and I watched closely as tiny lines of pain appeared between her brows. She groaned and brought a hand up to press against the space between her eyes. I rolled left and grabbed a couple of pain tabs from the drawer next to my bed. I put one under my tongue and held the other out to her. "Here, this should help."

Niko groaned again. "My head feels like someone has taken a bolt gun to it. It's never hurt like this before." Her eyes were still shut so I gently pressed the stim tab against the fingers of her free hand. She placed it under her tongue and waited. About thirty seconds later she took her hand away and the lines of pain began to ease.

I cautioned her, already having guessed the cause of her pain. "I wouldn't try talking mind-to-mind right now. I think you may have overexerted yourself today." Those blue eyes still carried discomfort when she looked at me. "Do you need another tab?"

She paused for a few seconds to think it over and I watched as Niko gritted her teeth. I already knew what she was going to say because Niko was a soldier and they were all the same. "I'm good, thanks." No sooner had she gotten the words out and I was slipping another tab between her fingertips.

"Don't tough it out. This is completely new for you. If you work too long and damage yourself, it will only delay our training. I broke my cardinal rule and didn't set a timer when we started walking. This is my fault."

After placing the second tab under her tongue Niko took my hand in hers. We were lying side by side on my bed, hand in hand, and I wasn't afraid. I had never been so close to someone, never been so open, but I trusted Niko with my life. "Why aren't you in more pain?" I shivered a little when she spoke, her voice slightly husky with the late hour.

"I'm used to this. I've been walking for twenty-five years so my uh, mental muscles are built up I guess. But even I can overexert myself. And if you snap back into your body while you're walking, you can get a headache or worse. The farther away from your body you are, the more dangerous it is."

She grew concerned. "How dangerous? Like the night your parents died?"

I nodded. "Concussion-like symptoms, hemorrhaging, burst blood vessels, maybe even eardrums. I'm not sure of everything that can happen, I try to avoid it if I can. I just know that it was traumatic when I did it a decade ago and not something I want to repeat."

We lay there for a few minutes longer, both of us processing the dangers to what we could do then Niko abruptly sat up and ran a hand through her hair. "I should—we should probably get some sleep. I'll leave you to your space."

Panic gripped me, but it was diametrically different from what I had always felt in the past. I had never been worried for someone to leave my presence before. But I didn't want her to go. I reached out with a tentative hand and drew her back down to the bed. She let me, eyes never leaving my face. When her head was back on the pillow next to my own I smiled at her, knowing she was trying to understand my usual need for space and my sudden want for company. "Stay."

She rolled to her left side and watched me intently. "Why?"

"Because you're part of me now. I'm comforted by your presence and soothed by your little analyzing looks and your touch. Niko, I never knew exactly how lonely I was until I met you and found myself no longer alone." I sighed and reached out to take her hand again. "When I said I'd never ask you to leave, that wasn't a passive declaration. That was me saying that I want you here and that I like being part of you."

Niko brought her hand up to touch the skin of my lips, then moved her fingertips to that scar in my eyebrow. "Even with so onerous a past between us, between my family and yours, my career and your life? You like being linked to each other when our future is uncertain and I've brought even more danger to your life?"

My eyes fluttered shut when she stroked the fine hairs of my left eyebrow. Finally I opened them because I really needed her to see it all. Despite the possibility of pain, I opened everything I had been keeping inside and pushed it toward her. "I only had existence before and my existence has always been fraught with danger. But you are the first person who offered me life, who has brought me to life." I gently took her fingers into my own and guided her hand to the center of my chest. "You woke more than just my power, I—" I didn't know how to say it. I couldn't say it. Some words had power beyond their base meaning and I wasn't ready to give all the power away, but I didn't have to. She knew.

"I understand." Niko's smile was the sweetest thing I'd ever seen and when she kissed me I felt an unfamiliar emotion burst through my skin. I knew that instant that she felt it too because she stiffened against my lips and clung to the front of my synth-suit. The word that coursed through both of us whispered from her lips. "Hope."

I reached behind her neck to seal us together tighter and risked the pain of two more words. *Yes, hope.*

Chapter Ten

The Rise of Us

"HOW DOES IT feel?" Ryan had tried unsuccessfully to surprise me as he walked up but after a month and a half of training with Niko, I felt him approach in my head. Just as I promised her, my request for a trainee was approved with no issues, only shock. Ryan immediately asked if we were lovers and I couldn't help blushing, which of course answered for me. I'd known him for a long time but he never really knew me. He gave me a strange smile and made a grand show of welcoming on the first day I started training at the facility with her. The in-facility training wasn't anything Niko couldn't handle. We used the strengthening equipment and I learned more defensive and offensive techniques from my trainee than she did from me, which seemed incongruous with my position.

Ryan was still looking at me expectantly and I returned his look with the slightest smile curving my lips. He was referring to the completion of Niko's internship. It was the first time I'd ever trained a courier so he was naturally curious. "It feels fine. She was an excellent student, very capable and intelligent." Out in the field was where I did most of my teaching and that was where I based my opinions on Niko's performance. To facilitate with her training I was given a variety of jobs that would take us to every Vanguard facility within a hundred mile radius of Chicago. We practiced different routes to all of them. She memorized both the delivery and security protocols and met all the researchers who would receive the data or prototype tubes. To say that the people at the satellite facilities were surprised to see me turn up with a trainee would have been an understatement. But Niko met each challenge with enthusiasm and grace. She had more than her fair share of confidence and charisma as she joked or just socialized with every new associate we met. We were very different people and she mentioned it more than once.

My thoughts were brought up short again as Ryan spoke. His voice was full of good- natured curiosity and I had to fight that familiar urge to shut down and close him out. Niko wasn't the only one learning over the past month and a half. "What will she do now? I hear there are a few veterans who have already put in a request to have her join their team." Ryan was a gossip and he often kept me informed of upcoming jobs and hot item information at Vanguard headquarters, the courier division in particular. And he never seemed to mind that the information only ever flowed one way. By keeping mostly to myself, I rarely had any news of interest so the point was usually moot. But I let my smile widen as he stood staring at me. His eyebrows went up in astonishment. "You?"

I nodded. "Yes."

"Of course, I should have known. You've certainly changed, Jules." My brows drew down with irritation, wondering what his comment meant and he held up his hand with a laugh. "Cool off there, courier. I meant that in a good way. I've always suspected there was a living, breathing human beneath that black suit. It's nice to have my theory confirmed. Did you get final approval or are you still awaiting Yates's decision?"

I couldn't help laughing at his ridiculous statement. "I suppose I am human indeed. But yes, I've already spoken with Karen about it and she seemed delighted to team us up. She's going to let Niko know her assignment at the end of the review."

"I bet she's creaming her synth-suit to have the best team in the country under her purview! Between the two of you, every job will be a surety."

I turned and punched him hard in the arm. "Every delivery with me was already a surety!" He rubbed his arm and nodded, accepting the mild physical abuse for subtly disparaging my perfect record.

"Yes, but the city has changed with so many BENs on the streets now. I hear they're even starting to harass the papered wagers and I have to wonder if couriers are next. They're looking for someone but it seems to be top secret who it is. Some say it's a defector from the General's inner circle. And right now we've got someth—" He abruptly stopped talking and furtively glanced around.

In an unfamiliar show of friendship, I tentatively placed my hand on his forearm. "It's okay, I've already heard something hot is coming down the pipe. They're worried the government will get their hands on it, aren't they?" He nodded. Perhaps one of the best kept secrets in all the courier division involved one of the biggest gossips. I had re-conned most of the upper managers within my company and discovered something very interesting a few years back. Ryan and Karen Yates, our manager, were lovers. That meant he was often privy to a lot of information that should have been well above his level. He rarely abused the knowledge he learned from our boss. Usually it was just to give me a heads up on a job. And any information given to me never had an outlet because I had no one else in my life. "Is it that big?"

He whispered the answer and the look on his face said that he had even more information to pass on. "It will change the world." Ryan looked around one more time and I sensed he was going to tell me the true nature of the project. "They've developed artificial leaves that filter the air at an unprecedented rate. The chloroplastic conversion is fueled by sunlight alone." He leaned even closer so that he was almost whispering in my ear. "Beckett has ten prototype trees in the main lab right now, sitting under solar lamps. They're filtering pollutants and creating oxygen at such a high rate that they've shut down the filters in that wing and are pulling air from the lab alone. Becket also says that we only need to dedicate fifty percent of our production facilities to the new tech and that will produce enough of the eco-trees to eliminated the need for helmets in North America within a decade."

Shock rippled across my face. He hadn't been lying. Eliminating the need for filters within a decade would bring health and freedom to so many people. It would change everything. Another realization came across my consciousness. "The government, specifically the General, won't like that."

Ryan looked startled at my words. "I guess I never thought about it like that but I think you're right. People won't be so easy to herd or track if they don't need suits to go outside. The possibilities for our future are staggering."

I nodded and thought to myself that a lot of things had changed the world. Changing the world was not always a good thing and I also wondered what a scared Rennet would do. But the tech Vanguard had created would certainly flip our society on its side. And Ryan's words — there was such a push of promise to them that I couldn't help wishing for something good to come of it. Only time would tell. I was deep in thought, considering all potential problems with a deeper BEN probe of all travelers for another five minutes until I jumped a little when words filtered into my consciousness.

Did you know?

I snorted with laughter and Ryan stared at me so I pointed at my ear to indicate I had a call on my cochlear implant. I didn't of course. Niko and I had been communicating a lot since the initial discovery of our telepathic ability. It frustrated her to no end that my twenty-five years of mental discipline had given me a distinct advantage when it came to keeping secrets from her, despite our mental connection. *I knew. Surprise.*

Her excitement was palpable through our connection and if I had to assign it a flavor it would be light and sweet. *So we're permanent partners now, not just temporary?*

I smiled as her joy came through. *For as long as you want.* Before Niko, sharing myself had been limited to my dreams and never involved such an exchange of emotion. Our newly realized mental powers of communication extended beyond mere telepathy to encompass empathy as well. I had no clue how it could be between two people and I never wanted to be that bereft of feeling again.

Her voice sounded in my head again and I shivered. She was right, I liked the way she felt inside me. *We're nearly finished here. Be out in a minute.*

As if he could hear our inner conversation, Ryan chose that moment to speak again. "Shift's almost done and Niko should be out soon. What do you two have planned? Going to try for an early dinner somewhere?"

I stared at him in admonishment. "What do we look like, white wagers? Besides, with curfew in place we'll be lucky to get home in time. We've got the next two days off and I don't want to bunk here simply because we can't travel to my apartment without papers."

He sighed. "Yeah, good point. I didn't think of that." Just then Niko emerged from the hall that led to the courier manager's office and my eyes were drawn to her. She continued to keep her hair longer on top and clipped short on the sides. I counseled her against having something so long when she spent the majority of her job in a helmet. But much to my pleasure, she stubbornly refused to listen. Watching the black suited figure come toward me I was reminded of just how strong she could be, in and out of the exercise facility. My mouth went dry as I remembered how her muscles and smooth skin felt beneath the tips of my fingers. An indrawn breath followed the memory of her surging into my hand after an intense session of psychic walking. Something must have shown on my face because Ryan nudged my arm and smirked down at me. "Something tells me that, white wage dinner or no, you'll be celebrating her promotion to full courier this evening."

I reluctantly pulled my eyes away from Niko and turned a familiar darkened look to my longtime co-worker. "That data is level 10 access only." He snorted and rolled his eyes. It had been a point of competition for years that I had jumped ahead of him in rank, but he never held it against me. Why would he? He had achieved the job he ultimately wanted as the training manager, and he was sleeping with the boss to boot. We were all happy.

Niko made a brief stop to exchange her trainee badge with her new Level 2 courier ident. It was quite a surprise when she did so well during training that they skipped her a level. I wondered if that had more to do with our future assignments than actual training performance. After picking up the badge she made her way over to where Ryan and I were standing. "Congratulations, Niko. You'll make a fine courier, despite being trained by the antisocial night owl." He jerked his thumb at me and I took it in stride.

Of course she smiled. "Thank you, Ryan." He was called away when one of the assistants popped her head out the door of the training facility. Niko looked at me with a smirk. "Antisocial night owl?"

I shrugged. "Well I am."

"You were." I leveled a look at her, very close to the one I gave to Ryan minutes before. I was caught by those blue eyes as they softened toward me. "You've changed, Jules, and people are starting to notice. You even cracked a joke with Dr. Bosche the other day."

Her statement made me wonder. "I don't feel that different. You are the social one whenever we make a delivery or train inside the facility."

Niko put her hand on my arm and I felt it all the way through my solar suit. Her mere touch energized my dreams. "You don't see it because you're too close to see the slow change. You're on the inside looking out."

"You're just as close, living and working with me every day."

The look in her eyes made me shiver. "I see everything, Jules."

A bit of my solitary defense reared its head and I couldn't hold in my stubborn words. "You only see everything because I allow you inside."

She smiled then and I didn't have to be a mind reader to know I had just won the argument for her. "Yes you do." Two months ago I would have killed rather than allow someone inside. I had killed.

I sighed. "Come on, partner. We have to burn sun if we're going to make it back to our apartment before curfew." We raced the streets home as the sun slowly faded over the west side of the city. Luckily we didn't have to cross any bridges but I was still glad to pull into the safety of the parking structure space. The parking garage was pretty secure, needing a security code to open the door. But for the courier tenants that had personal vehicles, each apartment had essentially their own locked garage within the garage. It cut down on tampering and thefts by the degens. Niko's excitement was palpable as we unlocked and entered the apartment. I couldn't help but be caught up as we put our kit away. While the solar suits, gloves, boots, and helmet were not all individually heavy, it still added up when wearing them all day. It was good to get my kit stowed and walk around in the relative freedom of my synth-suit.

Or you could walk around without.

Niko typically didn't startle me any more when speaking mind-to-mind unless I was deep in thought on something. And in the past month we had learned a lot about the different levels of privacy we held for our thoughts. Some thoughts were like office chatter, and if we listened we could hear them easily. Those were the thoughts that we could block with a complete wall. Others were buried a lot deeper and took work to get to and we decided early on that those would be off-limits. We both still needed some semblance of privacy no matter how much we craved our connection. I was the first to figure out how to build a wall around just those inner thoughts, thus still allowing communication mind-to-mind. Niko, of course, picked up the knack quickly. But as much as we marveled over the mental connection we shared, nothing could ever compete with the physical one.

When I didn't answer her suggestion, Niko stepped even closer and I shivered at her nearness. Personal space had become a thing of the past, just like the walls I had kept up between us. "You have no answer for me?"

Her hair had become tousled while in the helmet and I reached out a hand to run my fingers through the silky strands. Niko's eyes fluttered closed and I lost myself in the nearness of her. "Do you need me to say the words aloud?" In her head I spoke again. *Do you need me to say it at all?*

She opened those amazing blue eyes and smirked at both my statements. It was a smile that I had loved to hate and hated to love when we first met. I pulled her in and our mouths met with that familiar burn of passion. She opened herself further to me as we stood in the middle of my living space. There were no secrets between us and I knew her excitement was born of accomplishment. Niko didn't care that she had once been a captain of the General's private cadre. She didn't care that she was a former prodigy and a high level genius. She was excited that she passed into a level 2 courier position. Like the proverbial cat, she had landed on her feet. I was so distracted by her excitement that I never noticed her hands moving down my chest until the distinctive sound of Velcro drew me from her lips. The material pulled apart all the way to the apex where my legs met the body of the suit. Taking advantage of my momentary surprise, she quickly pulled my suit down over my shoulders then the rest of the way down my legs until I could step free. I removed my undergarments and felt suddenly exposed. My hand reached out to her and gently tugged the open collar of her suit. Arousal had stolen my breath, leaving my voice strangely quiet. "You too."

Her eyes held mischief as she took in my slightly parted lips and shining eyes. They were shining for her. When she was stripped down to match me the breath froze in my throat. Despite the similarity in height, I looked at Niko and compared her to the ancient Greek goddesses I'd read about in my comp literature program. She watched me watching her and I felt her excitement build. After undressing there was too much space between us so I quickly closed the gap and pulled her into the circle of my arms. The kiss started light, just a gentle caress of her tongue against my bottom lip. From there she brought us together over and over until I finally granted entrance. I brought my hands up to grasp the back of her neck and tried to pull us even tighter together. "Niko." I breathed her name from one kiss to the next.

Without any warning, verbal or otherwise, Niko suddenly bent down a little and grabbed me in that juncture where my ass ended and my hamstrings began. She lifted me into the air until I could wrap my own legs around her waist. Her strength amazed me and turned me on more than I'd ever been in my dreams. She started walking us toward the couch but I wanted more room. *Bed!*

Then I tried something new that we hadn't even talked about yet. I attempted to project the image of us on the bed, our bodies entwined and beaded with sweat. Niko almost dropped me as she ripped her lips from mine. "Fuck, Julia! You're going to make us fall!"

The back of her head had just enough hair to get a tight grip, so I did. "I suggest you walk faster!" She complied but I got her again as we reached the bed. When I sent an image of her lips kissing me much lower she did drop me then proceeded to make my vision a reality. I writhed beneath her touch and with every stroke and caress to the most tender parts of my body I spiraled higher. The pressure built beyond my ability to hold it all in and in a matter of heartbeats I came undone. A primal scream tore from my lips and so too the heart and soul of me. Even as I died and was reborn, shaking and convulsing on the bed below, I rose higher and higher through the ceiling and above the apartment building. Dark had fallen over the city, but there were still lights in buildings and along shipping routes. I stopped rising and spun in place to watch the world in wonder. It was beautiful and perfect and — lonely. As if I had summoned her by thought alone, her form came speeding upward until we floated on the same level. "What took you so long?"

Niko gave me an incredulous look as she drew me into her arms. Our dream selves were clothed once again but there was something about floating high above the city that kept the moment intimate. "It wasn't like you left in a calm moment. I watched you leave your body, Julia. I thought for a second that you'd died the way you flew straight up." She made a face. "It took me a minute to calm down enough to follow."

I spun us slowly so we could take in the night view. "This is beautiful."

"You are beautiful."

The only light at the top of the building was from the beacon that warned air transports and drones away from its height. Even in the darkness I could see the look in her eyes and it made me uncomfortable. With a free hand I rubbed my short-cropped hair self-consciously. "I — I'm not. I'm just me, Niko." I looked away from her, down at the city below where they hunted us like dogs. I thought about the scars on my body and mind from years of testing. My entire life had only ever been about loss. Niko's words and emotions that filled me were contradictory to everything I had always known. Not for the first time I wondered how much of what Niko felt for me was her own emotion and how much was due to the situation we had been thrown into. Was it possible for one mind to overwhelm the other in our dreams?

"Julia." She called me so softly but still I heard. When I looked up her eyes seemed deeper somehow. It could have been a trick of the light, or something that was just her alone, but the look caught and held me. "I love you."

It was too soon, it was too much. I shook my head back and

forth trying to deny words that my heart already knew. "No—"

She caught my hands and pulled me even closer then started dragging us back down. "We have to go back."

I let her pull me but regretted the rapidly fading height and view of the capital. "Niko, why?"

It was almost like we were in a fairy tale, with two lovers flying through the city at night. We passed quickly through the building below us until once again settling into our bedroom. She waved toward our bodies where they lay collapsed on the bed. "Please." I nodded and slipped back into myself. The first thing I noticed was that she was still inside me. When she stirred coming back to herself I gave a little whimper. She whispered to me as she slowly withdrew her fingers. "Sorry." Before I could say a word she quickly crawled up the bed until we lay on our sides facing each other.

Curiosity was a powerful thing and I was not immune. "Why did we have to come back? What was so important that we had to leave such a beautiful view and return to the reality below?"

Niko reached up with a tentative hand and caressed my cheek. I closed my eyes and sank into her touch. *This time it's you who doesn't understand.*

My words were loud in the silent room. "What don't I understand?" I tried to push her again. "Why did you say those words?"

"Drop your walls and I'll tell you." I looked at her skeptically and she elaborated. "All of your walls, Julia."

The breath caught in my throat. If I did as she asked, it would be an invitation for her to come inside and see the very heart of me. "And if I don't?"

Niko shook her head sadly. "Then you will never understand."

I swallowed the lump in my throat and shut my eyes. It didn't take long, and the process wasn't extensive that allowed me to be completely open. It was just very—specific. When I was done I looked at her again and those smiling blue eyes caught me. I wasn't sure what to think of her words or actions leading up to that point but I never expected her to just step inside. It was more than a simple mind reading. I felt her within and the fullness was strange. Then the fullness began to expand. *What...* Words failed at the immense pressure of love that poured from her into me and expanded my sense of self and the feeling of us. Her love burned the last of the shadows that I kept hidden away and sealed the wounds of my past.

This is how I feel. There is more to you than just your body. There is more to any of us than our past. I see all of you and I think that you're beautiful.

Niko was beautiful light inside me and the crack she had opened months ago was suddenly and irrevocably split asunder. I met her thoughts with my own. *Love isn't a gift to be passed around like stolen gold. It is a tidal wave that forces you off course and takes you to distant and exciting lands.*

Dylan Emery

I nodded and let the word fall from my lips. "Yes." Then before she could get away, before she could pull out of me completely, I found four more words to give. "I love you, too." And like two people possessed, we proved those words over and over throughout the night.

Chapter Eleven

The Promise

"WHY WON'T YOU teach me?" Frustration colored Niko's words as she faced me in the center of our apartment. I could not only see the slow burn of anger just behind her eyes, but I could also feel it. She was angry that I refused to show her what she considered a vital weapon against the Network. Like me, she had killed too many times in her line of duty. But how could I explain what it was like when you killed another person while dream walking, killed them with no other tool but yourself? How could I tell her what it was like when your mind was inside another living being as they died? A little part of you died with them. I never struggled with the morality of it all before Niko. It was just a matter of survival. But she had opened more than just my ability to love and to see without sight. Could I let her feel the horror that accompanied a psychic killing? She still hadn't mastered the newest trick I learned, which was how to slip free from our bodies when not in a calm state, although the psychic walking had gotten easier for both of us with each day that passed by.

Decades of practice made the transition from dreams to reality as common as breathing for me, but I was intimately familiar with mental control in all its forms. That was not the case with Niko. Some things she would pick up quickly, but others were more difficult concepts to grasp. I suspected she was still too tied to her notions of self and the real world while in the dreamer plane. I'd been operating with one foot in my head for nearly my entire life. I scrubbed a hand over my scalp and blew out a sigh. "Why do we have to keep going over this?"

"Because you're being stubborn! This could be life or death for us, and you know it."

Things were so perfect on every level with the exception of this one divergence of opinion. Our lives slipped seamlessly into each other, though truthfully she mostly slipped into mine. But it was the little things that kept us happy. We were simple and similar in so many regards. I discovered that she liked to read, just as I did, although I should have known that from the beginning by her ability to dispense quotes for any occasion. We both trained hard and were driven and dedicated when it came to our jobs. And Niko had a way about her, a passion that taught me things I never knew about myself. Our compatibility ran deep, both physically and mentally and it fueled the connection we shared.

My thoughts were interrupted by the vibration of my wrist comp and I knew I had found my reprieve from the familiar argument. "We can talk about this later, but for now we have to go." Her anger increased, battering at me in pulsing waves. I knew she hated being put off, and every time I told her no, the discontent dug its way deeper inside her. But we had a job to do, perhaps the most important of our career, and I couldn't afford to be distracted. With that singular thought in mind I blocked her out.

Niko felt it as soon as my wall went up and her face went from one of displeasure to stricken. It had been months since we confessed our love, and I had not once closed myself off from her. I felt the loss as acutely as she did, but it had to be done. "Why?" Her voice was quiet in the hum of the apartment filters.

My face fell into that familiar mask of coldness, that old indifference that I had thought gone forever. "We have a job to do. Now is not the time for this discussion and continuing this argument will only make us distracted on the job. A job that can be life or death for us. You've read the memo. The samples will be a beacon to everyone from Vanguard's competitors to the government. This is important enough that they're sending out a couple different courier teams with empty tubes as a distraction. You have to focus, Niko!"

"Fine!" The word ground out between her teeth and she stalked by me to don the rest of her kit from the closet. I already had my boots and gloves on. I just needed my helmet.

Niko maintained silence all the way to Daley, not even asking my plan for the upcoming deliveries. She should have been full of questions simply because we were making multiple deliveries instead of just one. When we arrived at headquarters I didn't pull into the parking structure as normal protocol dictated. My instructions arrived on my wrist comp right before Niko and I fought in our apartment and I didn't get a chance to tell her the change in plans. I led us around the block to the research bay and her voice finally came over my helmet com. "Where are we going?"

I glanced over at her but saw nothing of her expression because of our blacked-out face shields. "Change of protocol came in right before we left. I didn't get a chance to tell you and I'm sorry." We paused to wait for the secure dock doors to open and I glanced off to the west. The sun was setting and while it was visible for once, it was also disconcertingly blood red. I hoped it wasn't a sign of things to come.

"Hey."

She called to me as we waited for security clearance and I looked over at her. Niko's faceplate cleared and I saw the turmoil she was in. Her voice came through my inside com. "I'm sorry, Jules. I don't like blocking from you — or being blocked. I know you, and you wouldn't be so adamant if you didn't have good reason. Sometimes I push and it doesn't always have a good result."

I cleared my own shield and shook my head at her sad blue eyes. "No, it doesn't." I paused and conceded my own apology. "I'm sorry too. I should have tried to explain better but I promise we can talk more when this is done."

She nodded and our attention was caught as the security door slid open in front of us. Without another word we rode forward and joined the five other teams inside. We left our bikes parked in the loading bay and walked over to the rest of the group. I was shocked that there were no other people in the normally busy bay. My eyebrows went up at the gathering of so many couriers since I was only expecting one or two other teams besides us. If that wasn't enough to surprise me, the presence of Goeta-sen surely did. He stood in a cluster of top managers that included William Becket, the head of research, our boss Karen, and James Carville, the North American Director of Production.

Two techs stood off to the side with carts of carrier tubes and chip feeders. My conversation with Ryan came back to me and I had a feeling that our biggest threat in this job would be from the government agents. Vanguard was certainly acting as if that were the case. I felt a tendril of curiosity flit through my head and I looked at Niko and shrugged. Part of me wanted to dip inside to read one of them. Emotions were easy. They were like pulsing waves that emanated off people when they were strong. But thoughts, you had to kind of push inside to read the thoughts of a sightless person unless they were asleep. It was exhausting but Niko and I had practiced on various people while working out at the courier facility. We didn't want to be unethical so it was only to skim surface thoughts, but it still took a lot of mental effort. It was effort neither of us could afford to expend when the answer was about to be made known. Karen was the one that called us all to attention.

"I want to thank you in advance for your excellent years of service to Vanguard and apologize for the strange change of protocol at the last minute. You're all here because you're the best and you've proven yourself to this company."

A voice called out from the group though I couldn't see who it was with all our helmets on. "The hotshot newb hasn't proven herself yet. Why is she here?"

Our boss's response was deadly serious. "Not only did Ms. Jones score perfect on the Vanguard placement chart, but she's paired with our most senior courier, who also happens to be the only courier with a perfect record. Now if we can get back to the matter at hand, this delivery is more important than simple rivalries and petty sniping."

The helmet on the far side of the group glanced our way and gave a single nod. "I apologize." I recognized who it was then— Canfield. I turned him down years ago when he requested to partner with me. Even if I hadn't been set on riding alone, we would have never been a good fit.

"Good. I'm going to turn it over to Goeta-sen now to explain this particular delivery."

She stepped back and Goeta-sen moved forward. I was struck again by his small stature and penchant for corrective lenses. Defying his unassuming look, Yasushi Goeta's voice was loud in the cavernous space. "Today's delivery is not something to be taken lightly. It is the most important advancement our company has ever created. That is why we have concerns about the security of getting the prototypes and blueprints to the production facilities that are nearest to the capital. We have called in six teams instead of the original three to cause confusion for those looking to stop our couriers." Murmuring ran through the small crowd of us and he held up his hands. "Senior couriers will be given the prototype tubes, and junior couriers will be chip-loaded with the plans. All teams will make deliveries to the six Chicago region plants, and each team will have a different order of delivery. Any questions?"

A hand went up, a level 7 named Janna Smith. "Are we more worried that our competitors will steal the tech, or the government? The BENs are thick right now and have been for months. Is this tech the reason why?"

The director shook his head. "I'm afraid that has nothing to do with us. But the government are the ones we are most afraid of with this tech. We cannot let it fall into their hands."

Uncharacteristically, I spoke up in the crowd. "Is it that bad?"

He smiled and it was the same smile he bestowed on me the first time I met him after he learned I also had a perfect Vanguard score. "No Jules-sen, it is that good. Now, I'll let William-sen explain the procedure for this delivery."

The head of research wasn't a broad man, but he was tall and lanky and wore a perpetually serious face. While not as loud as the director, his voice was still easily heard over the large overhead filters for the research bay. "When we get started we will call each team up to receive their delivery schedule, chip loads, and Courier tubes. Seniors will get a security load only to protect the tubes while the junior courier will get the data load and a set of dummy tubes. Any questions?"

Another hand went up. "Why are we doing it like this?"

He sighed and I practically felt the worry seeping from him, despite keeping myself partially shielded. "Because we ran the numbers and statistically speaking, this has the greatest chance of success without the government co-opting our tech. Any other questions?" The crowd remained silent and he gave us the first smile I'd ever seen from him. "Now before you get your details, I'll give you the good news. Upon the delivery completion of all six live tubes, each team will be given a twenty thousand cred bonus."

"Fuck!" I didn't know who said it but I certainly shared their sentiment. That was half our yearly pay. Teams would have to split it, but still.

That's a lot of money for new tech, especially if all six teams deliver.

I looked at the nervous techs then back at the white wagers and answered Niko's words in my head. *It certainly is.* I glanced at my lover and issued a warning. *We're going to have to be especially careful with this one. It will involve a lot of checkpoints. So far your ident has held, but it would only take one soldier at a checkpoint who actually knew you to blow it all to fuck.*

She smiled at me through the clear plate. *Luckily I didn't socialize much outside my inner circle. We were an elite group that traveled with him all over the country, specializing in the General's personal safety. So I didn't fraternize with the common grunts that went out on patrol*

I grinned back at her and keyed my internal helmet com. "Lucky you."

"JP-10!" I looked up as our team ident was called. We had

been caught in our heads long enough for half the teams to be loaded and gone. Niko was directed to the tech on the left and I to the one on the right. There she received her chip load and holder with six empty tubes. I held my arm out to get my own chip load as Karen walked up.

"Just another day, eh Jules?"

I have her tight smile. "I wouldn't exactly call it that."

She nodded toward Niko as she imprinted with each tube. "How's she doing?"

With those words my smile turned open and warm and I raised my face shield completely so we could talk better. "She's the best I've seen. If routes are closed down she always knows the alternate way to go, even without bringing it up on the HUD. I think she memorized a map of the city in her first week."

"Better than you?" A wash of pride swelled up inside me and I couldn't help letting a little of it out in my expression. Karen laughed. "Ah Jules, you've certainly changed."

I started imprinting to my tubes but spared one last glance at her. "So I've heard." It was a nice touch that Goeta-sen took the time to shake all of our hands before we left. But with the schedule being so tight, I wasn't surprised that they dangled the carrot of such a bonus. I wondered if some of the couriers had realized yet that we had to maneuver all the checkpoints to make our deliveries, some of them two hours out from the Daley center, all within our twenty-four hour delivery period. I watched the tube set. They never changed the times. And out of the entire lot of them, there was only one team besides ours that made regular midnight runs. After we had each stowed our tubes in the secure paniers, we mounted our bikes but I held Niko back. "Wait."

Her face shield was still clear and she gave me a curious look. "Why?"

I nodded toward the last two teams that were stowing their tubes. "I want to let them leave first." We waited as first one team left, then the other. *I also wanted to do this while we are still safe.* Before she could ask I dropped the walls between us. I knew that letting myself be so open would show her the depth of my fear.

Why are you so afraid of this job?

She had seen it but not known the reason why. *I'm afraid for you. I'm afraid they'll find you and take you away from me.*

She smiled at me and I was taken back to that place in our dreams, high above the city. Her words in my head interrupted the image of that transformative moment. *You only used to be afraid for yourself.*

I laughed in my helmet and keyed the com between us. "Apparently I've changed." I glanced up and gave a nod toward the door where the techs were waiting to shut and secure it again. "Let's go." I had memorized the delivery schedule then destroyed it before we even mounted our bikes. Our drop order had mid-range deliveries first then back into the city and finally ending with the facility in Milwaukee. That one was about a hundred and forty kilometers north of the capital, but at least the drive would take us along Lake Michigan, not that we'd see much but the big shippers at night. Outside Chicago, the checkpoints were few and far between, just open road. I felt secure enough to run with high beams on most of the way, rather than our night vision. The first drop was Michigan City, which followed the highway southeast around the big lake. We passed through two checkpoints just to get out of downtown and on the highway. We hit another about halfway there. After Michigan City, we came back down to the Gary plant, passing through another checkpoint. The third stop was a little farther out, roughly southwest of Chicago. It was about another forty-five minutes over to Joliet, so we didn't arrive until 0040 hours. We took our first break at the Joliet facility, grabbing a pre-pack from their canteen and downing a stimulant. There were very few people around as we refueled our bodies and Niko's voice was hushed in the large cafeteria. If the other late night diners in the plant didn't know we were couriers by the black suits, then the helmets sitting on our table would have surely given us away.

"We're making good time. It's been surprisingly smooth through all the checkpoints outside of Chicago. Maybe their net isn't as wide as I thought. Or maybe they think I've already fled north."

I thought about her words and shook my head. "It's almost too easy."

Niko looked at me curiously. "Why do you say that? My ident is good, and I look nothing like the picture they have on their readers for Nikolette Morgan. I saw it at the highway checkpoint coming out of Chicago. Souza's alteration was perfectly smooth because they don't even realize the image is wrong. They're making us clear faceplates and they haven't made a match yet."

Leaning closer, I stared into those blue eyes that I would be lost without. "That's the problem. They're still really hot on you and sooner or later someone who knows you will see your old net ident and realize the image is wrong." I sighed and dropped my head into my hands, rubbing the stubble nervously. "I hate this. Every single checkpoint is like playing Russian roulette right now!"

"Jules—" Niko lowered her voice and the emotion behind it made me tremble. It made me fear what she would say next. I lifted my head from my hands and met her too serious eyes. "We need to plan for the eventuality that they figure it out."

Fear coursed through me at the thought of being in BEN hands. "I won't let them take either of us!"

She reached over and touched my hand and tried her best to soothe my fears through our connection. "The fact is that they're primarily looking for me right now. They know who they're looking for. Yes, they want Dreamer Zero too, but they don't know who she is. If the time comes that my game is up, you need to get away. You'll have the best chance and you can't fall into their hands. I trust that my mother will protect me from the worst that Rennet would do."

In my very deepest thoughts, farther down that Niko ever penetrated, I knew that her mother would do no such thing. The longer the manhunt went on, the more I suspected that Dr. Morgan wasn't as innocent as Niko had been hoping. "I don't want to leave you."

Julia, no matter what, we can't let them have both of us. Promise me that if I'm nabbed, you'll run far and fast. I shook my head at her silent words. *Promise!*

Her image wavered in front of me, watered, and I closed my eyes to the sorrow that spilled out in acknowledgment of her words. *I'll promise if you'll do the same.* Niko nodded back to me and I shivered at the thought of a future without her. Before we left I instructed her to wrap her arms around me from behind. It was more than just a hug for comfort. I positioned her arm to synch her chip to my backup so that I held the design data that matched the last three tubes.

"That seemed like a very specific hug. What were you doing?" I looked around to make sure no one was watching then I carefully unzipped my solar suit and opened the Velcro of my synth-suit beneath. Then I took her hand and gently rubbed her fingers across the chip that sat just beneath the skin and under my breast. "What is that?"

"I just stripped your chip." Her face changed to one of shock and fear and I quickly tried to reassure her. "You said it yourself. You are the primary target for the BENs. And when we leave here we'll be heading back toward the city where the greatest danger lies. I'll pass it back before we get to each facility. This is just a safeguard to make sure nothing falls into government hands. Okay?"

"I trust you." I smiled at her and could feel how fragile it felt on my lips. She smiled back the same way.

After Joliet we made our way north to Naperville then back into Chicago to the Lincoln Park building. It was 0300 hours when we met with a familiar duo. Dr. Bosche grinned at Niko when we walked up with the tube. "I see you haven't broken her of those night owl ways, Niko."

Niko laughed. "Now why would I do that when I get to see you and Dr. Rook looking so bright-eyed and bushy-tailed in the wee hours of the morning?"

For the first time in ten years, Dr. Rook actually rolled her eyes and cracked a genuine smile. "Well you've seen us now so can we get this transfer completed? I still need a little more bush in my tail. These 0300 meetings start to wear on a body when you're my age."

"Hey, I'm older than you are and you don't see me complaining!" Dr. Bosche joked with her, seeming to be as surprised by her humor as I was. She just shook her head and made a hand motion to get on with our job.

We completed the tube and data transfer to the scientists at Lincoln Park then I pulled Niko aside as they walked back through the security doors into the main wing. "Do you want to take another break here or just push on?"

She thought for a second then glanced toward the door to the facilities. "As much as I want to finish out this last tube, I think I need to take five. You have another stim tab?"

I nodded. "I have a handful, but I was going to save them for the trip back from Milwaukee."

"That makes sense. All right, off to empty my bladder then."

It took longer getting back out of the city the second time than when we began our trip. But once we hit the open highway north, we didn't see another checkpoint until around 0400 and that was a cursory inspection of idents, papers, and facial match. There was no one else on the highway so I assumed it was a pretty boring post. "They rotate posts on a daily basis. So that particular team won't be stuck out here tomorrow."

Niko's voice through my helmet com startled me. "Were you just listening to my thoughts?" I glanced to the right where she rode beside me on the highway.

Her voice came back sounding like a kid who'd just been

caught doing something wrong. "Sorry. It wasn't on purpose. You were thinking kind of loud over there."

One of the things that made us so compatible while working is that she never felt a need to fill time and silence with sound. I had been a solo courier for a long time and I preferred a lot of quiet while on a job. Perhaps her years as a soldier meant that she was used to quiet focus when performing her duties too. I never really asked. "Thanks." Once safely out of the checkpoint zone, we kicked back up to one hundred and thirty kilometers an hour, high beams illuminating the highway ahead of us. I checked my HUD for power and we were still well within the green. Sometimes I felt like I could go forever on a full battery. The rest of the trip was easy after that. There was only one more stop on the way into the city and immediately after handing off the last tube both our wrist comps vibrated.

"Holy shit, they weren't lying!"

I touched the screen and checked my balance. No, they definitely hadn't lied. Not only did we each get ten thousand creds as a bonus, but we also got paid for delivering six tubes within the twenty-four hour limit. Relief coursed through me as well as a fair bit of exhaustion. It was after 0600 and we'd been running for nearly ten hours straight. I smiled softly at Niko. "Ready to go home?"

I got a lascivious grin that morphed into that smirk I loved so much. "Absolutely!"

It was nearly two hours to the first checkpoint outside the capital, and we had no problems passing through. As the sun lifted above the horizon, so too did the nightly curfew. We were coming back in on the I-90 highway so our closest exit was actually quite near the bridge on Roosevelt. There were only two BENs at the checkpoint at the bottom of the off-ramp. Per their standard routine, one kept the bolt gun ready and the other did the check. I noticed the rifle wasn't standard issue though and briefly wondered if they were armed with tranqs. After all, they wanted to bring in Niko alive, not dead. The shorter soldier scanned my ident and checked my papers first, handing them back when I was done. Then I was asked to clear my faceplate to compare against the image on the handheld tablet. "You're clear, Jules Page." I was just getting ready to release my brake when he held up his hand again. "Wait!"

"What's the delay?" The BEN with the rifle sounded annoyed, possibly because there were more riders coming down off the freeway, which would cause a backup with only two BENs on duty.

"Save your gas, Dan, I'm getting an update."

I glanced over at his pad and the coldest tendril of fear started my heart racing. The image Souza had put into the system disappeared and resolved into a picture of Niko, older and obviously in a more private setting. Someone had figured it out and replaced Souza's image in the system. Feeling my terror, Niko glanced my way. I cued our helm to helm com in a panic. "They know!" Without even waiting for a reply from her I took off, my bike leaping ahead with speed that only Souza could arrange. She was right behind me and I could practically feel the bolt aimed at my back. Niko yelled through the com at me.

"Weave! There are only two of them and we'll be harder to hit!" We made it about a block when Niko abruptly lost control of her bike. "They hit my tire!" I started to slow to a stop and could see the BENs coming at a fast pace with their hydraulic enhanced armor. I froze, unsure what to do. "Don't wait for me!" My gaze swung to where Niko was pulling herself off the ground. In the next instant she cried out through the com and her hand went to her back in slow motion. When she brought it in front of her again she had a small feathered dart between her gloved fingers. That impenetrable black helmet turned toward me and I felt her fear come through our connection. Making a split second decision, I turned my wheel to go back for her but stopped as two words from my past collided with the present. *Julia, run!*

She was twenty yards back from my position and the BENs were only seconds from reaching her. *No, I won't leave you!*

Niko glanced back to see the approaching BENs and I could feel her start to fade in my mind as the tranquilizer kicked in. *I love you. You promised.*

I had no choice, she left me no choice. "Fuck!" I screamed in rage as I kicked the bike around and accelerated away from them. There was a moment of panic as I felt the lightest prick on my left arm, but I was already too far away and the dart barely penetrated my suit. It was fast stuff though so I hit the button on my adrenaline pump to shake off the lethargy that threatened to drag me down. I knew I had to get out of sight before they called in the transports. They'd find me for sure if I stayed on the street longer than a minute or two. I brought up my HUD and realized that Souza's warehouse was three blocks away. Racing the distance with murderous speed, I nearly took my head off by not waiting for the door to go all the way up. I didn't breathe easy again until it shut behind my bike, camouflaging me from the

BEN patrols and closing my path back to Niko. Once I cycled through security, I tore into the main garage and came face to face with Souza and six armed guards. I ripped off my helmet and the expression on his face was one I'd never seen before.

"Jules. What have you done?"

Chapter Twelve

Dying With Every Death

I LOOKED AT him feeling a mixture of hopelessness and resolve. "I've done what I do best, survive at all costs."

He shook his head and I was suddenly able to read the look. It wasn't anger that came crashing through to me. It was apprehension warring with loyalty. "Whatever you've done, it's white hot out there right now. Niko's capture and your escape just came through all the comps and coms. They have your image and ident in the system, which means your job and apartment have both been compromised. And every second you stand in front of me risks my entire operation. I'm sorry, but you can't stay here."

I quickly glanced at my wrist comp and brought up my corporate balance. Taking a chance, I did a transfer that would take my total cred sum and route it through five different out-network systems and dump it into an untraceable account. The same account I had my parent's life insurance money stashed. Freezing accounts was one of the things the Network did when they apprehended someone and I felt a small thrill that I'd beat them to it. I looked back up at Souza and his guards. "Do you trust them?"

He glanced over his shoulder and gave a discreet wave. They quickly marched back inside and left us alone. "What do you need?"

I cocked my head at him because he was a master at summing up a situation. "I need a way to hide near the compound and dry-pack rations for a week."

I waited as he thought about my request. "Impossible."

Things were never impossible for Souza so I continued on as if he'd just agreed to my request. "I also need weapons. At least two bolt guns, a lock breaker, and a badge that will get me inside the BEN main facility." The look on his face told me that I'd requested too much so I sweetened the deal. "I'm not going to call in my marker, Souza, because I may need it someday. But I can give you creds."

He shook his head. "As you've stated before, I've hacked your accounts seven ways to Sunday and I know you don't have enough creds for me to take all this risk."

"How much, Souza?"

He lifted his chin at me and I chaffed at the time we were wasting in barter. "Half a mil."

That made me raise an eyebrow at him and I countered. "Quarter mil."

Souza shook his head. "You're bluffing. You don't have that much unless your paniers are stuffed with cred chips."

"Are you accepting a quarter?"

He pressed is lips together in consternation. "Three-fifty."

"Three hundred final, yes or no? We're wasting time here."

I waited as he mulled it over then his dark face creased into a smile. "Deal. I want the cred now because I'm still not convinced you have it."

"Give me an account." He rattled off one I'd used before when upgrading my kit and with a few entries on my wrist comp, I transferred three hundred thousand creds to his account. "Check your balance." He brought up his own wrist comp and surprise washed over his face. I smiled at him but it was forced. "You don't know everything about me, as much as you'd like to."

Souza and I had always had an interesting relationship. I saved his life once and saved his business twice and for that I was trusted more than most in his life. And he definitely owed me. He knew some of my story but not all of it, and I wanted to get through the situation without a long tale if I could. His eyes looked on me with newfound respect, although I supposed nearly half a million creds would put that look on any face. "I need a place, Souza. Somewhere that I can't be bothered by anyone or anything."

He let a few precious seconds tick by then drew in a deep breath. "I have a few safe houses scattered around. Just in case I ever needed to run. How close do you need to be to the compound? Are we talking meters or kilometers?"

I thought about his question. The truth was that I could be anywhere in the city but the greater the distance, the more strain I'd be under. "Less than ten blocks would be best."

Souza smiled at me, and it was a very telling look. "Oh, I think I can do better than that, although it's not as nice a place as I have here."

"I just need a place with facilities, a bed, and supplies."

He tapped his earpiece and spoke into the space between us. "I need a code five kit brought to the basement...two weeks. Just bring it all down." His eyes focused on me again and he nodded.

"Your kit will be downstairs. Now let's take care of the rest." He turned and walked rapidly back to the security door leading into the guts of his operation. I knew he wanted me out of the building as soon as possible. Even though he had the cams hacked for the entire neighborhood there was always the possibility that the BENs would start going door-to-door in their search for the fugitive, in search of me. Once inside he took me to his heavy weapons room. I'd only seen it once before, when I picked out the bolt pistol that I kept in my desk drawer. It took less than ten minutes for Souza to equip me with two pistols, including a belt with cross draw holsters, and one rapid-fire rifle with an extra capacity bolt magazine. I also got extra ammo and half a dozen canisters to power them all. The next stop was his comp room. He went to a secure cabinet and removed a small nondescript box. "This is a lock breaker. You just fit it over the biometric scanner and it will hack the system with an ultrasonic frequency randomizer. But once you're in, they're going to know it. It would probably be just as subtle if you blew a door in with C."

I raised my eyebrows at him. "Do you have any of that?"

"No. I can procure it if I have to, but I don't deal in it." He led the way back out of the heart of his operation and to an elevator. I watched the numbers go by as we dropped four levels and the doors swished open. As we stepped out he tapped the screen of his wrist comp a few times and my own vibrated. "I can't give you a badge. They'll go to bioscan now for sure, and you've truly poked the nest with this one. I've just sent you the map to my hidey-hole. You can push it to your helmet once you're loaded. Level eight NFC access code for all the doors there."

There was a full pack sitting on the concrete just outside the elevator, and my bike was parked next to it with the helmet sitting on the front of the seat. I turned to him in surprise. "How did you—" Souza stopped me with a look. "Of course, you sold me the bike therefore you have the access codes for it." I bend down to grab the pack and strapped it to the rear of my seat. It wouldn't be a comfortable ride, but I knew I'd manage. When I turned around again, Souza was standing there looking strangely hesitant. "What is it?"

"We have an odd friendship, don't we?"

I thought about his words and intent then nodded. "I suppose we do."

He held out his hand and I did not hesitate to accept the shake. "Jules, in case you don't come out the other side of this, or the entire city just burns down around us, I just wanted to say that I was glad to have known you."

Despite not having a close relationship, I had come to consider him a friend. Both the words and the emotions coming from him had me feeling strangely melancholy. "Thank you."

Before he let go he gave me one last Souza grin. It was particularly bloodthirsty. "I expect you to kick their asses from here to hell and back. Let them have their final sleep...Julia." Shock washed through me as my heart thudded painfully in my chest. He knew. Perhaps had always known. He didn't say another word though, just nodded in acknowledgement of the look on my face. Fearing any more revelations from him, I got on my bike, pushed the map to my HUD, and took off down the tunnel.

I arrived about thirty minutes later and found myself facing a concrete wall. At a loss, I read the instructions he had included with the map. The door was like the entrance to the warehouse from the street above, so I pushed the security code he gave me with my helm's enhanced NFC and the door silently slid open. My first thought was that his bunker was larger than I expected then I remembered that it was Souza's personal safe house and he probably had it kitted out for comfort during a long stay. Lights came on when I rode the bike inside. There was an antechamber of sorts where I left the bike, helmet, and gloves. There was a kit rack where I could even plug in my helmet and suit to charge the power packs. I quickly removed the pack Souza provided and walked into the living space proper. There was comfortable furniture, a small kitchen, and two other doors. Upon investigation, one door led to the facility and the other to a bedroom. I brought up the safe house layout on my wrist comp and saw that he had one wall marked with red on the map. The brickwork matched all the others and I grew curious. I moved the chair that was in the way and used my wrist comp to push the NFC code again. Part of the wall dropped back away from me then slid to the right. There was a tunnel on the other side. Trust Souza to always have a backup plan, even for his backup plans.

Thinking of Souza's plans made me realize I needed my own. After stowing the rations in the surprisingly stocked kitchen, I ate a couple of power bars and used the facility then went into the bedroom to lie down. There was a convenient charging port next to the bed so I immediately plugged in. Both the suit and helmet batteries were fast charging and held a lot of power but I always liked to be prepared so I topped them off at every opportunity.

After settling onto the comfortable bed I mentally prepared myself for what was to come. I needed to know where Niko was and I needed to know if she was okay. Souza's location was everything he had promised. I was about three stories directly below the block where the compound was located. The Dream Walkers above were going to have a very bad day. There was no time to regret not showing Niko how to kill in her dream form. There was only time to act. My steps were clear in my mind. Location, communication, retribution, and rescue. If I had any luck at all on my side, all four tasks would go in my favor.

As soon as my eyes were shut I flew up out of my body. I rose quickly through the levels above me, passing through two other tunnels and a sub-basement of the compound itself. I had never walked the main Binary Enforcement Network headquarters because I assumed the risk for being seen by another Walker would be too great. But if there was ever a moment for risk, it would be now. Rather than waste time and energy searching the halls and corridors, I rose all the way up and out of the building at the speed of a bolt. From there I searched the perimeter until I found the BEN patrol entrance. There was a parking lot on the south side of the building and I watched as a transport pulled up and a mobile bed was wheeled out the back. The mobile bed was fully enclosed to avoid having to suit up a tranquilized black BEN while they were on patrol. The BENs could move in and out of the transport without threatening the health of the Walker. A machine and monitor was mounted to one end and the head of the bed itself had a clear poly cover that hinged open for easy access to the black BEN's body. Multiple wires and tubes were leading from the machine into the man lying inside the enclosure. Being four stories above them all, the Dream Walker standing next to his own body never even saw me.

I started to second-guess the morality of what I was about to do until an image of Niko flashed through my mind. That was the moment I lost my doubts. Silent as an avenging angel I flew down from above until I was close enough to just flash the remaining distance to the Walker. I grabbed him from behind in a headlock and spoke directly into his ear. "Where did they take Captain Morgan?"

His loyalty had clearly been washed deep because he stiffened and tried to fight free. "Eat a bolt!" I pulled some of my precious inner strength to keep hold of him because he was a strong man, even in his dream state. I couldn't wait for him to tell me. It was time to try an experiment of my own. I didn't want to kill him yet. I needed more than just his death. Slowly, I pushed my mind inside his, letting the weight of the man's thoughts press all around me. "Wha—what are you doing?"

"Where is Captain Morgan?"

Panic was thick inside and rose fast around me like a flood. "I can't tell you that, they'll kill me!" I pushed farther in, seeing a glimmer of answer just out of reach. "Ar—are you in m—my head? Get out of my head!" He tried to struggle more but I just held on tighter.

"I won't ask again. Where is Captain Nikolette Morgan?" As her name fell from my lips I saw the room in his mind and the nameplate outside on the wall. I didn't retreat from his head when the information was completely mine. Instead I pushed all the way in and just flexed. Agony filled both of us, as well as fear. The scream that left his lips disappeared with his Walker projection. At the same time alarms sounded on the mobile bed. BENs scrambled into action, not even realizing that the body they were transporting was already gone. They took off at a run toward the airlock doors of the building. I had never killed in that manner before and I had to admit that while dying inside his brain with him was a horror of another level, it still didn't match the psychic executions of my past. The man's death was personal, more intimate, but it wasn't the system shock of the other method. Both were guaranteed to give me nightmares in a normal sleep. "Goodbye, Devon Cass, I'll see you in my dreams."

I knew there would be more Walkers out on patrol as well as the ones I'd find inside. I had no idea how large the project had grown under government control, but I was about to find out. In a blink I was inside the filtered air lock at the front of the BEN entrance, ahead of the desperately frenzied soldiers. As soon as I was inside I floated upward through the next three floors until I was on the fourth level. The nameplate read four thirty-seven D so I made my way down the hall to seek it out. Truthfully, I had no idea if Niko was still alive. I was sure she would go walking as soon as she rose above the deep sedation and I wanted to be there to greet her. As I turned one of the many corners in the labyrinthine facility I came face-to-face with another Walker.

"Who are you? How did you get in here?" The woman was tall and broad-shouldered with shaved hair much like mine. Her eyes were dark and angry.

As I willed it, I appeared behind her and put her in the same headlock that I had used on the other Walker. Rather than wait to see if she would answer my question aloud, I pushed inside her mind. *How many more Walkers are on this floor? How many in the facility?*

She immediately froze and trembled in my arms, her terror running a completely different route than Devon Cass. Perhaps it was because she wasn't a BEN. She was one of the lab rats kept by the esteemed Dr. Morgan. She spoke aloud in the dreamscape. "What are you doing to me?"

I pushed in a little farther and saw the truth of who she was and spoke the next words aloud in the dreamscape to reassure her. "Amelia Fanchon, tell me if there are any other Walkers on this level and I won't kill you." I didn't want to kill her. She was no different than the child me. Just another pawn in the war.

"I—I think there are only seven of us on the floor right now. I'm sorry but I don't know how many are in the facility. They have the test subjects split up into different rooms and move us around during the day for testing then bring us back to sleep at night. I don't know where the BENs sleep. What are you going to do?"

I had to organize my thoughts for a second. "So there are no BENs up here right now?"

She shook her head. "No, two are black BENs up here for monitoring and field rest."

"Okay, think really hard for me. What do those two BENs look like?" I pushed a little farther and she cried out. "Focus, Amy! What do they look like? Show me in your head and I'll get out and let you go."

The images of both appeared in my mind. About the same height with matching brown hair and eyes, the man and woman could have been siblings. And who knew, maybe they were. "Thank you." I withdrew from her mind as quickly as I had entered and her dream-self sagged within the circle of my arms. After a few seconds of recovery, she stood straight again.

"Who are you?"

I smiled at her and it was nothing less than wicked. "I'm Dreamer Zero." Amy took off running back the way I had just come from wearing a well-earned look of terror. I proceeded down the hall and when I reached the middle, a woman walked through the door next to me. Despite the surprise etched on her face, she matched the image I had just stripped from Amy. As a black BEN, I knew she'd probably be monitored and have a way to communicate with the scientists in the room, just like they could communicate with their teams in the transports. I rushed her, too fast for her to react, and pushed into her head just far enough to see her truest heart. She alone had been responsible for bringing twenty Walkers in for experimentation and seemed proud of her record. Her mind screamed at me in defiance. *Get out of my head, you bitch!*

The read took mere seconds of my time. She didn't even get a chance to react to my presence before I held up my hand and willed a spike into existence, the same way I once showed Niko how to create a helmet. It gleamed nearly white and it was nothing more than the focus of my power, a concentrated piece of self. Her eyes widened right before I shoved it straight into the back of her brain. I found myself inside her mind as the agony flared white hot then I died and was back to me again when the Dream Walker disappeared. I shut my eyes as my Walker body trembled with the shock of her violent and abrupt death. Until Devon, the psychic execution was all I knew how to do and that was what I didn't want to teach Niko. Every single one took a little piece of me with them. One down, one to go.

Drawing in a metaphorical breath, I walked into the room that the black Walker had exited. A machine in the corner was screaming with the death of the woman I had just killed. There was a Walker with his back to me, staring at the lifeless body on the mobile bed. I immediately knew who it was and didn't even give him a chance to turn around. I killed him the same way I did the other and took precious seconds to absorb the system shock as the next mobile bed alarm sounded off.

Scientists ran from bed to equipment in a panic trying to save the bodies whose minds were long gone. One still figure took it all in with a calculating look and immediately touched her wrist comp. Before I could wonder what Dr. Morgan was doing, her voiced sounded over the building's com system. "Attention, security breach. Lockdown initiative Zeta, Walker initiative Psi-Surgere!" She was calm and so very cold. And looking into those blue eyes, I could easily see Niko's intelligence inside. I didn't know what the specific lockdown procedures were but if I had to guess I would think it would involve waking all the Dream Walkers currently within the facility. I said a simultaneous thank you and apology to Souza because the BENs would surely begin their door-to-door search now that I'd gone on the offensive.

Before I could dwell more on the consequences of my actions, a tech burst through the door as well as a BEN team pushing a mobile bed. It was the same Walker I'd killed in the parking lot. "Dr. Morgan, he crashed just before coming inside. There's no com from him and we couldn't bring him back from the flat line!"

Olivia Morgan used her foot to stop the approaching bed and shoved it back away from her. "That's because he's dead. Take him to the cooler, I'll examine the body later." She pointed at the other two beds with flat-line alarms. "Take those with you." She turned to the BEN team lead that stood at the head of the mobile bed, still in his heavy armor. "Right now you need to send word to all the field teams that Dreamer Zero is the insurgent and all Walkers need to be brought out of sedative immediately. We can't take any chances right now."

He looked at her questioningly. "Are you sure it's not the new one we brought in?"

She smiled back at him and cruelty stained her lips. My fear for Niko skyrocketed upon hearing he words. "That would be quite impossible. The newest subject has been stimmed up since we brought her in. We don't want her walking away, now do we?"

I rushed past her and through the door at the far end of the large room. On the other side I found a hall full of doors. Two guards flanked the door at the very end and I knew she would be there. Nothing prepared me for what I felt when I walked through to the other side. Niko wasn't even given a bed. Her body was lying on a table surrounded by a collection of machines and screens. She only wore her undergarments and was clearly chilled if the goose bumps were any indication. Wires and electrodes were attached to her head in a halo, and others led off to all the major muscle groups of her body. Intravenous lines violated her at the back of each hand, her foot, and the left femoral artery. She didn't look at me as I came in, just continued to stare straight up at the ceiling. I had no idea why. "Niko!" I called and still she didn't move. Her eyes were open but she gave no response to indicate she was awake as she should have been in her stimmed state. Niko had always been able to see and hear my Walker and I feared what the loss of that ability would mean. Two meters from the door to the table, and I covered the distance in the blink of an eye. Then I slowly floated above it so I could look down at her face. Horror-filled blue eyes were open and tears streamed down the sides of her face. How could I have missed the tears from a few meters away? I wasn't sure what I would find but I concentrated and slowly pushed inside her mind. Her voice to me was immediate and reassuring.

Julia!

I sighed, wishing more than anything that I could take her hand. It was hard pushing my way in when she was so stimmed up. The waking mind was a hive of activity and hard to pin down individual thoughts. Normally I had no problems speaking mind-to-mind when we were both awake, but we had never tried it with one of us walking. I suspected the stimulant she was on did more harm than anything else. "Can you hear me?"

Her eyes didn't even blink, just continued to release a steady stream of tears. *Yes. I'm sorry though. I can't move.*

My eyes widened at the true misery of her situation. She was trapped in her own body and stimmed awake. Both paralyzed and aware. "How?"

Neuromuscular block. I don't know exactly what they gave me, only that allows for autonomic function but seems to be targeting my other muscle groups. I can't so much as turn my head or blink but they didn't intubate me.

"I'm going to get you out. I just need time. Think, how long can you safely stay stimmed?"

I waited for her answer, disconcerted at the lack of expression on her face. If only she had mastered the art of walking while not in a calm state, perhaps I'd be able to touch her, but she had not. I felt like a failure on so many levels. *Sleep can be found in the hardest bed and lost with a single smile.*

I shook my head at her quote. "I don't know that one. Who is it?"

Brady Kirk, sleep researcher of the past century. And to answer your question, no one really knows though twelve days is the assumed safe limit for such things. Studies have been conducted off and on over the past hundred years but the twelve days was only hit in a controlled environment.

I looked up at the room around us. "Well you can't get more controlled than this."

Julia. Her voice was quiet in my head, meek and broken. I looked back down into those pain-filled eyes. *She's been testing me – she did this. My own mother. I thought I knew her.*

My eyes closed to the anguish that she wasn't even allowed to show. My dream-self whispered the words through my hurt. "I'm so sorry." I was starting to feel drained and I hadn't set the timer on my wrist comp so I knew I had to get back. But I took a chance and used a little more of my internal energy to push into her mind again. As gently as I was able, I shared with her all the love and hope I carried within.

I love you too.

I looked down at her and felt the loss of her in every part of me. *I have to go.*

Niko's mental sigh tickled through my brain and I tried to hold onto my control. *I know. Be safe.*

I pulled away then, missing our connection. I looked down at her still body one last time. "I'll be whatever you need." Then I left the room and made my way back to where I started. I ignored the frenzied activity that seemed to infect every hallway and room of the massive building. I ignored my aching heart. I had to get back to my body for some real rest because the onset of night would bring the second phase of my plan. When I had slipped back into myself I opened my eyes despite the wave of exhaustion and headache that settled over me. I could hear filters running and briefly wondered where they vented to. I checked my wrist comp and set an alarm for later. I made a promise into the empty room and the blackness around me swallowed the words. "I will be your nightmare until she is safely back with me. You can't fight your dreams." I shut my eyes and before I succumbed fully to the sleep I desperately needed, I built the tightest wall I was able. I was safe as I could be for now. It would have to do.

Chapter Thirteen

Tell Them I'm Coming

MY WRIST COMP woke me at 2200 hours and I felt somewhat refreshed, minus the headache. I was fairly lucky in that, despite being a Dream Walker, I rarely ever remembered my real dreams. Though it was probably a good thing considering all I'd been through and seen. The first part of my plan was set and I considered my late morning actions while walking a success. The Walkers were afraid of me, afraid to go to sleep. And the Network, especially Dr. Morgan, wouldn't want to lose any more so they'd be stimmed just like Niko. Rage swamped me when I thought of my strong soldier looking so helpless on the table. I remembered my own time spent at the hands of her mother and shivered. No one should suffer like that, especially at the hands of their own kin. Eyes open or closed, the blackness of the room was complete so I lit the screen of my wrist comp to find my way to the facility. Angry focus had me running on autopilot, and I went through my routine without any thought at all. Scrubbing, eating, changing into a clean synth suit, and then putting my solar suit back on. It wasn't comfortable to sleep in but I wanted to be ready in case one of Souza's tunnel alarms sounded and I had to leave fast.

After nearly an hour I went back in to lie on the bed and a second later I was floating above my body. I immediately changed my dream appearance to one where I was covered from head to toe in black. I wore my solar suit, gloves, boots, and helmet because I didn't want them to see my face. It was time to begin phase two, introducing them to the beast in the closet. They wanted Dreamer Zero, they were going to get her. In no time at all I was back within the walls of the compound. The front courtyard was well lit and it must have been near shift change because BEN patrols were rolling out to cover the city. I smiled when I realized none of them carried Walkers. It didn't take long to find the line of buildings that made up their barracks. I went into the first one and it was massive, housing more than a hundred men and women. About a third of the beds were empty and I smiled with cruel joy at the remaining sleepers. I whispered the words of a quote that I was sure Niko would know.

"Demons scald the sweetest sleeps when our angels are afraid."

I wasn't sure why I whispered. It wasn't like anyone was left to hear me in the Dreamer's plane. It was time to begin so I went to the very first sleeper. He was a man, young and hale. I glanced around and realized that most of the BEN soldiers were younger, between twenty and twenty-five years. Shaking my head I decided that age didn't matter because we were all responsible for our own actions. With a minimal amount of effort, I slowly pushed inside his thoughts. I purposely didn't go deep, just far enough to see his dreams and to get a feel for the man he was. *BEN!*

The equivalent of a mental yell caught his attention but he didn't wake. He just assumed he was dreaming. *What?* I could see him. The current dream faded and he looked around. I appeared to him then in the black suit I had chosen. He couldn't see my face but I witnessed the fear wash over his. *Who are you?*

I ignored his question and distorted my own voice as it sounded through his head. *What do you fear, BEN?*

He looked at me curiously. *My name is Andy, not Ben.*

Who do you fear BEN?

Andy shivered and his face went pale in the dream. His voice was a whisper. *You – I fear you.*

I nodded. *Do you know who I am?*

The man swallowed, his Adam's apple bobbed up and down below a barely shaved chin. *You're Dreamer Zero, the insurgent.* I nodded at him, a motion he could see despite the intimidating helmet on my head. *Ple – please don't kill me.*

I walked toward him in his dream and he started to back up. When I kept coming he turned around and started to run. I didn't chase, but rather I suddenly appeared in front of him and made my dreamer self into an impenetrable wall. He bounced off the front of me and landed on the ground with a *whump*. I looked down at him as he froze in fear. What's the worst thing you've ever done, BEN?

The man on the ground squeezed his eyes shut and shuddered with memory as I dove in deeper. A woman appeared nearby and another image of Andy was standing with her. I watched as months of time compressed into mere seconds. They dated, they had sex, and then he cheated on her. His girlfriend and the other woman were both BENs so it wasn't hard for his infidelity to be exposed. In the dream within a dream, Andy cried when the woman left him and I felt the sorrow he still carried within his heart. The Andy on the ground in front of me cried too. *I made a mistake – I'm so sorry.* He shook his head back and forth as if he were trying to shake his betrayal loose. He wasn't what I was looking for.

Andy! I shouted at him and he finally looked back up at me, eyes red but focused.

Will you kill me now?

I took one step away from him then another and shook my head. *No Andy, but I need information. Who is the worst among you? Who do you fear besides me?* People started to fill the dreamscape around us. Dr. Morgan and General Rennet I recognized right away. Others I had to focus in on name tags and armor serial numbers. There were about a dozen and I memorized every name and face. They were the ones I was looking for. *Thank you, Andy.* I nodded again and disappeared from his dream.

After that I systematically went from bed to bed in the barracks, reading the true nature of each soldier and inquiring about their fears. Not surprisingly, the same faces came up again and again. And when I got to those soldiers that the others feared, I didn't bother with the questions. My wrist comp had vibrated hours before but I ignored it because I knew I had to finish the building I was in. Something drove me and I could not go back until I had finished. The second to last bed held another one of the feared BENs. I slipped into his dream and saw red at the images I found there. He and two others held down a woman on the bed of her own home. Raymond Felix had his helmet on but had opened the front of his armor in order to perpetrate his violation of the sobbing Walker. When he was finished he turned to a small child that peered out of the closet door. "Your mother has been found guilty as a criminal Walker and this is what we do to criminals. If you tell anyone about this, I'll come back for you!" Terror filled the little girl's face as she ducked back out of sight. Rage drove me to scour away the dreamscape around him.

I stripped him next until he stood nude in the center of nothingness. *Ray Felix! You have been found guilty of crimes against Dream Walkers. You have been found guilty of crimes against children. What do you have to say for yourself?*

When I first appeared I could tell he was afraid, but after I finished speaking he stood a little straighter and a smile spread across his face. He stroked himself right in front of me. *What's the matter Dreamer? Are you jealous I didn't save any for you?*

Faster than a thought, from one stroke of his calloused hurtful hand to the next, I was in front of him taking his head within the cage of my clutching fingers. Before he could say another word, I pulled power and dug straight into his skull. I split him asunder, thus shredding his very psyche with my bare hands. White-hot agony enveloped me as we died then I was forced out of the body and back into the dreamscape. He slept without covers and I watched in fascination as his body released all autonomic function and a stain spread across the bed below him. Exhaustion threatened to drag me into the deepest pits, tried to pull me back to my corporeal body, but I fought on. I quickly dipped into the last sleeper and saw she was of no consequence, not one of the feared BENs. But I left her with a warning. *Tell them I'm coming.*

I knew I was at the edge of my limits, but I still had one more thing to do before I could go back. The sky had begun to lighten in the east, meaning I had been walking longer than I'd ever done before. I quickly made my way back up to Niko's room before I could dwell on how much I wanted to return. I didn't run into any fellow Walkers on the way. When I peeked into one room I could see half a dozen inside engaged in various activities. A pack of stim tabs sat on the only table in the room. They were stimming willingly. It wasn't being administered. They were afraid. Making a split second decision, I stepped through the door into the room. All action stopped as their heads swiveled in my direction. They couldn't see my face, just a person in black. "You're not real!" One woman spoke up and pointed at me with a shaking hand.

I waved at the rest of the Walkers. "Ask them if I'm not real. Ask your friends if they see me too."

Another man who was seated in front of a game of some sort nodded. "I see her, Jen. She's real."

Another voice, off to the side of the room. "But how?"

Laughter preceded my words. "That is for me to know, and you to learn when sleep next finds you. But for now, tell them my message."

"Tell who?"

Anger rose with my words and I projected that rage at every individual in the room. "Tell Dr. Morgan and General Rennet that I'm coming for them." I disappeared back into the hallway while they still shook in fear. I couldn't touch them while they were awake, but they didn't know that. They had no idea what I was capable of.

I made my way to Niko's room next and moved to float above where she lay immobile on the cold metal table, still awake. She was awake but I sensed that her mind was unfocused so I called to her. "Niko!"

Julia? You're really here? I thought it was a dream – but I'm awake. How could it be a dream?

I felt the tears well up as sorrow ate at my heart. "I'm so sorry. I'm working on getting you out of here but it's going to take a few days. There is so much to do and..." A wave of weakness sent blackness through my vision.

What's going on, you're – fading?

Shaking my head, I reached out a hand to touch her face. It was a hopeless gesture but I longed to feel her skin again, craved her embrace. "I'm sorry, Niko. But I have to go back. I'm so tired..." Just when I thought I would not even make it back to my own body, a wave of strength and love pushed through my mind. I shook my head in wonder as she gave me something she couldn't really spare. "Thank you. Now I really have to go!" I sped back to the corridor and down all the levels to the first floor. Pain started to throb through my head like a spike being hammered in to my frontal lobe. I sank levels into the ground until I once again found my hiding place and my body. I dove in, feeling like I only had seconds left and bowed my back as agony froze every muscle. A scream tore from my throat at the blinding pain that threatened to split my head in two. I opened my eyes in the darkness and felt wetness on my face and cheeks. Having no choice, I rose and staggered into the facility to look at myself in the mirror. My skin was pale and gaunt. Blood streamed from my nose and stained my cheeks where it had run in rivulets down the sides of my face. Tears had dried in tracks at the corners of each eye, much the same way. The swollen eyes and whitish salt brine was testament to the pain and emotional anguish I felt over the past six hours. I had clearly over-extended myself and knew I'd have to be much more careful in the days ahead. I quickly cleaned up and went for another round of deep healing sleep. I would get her back or we would all die with my effort.

I woke sore all over, with hunger digging into my belly. I squinted at the display on my wrist comp and understood why. I had slept for ten hours straight. With the way my body felt I knew it was in desperate need of food and hydration. It was late afternoon in my second day of hiding. Souza had a comp with a large monitor in the main room. So after taking two pain tabs, I heated some food and brought up the local broadcasts while I ate. I shivered when I realized that my face was on every news site. There were reports of BENs going block to block, searching every single residence. I briefly wondered if they would have obtained warrants for my personal belongings and records at Vanguard then realized the depth of my foolishness. Of course they would have. My past had been compromised and my future was in jeopardy. I had nothing left. Nothing but Niko and my anger.

I looked down as I ate and saw the pronounced bones of my wrists and knew that expending so much energy during the long walk had drained me more than was healthy. I ate as much as I could hold and forced water into my belly until I felt the gurgle of it. I napped after that and another handful of hours later, I did it all again. I had just taken two more pain tabs for my head when an encrypted call came through the comp in the main room. I answered and Souza's face came up on the screen. He was in a transport of some type and sparse northern trees passed by outside his window.

His voice was equal parts amused and frustrated as it sounded over the speakers. "Hello Jules, how are you enjoying the accommodations?"

"Considering they were intended for you, they are perfect and you know it. Is there a reason for your call, Souza?"

The grin dropped from his face. "I see you've taken my words to heart. My warehouse has been compromised and the city is untenable for me now." He paused at the look on my face and rushed on. "Don't worry Jules, your location is safe. My entire system was scrubbed and access to the lower tunnels was sealed before I left."

I considered the view behind him. "You heading north?"

Souza nodded. "Just to Toronto. I've already got control of the dark market there and have a satellite facility set up. It made the most sense. The capital has become too hot. Maybe once you clear the rats from the warren I'll come back."

I nodded at him. I didn't need any words and Souza didn't need psychic powers to know that I would do the job I set out to do, or we'd never see each other again.

Deciding to attempt another daylight visit, I went back into the bedroom to do some walking. I wanted information. I wanted verification that my warnings of the night before would be heeded. I arrived at the compound and checked the barracks for sleepers and was disappointed to find that my warnings had been for naught. A number of bunks were full of the midnight shift BENs catching up on their rest. Anger followed me inside and back up to the fourth floor, the Dream Walker floor where I sought them out. I found a bigger room with more stimmed Walkers inside. They looked — rough. They'd all been awake for two days and the strain to their bodies was beginning to show. These weren't the test subjects. I passed that room at the other end of the wing. They were strapped to hospital beds, wide-awake. The room full of Walkers that I was in were all BENs. "You!" A woman pointed at me, one of the smaller group from the night before. "You killed them, didn't you?"

"How can we see you?" He waved toward the original group "They said you came, that you warned us but we've never been able to see a dreamer while we're awake and Dr. Morgan didn't believe them." His words made me re-evaluate my theory that all Dream Walkers could see each other, awake or no. I surmised that living in such close quarters with each other, they would have already been aware of the possibility. Perhaps it had to do with the strength of the Walker then.

My helmet voice came out warped and angry, just as I felt. "You've all been warned, whether they believe you or not doesn't matter to me. You can see me because I'm Dreamer Zero. As of right now I consider you all traitors to our people."

The same man spoke up again and I could feel his smug suspicion roll off him in waves. "You can't hurt us!"

Another man spoke from the group I had seen the night before. "But Dave, what about the BENs who died in their sleep last night?"

Dave looked at him with a raised skeptic's eyebrow. "General Rennet already said they had a security breach. Clearly Dreamer Zero is working with someone." He turned back to me then. "It's just as Dr. Morgan thought. You have no power over a Dream Walker who is awake." He smiled, clearly feeling secure with his realization.

In a blink I was standing right in front of him and when he scrambled backward he ran into the wall. His bravado was a front and I knew it. I leaned even closer then spoke to him with no helmet modulation on my voice. "You can't stim forever." And with that, I disappeared. I didn't go far because I wasn't really sure how, but I appeared in the hallway once again. I had one last stop then I would be able to rest again for a few more hours before evening shift.

Niko was in the same place and my heart constricted to see it. When I floated above her I got no response again. "Niko, I'm here."

Her thoughts came at me, disjointed and weak. *You're not*

real – nobody is real.

I tried again. "Niko, its Julia. I'm real and I'm here to see you. I'm sorry you're still trapped in this room."

The words in my head were wispy, yet heavy with disbelief. *Julia?*

"Yes!" Something changed in her eyes and if I didn't know her very well I would never have seen it. Or maybe I just felt it in my mind.

My Julia?

I looked at her tenderly as my heart broke into a million pieces. *Always.*

Tell me that I'm not crazy.

They had put some kind of gel in and around the edges of her eyes, probably to keep them from drying out. But as I watched the tears began to stream again and I knew that the new flood wasn't from her stimmed and paralyzed state. I forced my face into a smile for her benefit alone. *Only crazy for loving me.*

I felt her pleasure and warmth through my very core. *No, lucky. Please hurry, Jules – I don't know how much longer I can stay like this without losing it.*

Thoughts raced through my head and I knew I was running out of time. I had more preparation to do. *Niko, can you tell me how to counteract the neuromuscular block? If I can make it inside you'll need to be able to move. How can I move you?*

I don't know, hard to focus now...

"No, please! I need your help, anything you can tell me."

I could feel it as soon as she pulled herself together. When she spoke in my head again it was almost as if she were reading from a textbook. With her mnemonic ability, she probably was. *Neuromuscular blockades that are facilitated by muscle relaxants can be reversed pharmacologically or endogenously.*

I wasn't a genius of her level, nor a geneticist, and I certainly didn't grow up with geneticists as parents. I rubbed my hand across the back of my head, having gotten rid of the psychic projection of my helmet as soon as I entered her room. "I don't know what that means!"

She probably gave me turbocurarine and would most likely have a reversing agent somewhere nearby. In a lab cabinet somewhere. I want to leave, please – can you take me with you?

I sucked in a breath because I wouldn't be able to bear it if she begged me. "Niko, what is the agent called? Give me a best guess."

TEA

Bewildered, I spoke directly to her mind. *Tea? I don't understand!*

No, T-E-A! Its tetraethylammonium. I nodded but suddenly found myself with another problem. Not only was I speaking to her mind directly, I was also getting the full range of her emotions and her fear threatened to swamp me. I could feel her draining me the way I had drained her the last time I was in the room. *Please — Julia — I can't take any more. Let me go back with you, help me!* Her voice was a scream in my head and I brought my hands up in an attempt to stifle the pain.

"Niko, I'm sorry but I have to go back now. I'll come see you again in a few hours—" Another mental scream interrupted my words.

No! I'm begging you, please don't leave me! Don't leave me, Julia! Her words chased me from the room and continued to linger heavy in my heart long after I returned to the bunker.

Chapter Fourteen

Until Tomorrow

I SETTLED BACK into my body as hopelessness and exhaustion hit me like a tidal wave. I was never going to get her out, how could I? There were so many soldiers within the compound that I would have to kill them all to get through. I wasn't a soldier and I knew after being in some of their heads that I couldn't kill so many. Who was I to take their lives when some of them were completely innocent? Many I touched had no idea what happened inside the lab area. They thought the Dream Walkers they brought in were all recruited into service. I had already killed too many since they took Niko. I wasn't sure if my mind would recover if I completely abandoned my conscience. If only I had allies or could win some of them to my side, but it was an impossible situation. My original plan was to make them so afraid they'd stim the soldiers and after a few days of constant paranoid alertness the soldiers would make mistakes. Those mistakes I planned to exploit to get in and get Niko out again. I would have to continue with the plan I had and hope that Niko could hold on long enough despite the pain and torture her body was going through.

Thoughts of Niko turned me to thoughts of her mother, Dr. Morgan. Somewhere over the past ten years she had changed. When Niko first told me who her mother was there was a big part of me that hoped the woman was being controlled by the government. But even when I was young I recognized that insatiable thirst for knowledge in her, one that seemed to skirt the boundaries of moral norms. Having the power and unlimited budget that the government afforded seemed to balance out the death of her husband and loss of her soul. I feared her decades ago for what she had done to me as a child, but I abhorred her now for her betrayal of Niko. The only person I wanted to see more within the power of my dreams was General Rennet. That man had been an evil canker on the skin of our country for much too long. I raised my left hand and checked the time on my wrist comp. It was 0550 hours. I needed rest, nourishment, and ideas about how to get into the compound and safely back out with an extra person. A person that may or may not be able to walk on her own. Perhaps I could take a drone in the same way Niko stowed away to escape. I needed to speak with Souza again. Years ago we had discussed the possibility of escaping the compound and I knew he had ideas. I pulled my aching body from the bed in order to eat, drink some water, and use the facility, then I went right back to bed. I needed rest or I would be no help to anyone.

I slept for nearly ten hours and woke hungry. It was disconcerting to be living below ground in a bunker where my only gauge of time was from my wrist comp and my Walker visits above. I rose and opted for some exercise before another shower and meal. Souza had stocked some high calorie foods as well as lean ones besides the ration bars. I decided to take the ration bars into the bedroom with me next time I was ready to walk. My head always seemed to have a low level ache to it, perhaps because I was walking for long periods two times a day. That alone was straining my system and that didn't even take into consideration the energy I had been expending by pushing into people's minds, extracting information, and killing. After looking after the health of my body I used the bunker's comp to contact Souza. He seemed only marginally surprised to be hearing from me.

"Jules, how is it going with the fight?"

I shook my head, not wanting to make small talk. "I need to know how to get into the BEN compound and back out again with an extra person."

His face fell. He didn't tell me it was impossible. He didn't smile and give me an answer. He just stared at the camera on his end. I watched him as he thought about the problem and my heart sank as he shook his head back and forth. "I don't know. It's certainly something I've thought about over the years, and we discussed it on occasion as well. But truthfully, I'm not sure of a good way in that would get you back out again too."

His words stripped me of everything good and anger was all I had left. "Well try dammit! She's fading, Souza—she's losing herself and won't last much longer in there!"

He cocked his head at me. "Niko?" I nodded and understanding dawned on him. "You're not doing this simply because they're coming after you. You're doing all this to rescue Niko. She's means that much to you?"

Tears welled up in my eyes. "She means everything."

He sighed and rubbed his smooth chin. "Give me a day, can you do that? I'll see what I can come up with on my end. And Jules..."

"Yeah?"

"If you do get in, I have a chip that may help everyone fear the Network a little less. In the top drawer of my comp desk, I have a variety of chip drives. You'll need the one that's in the sleeve labeled 'Proto-wipe.' If you can get that to a comp that's connected to the Network's system, it will do two things. First it will install a virus that will create network connections and will release all classified data to the worldwide network. That includes information about the Dream Walker project and the things that they've been doing to people in the labs."

I looked at him in surprise. "How do you know about that?"

"People talk, Jules, and I have ways of hacking systems that are connected to outside lines. But their main system is not connected to the web for security purposes."

I nodded. "You said it would do two things, what is the second?"

"It will install a worm that will wipe their system as soon as the data dump is complete. The entire Binary Enforcement Network will be crippled. With no coms, data, or systems, that might be enough chaos to get you and Niko back out of the building unnoticed. However, I'm not sure how to get you into the building so give me a day to think on it, okay?"

"I guess I don't have a choice. You're my only hope right now. Thank you."

He shook his head sadly. "Don't thank me unless I can help you get in." He disconnected and I was left sitting in the quiet hum of the room filters. It was early still but I couldn't stop until Niko was safe again. I went back into the bedroom with a canister of water and some power bars then reclined on the bed to start it all again. High above me, I made my way straight to the second barracks building. Inside I found some of the midnight shift BENs sleeping in their bunks. I systematically went through the men and women that were deep in REM, just as I had in the other building. I finished faster than before because I didn't spend so much time and effort with each person. I simply got a read on who they were and left the more innocent ones alone. I went through the rest of the buildings and by the time I finished with the sleeping soldiers, a total of twenty-three more were dead. I had stolen their life with a little bit of my own and I felt hollow inside.

One thing I wanted to try was to see if I could influence someone who was awake. I knew it would be hard and would drain me considerably, but I had to know what I could do, see if I was capable of more than just death. On the first floor I went to an area that appeared to control the security cameras for the compound. They had monitors for the streets around the entire city block, as well as screens that showed different floors and perimeter shots around the compound itself. I thought perhaps if I could make someone see something that wasn't there, then maybe when the time came I could make them not see something as well. I pushed into the mind of the man that sat at the security desk. I remained in his outer-most thoughts, reading his worries about the creds he owed a broker for a series of bad bets and about his boredom while working the job he had been placed on for the current shift. I focused much the same way that I had with Niko, willing the man to see a person in a black solar suit with a black helmet walking down the hall on the 4th floor. He blinked and rubbed his eyes then leaned forward and squinted at the monitor.

"Holy shit!" Shock rippled through his thoughts a split second before he hit the alarm button. He scrambled with the microphone to announce the alert com-wide. "Intruder on the 4th floor, Walker wing!" Alarms sounded that would bring the midnight shift BENs out of their sleep and then the real chaos would begin. Exactly as I predicted, more alerts sounded over the com system.

"Code red, agents down in barracks number two, multiple fatalities."

"Roger that, multiple fatalities in the others as well."

I floated up two floors and skimmed a technician that was working at a comp. I inserted the image of me, that same person in black, walking by the window of her room. She panicked and made the call.

"Intruder alert, level two research wing!" Red lights in the hallways flashed in time with the intruder sirens. As I watched a group of soldiers in full armor jog though the main entrance, I was glad to see that everyone was awake. They were awake and now they were scared. I wanted to go see Niko again before I left but I couldn't. I had enough energy, barely, but my heart could not take it if she begged me again so I left. I flew back to my body for more food and a few more hours of sleep. I planned to harass them again in the midnight hours and hoped that Souza could help me come up with something solid to get inside.

I wept upon my return to reality. In the dark cocoon of Souza's underground bunker I cried for the disparity of power and unfairness of the world. I cried for the childhood that I was never allowed, and I mourned the future that was slipping away.

With Niko I had found something that meant more to me than my own survival. I found a woman who loved me for who I was, not for what I could do for her. And I loved her the same way. After wallowing in self-pity for nearly an hour, I forced myself out of bed to take care of my basic needs. I ate, exercised, and cleaned myself in preparation of the night to come. I would need more sleep before waking up to do it all again. It was 2050 hours when I dropped my tired body back onto the bed. I set my comp for 0300 so that I could wake and return to the compound as my Dream Walker self.

REM sleep came upon me fast and I almost felt as though I were walking, but I knew it was a dream because the world was like none I'd ever seen. I thought for sure that I was imagining the future that Ryan had promised, one without helmets and breathers, but too many things were different. I was in Chicago still but it was a city of the past. I flew over people walking along the sidewalks, heads bare and laughing. There were cars, trains, people, motorcycles, and bicycles everywhere. It was amazing, and overwhelming. I aimed for the old stadium that had been converted to BEN training grounds decades ago and saw something I'd only read about in the history feed on my comp. Men ran across a wide green expanse playing a game that had gone away with the decline of our atmosphere and increase in daily temperatures. As I soared across the clear blue sky I felt the tears running down my cheeks. I dreamed of a past that I'd never seen and for the first time I truly felt hope for the future.

Vibration on my wrist pulled me from the dream and I sucked in a gasping breath as I was wrenched disconcertingly from that new world, that world that used to be. I both regretted remembering the dream and reveled in its memory. It filled me with a sense of happiness and peace, and I felt the loss of waking somewhere deep inside. I had to wonder if dreams were the only way most people could get through the dreary existence of life. There was no reason why I would suddenly remember a dream so vividly when most of my life had been slept in silence. I never needed my dreams before because walking had been more life than I'd ever allowed myself to live. As I sat up in the darkness I felt coolness on my cheeks. Reaching up I realized that the tears of my dream had followed me to the waking world. After wiping my face I went to use the facility then downed an energy bar and some water before reclining back on the bed. It had been a long day and an even longer night and I wondered what I would find on my return to the compound. I hoped to see the entire place wide-awake with hundreds of stimmed soldiers wearing down their sanity in the barracks.

As if the fates themselves were smiling down on me that was exactly what I found. Despite the fact that it was just after 0300 hours, the bunkhouse lights shone out of the windows into the night. I took the time to notice the surroundings, both around the compound walls and around the main building inside. I watched as the transports came and went then floated up into the air and observed some more. The transports had a large rack on top, perhaps for holding supplies on long patrols. If a person could get on top of the carrier it would be possible for them to flatten themselves enough to not be seen. That might be the best plan I could come up with. After scouting from the air I floated back down again and went into the nearest barracks. Men and women were lying on bunks watching the vid screen, some played games in a rec area and others read on handheld comp tablets. Everywhere I looked they were busy. They also looked a bit edgy. I moved closer to listen to two women speak as they played chess. Both were tall and muscular, a testament to their jobs and training. One had deep black hair and the other was medium brown, very close to the color of Niko's. I skimmed their minds to learn names.

Miri had the black hair and was also black on the chessboard. "Have you heard how long we have to stay stimmed?"

"Rory says that they're hoping to pin down Dreamer Zero sometime in the two days. Apparently the General has ordered a systematic sweep of the maglev tunnels because troops haven't found anything above ground and he thinks she must be nearby."

I grew alarmed at the news coming from the soldier named Carmen. General Rennet certainly wasn't stupid. He'd held his post for a long time. Depending on what tech they brought with them underground it was possible that they'd eventually find the bunker. I was going to have to move sooner rather than later. My greatest hope was that Souza would have a better suggestion for me other than sneaking in on the top of the carrier. Even though I would fairly blend in with the roof of the vehicle in my black suit, it would only take someone astute on the camera as drones came and went. Regardless of what I learned from Souza, I was already planning on making my attempt after my next REM sleep. After that I went back up to the fourth floor. I made my way down the hall, peeking into the various rooms and labs. The Dream Walkers had their own set of living quarters set up on the opposite end of the labs. Sleeping rooms were usually double bunked and there were various recreation areas set up in their wing of the building. The main building was enormous so I wasn't surprised that they made the call to house the Walkers inside. The general populous would have been nervous to have the dreaded Walkers sleeping so close to them.

I picked one lounge that had about twenty Walkers inside entertaining themselves, very much like the soldiers in the barracks below. The big difference was that while the Walkers were Binary Enforcement Network agents, they weren't soldiers like the men and women outside They definitely weren't at the same physical fitness level as the regular BENs. And the Walkers had been kept awake for two days longer than the BENs outside. They looked haggard with dull hair and dark smudges beneath their eyes. I could see just by looking at them that they were nearing their breaking point. I walked into the room wearing my traditional black suit and helmet and panic ensued. Even though I wasn't real to them, every single person could see me. A few faces I recognized from my previous visits. A voice near the vid screen yelled at someone on the comp. "Call security!"

I moved in a blink to the center of the room and faced the nondescript man. "And just what will security do for you, hmm? They can't hurt me. As a matter of fact they won't even be able to see me."

"Dreamer's right, Joe. We're the only ones who can see her."

The man named Joe turned back to me with a curious look on his face. "How have you been killing the soldiers outside? We know it's you, but we've never even been able to see other Walkers while awake, let alone do something like that."

I didn't answer his question. Instead I proposed one of my own. "Are you all volunteer black BENs? Were you all recruited into the Network and serve willingly?"

I watched a few people look away from me but the man's expression turned smug. "I've been an agent for five years! They treat me well so of course I serve willingly. The job is easy. It's not like I have to sweat and grunt like the pigs in the barracks. And I'm not a murderer like you!"

Looking around I took note of even more lowered eyes. "Is that the way the rest of you think? That you are innocent of all wrongdoing or harm?" I turned back to Joe. "Tell me, do you know what becomes of the Walkers you help bring in? Do you know the amount of pain and suffering that just doing your easy job leads to?" No one answered so I thundered my voice through the dream plane and everyone in the room jumped with the magnitude of it. "Do you?" To a sightless person, it would appear as if they all stared at nothing and spoke to nothing. No, security would do no good but I knew they would still arrive any minute. Taking a chance at wasting more energy than I should, I projected Niko as she was lying paralyzed on that table. The look in her eyes and the way she was nothing but a human receptacle for tubes and wires. I made sure they had a good view of the burn marks and bruises on her skin where tests had been performed. I showed them an image of other test subjects as they were strapped to tables, screaming as they writhed in pain. Then I showed what it looked like when Dr. Morgan failed to extrapolate any more data from her subjects. I showed how she terminated them with nothing more than an innocuous looking syringe.

"You're lying!" Another woman near the kitchen area stared at me with a face devoid of color. I moved without walking over to her, a mere blur to their eyes. When I stood right in front of her I pushed into her mind just a bit. It was hard, like walking in thick wet concrete, but I was able to speak to her mentally. *Look, I will let you see the truth in my head.* And I did. I opened up to her so she could see the truth in my words. I let her see what I had witnessed in the rooms in the opposite wing, what I myself had gone through as a child at the hands of Dr. Morgan.

The woman shook her head slowly back and forth. "She's not lying. What have we done?" Tears rolled down her face as she realized what she had been a part of for the past couple years. Then she sank to her knees and put her head in her hands. "What have we done?"

"Don't let her into your head, she's trying to trick you! We know the ones they keep for the labs were the criminals, were the Walkers that refused to obey the law. They were weak! Dr. Morgan said that there was something wrong with them and she was trying to find a cure. Her research is vital. She is the greatest mind of this century and I trust her completely."

His words fueled my anger and I floated into the air and slowly advanced toward him. "So you think they were weak, Joe? You think that the people in the labs who have been treated worse than animals are criminals? Do you know who the Walker is that they brought in a few days ago?"

He shrugged. "Just someone in the General's cadre, who cares?"

I advanced until I was right in front of his face. "That woman is Dr. Morgan's only daughter! And she has been running experiments on her since she came in. Now tell me how much you mean to the good doctor if she cares so little about her own flesh and blood? Her daughter was completely healthy and her only crime was in that she ran rather than becoming another rat in her mother's lab." I knew some of the black BENs like Joe would never change their mind. Their brainwashing had been thorough and solid. But looking around, I could see the doubt and horror linger on the other's faces. I had accomplished my objective with the black BENs, and the ones that were here would surely spread the news and the story of what I told them. They'd pass on what I showed them of the Walkers in the labs. Before I could leave the door burst open and five armed soldiers piled into the room. They looked around confused then the leader addressed the group as a whole.

"We had reports of a possible intruder. Where are they?"

One man pointed at Joe or at least where I was standing. "She's right there! You just can't see her."

The soldier in charge of his troop looked at the man as if he were crazy. "This isn't a fucking joke. We're on high alert right now! Filing a false intruder claim is a serious charge. Don't think your special status will get you out of punishment!" I was standing close enough that I quickly skimmed Joe's thoughts then wished I hadn't. If he had been sleeping in one of the buildings outside, he would have died sometime in the past two nights. He would be the perfect subject of another test. I moved to a different guard, not the leader. The guard on the far right was younger and looked nervous. He didn't like having to stay stimmed up day and night but he was terrified of the idea that soldiers were dying in their sleep. It took a fair amount of power to project in his head but the end result was well worth it. Even though not one person in the room moved, he clearly saw Joe raise a bolt pistol toward him so he brought his own gun up to bear on Joe in response.

"What are you—" Before the patrol leader could even finish his sentence I had the young soldier convinced that Joe was pulling the trigger. In a panic, he fired his rifle and Joe's head snapped back in a spray of blood.

I looked around the rest of the room at the horrified faces of the black BENs, my fellow Dream Walkers. "He was not a good man, and you have all been committing a crime against our people. From this moment on, I suggest you choose your sides wisely." Then I blinked out of the room before any of them could respond. My display with the Walkers had exhausted me immensely but there was no way I'd be able to skip seeing Niko again. I hoped that she would take heart in the fact that I was planning on coming for her the next night.

Dread preceded me down that familiar out-of-the-way hall that lead to Niko's room. Different guards stood outside the door than the last time I visited. Before I could change my mind I went through the door to the other side. I stopped just to one side as shock and pleasure cascaded through me. "Niko!"

She stood staring at the wall and she spun in place when I yelled her name. "You came!" I jumped from my place in front of the door to a spot near her and drank her down with my eyes. She wore a white synth suit again and seemed to be walking around with relative ease.

I looked into her blue eyes with wonder. "How?"

Niko seemed as lost in me as I was her because it took a few seconds to answer. "She came in earlier today and had technicians disconnect me from all the equipment then she gave me an injection that would counteract the neuro-blocker. She said that humans could only be on it for a few days otherwise they ran the risk of doing permanent damage to the subject." I heard the words come out of her mouth and I knew where the dark look on her face sprang from. "Julia, she referred to me as a subject." My brave soldier took in a shuddering breath and ran a hand though her hair. In a moment of strange humor I wondered if she hadn't picked up that habit from me.

"I'm sorry. I wish I could get you out of here right now but I can't."

She wasted no time pushing her own pain away and narrowing her focus on me and my answers. "When though?"

"I've been scouting and more these last few days. The good news is that all the Dream Walkers have been stimmed up as long as you have. They've also started stimming the soldiers over the past twenty-four hours. Souza has left me with a virus on a chip that will release all the classified information that the government currently has stored in their system. It will also bring down all their systems after the virus runs its course, thus crippling the entire Network. So that may be our way out."

Niko gave me a calculating look and I could see the genius waiting to tackle the problem of escape. "How long does the virus take to work? How are you planning on getting in?"

I shrugged. "I don't know how long it takes I'm waiting on another call back from Souza. He's bolted off to Toronto because Chicago has become unsafe for anyone hiding from the Network. I'm staying in a secret bunker about four levels down but my place may be compromised within the next forty-eight hours. So when I do get you out we'll be on the run. As for getting in, well I've got an idea about stowing atop one of the carriers coming back from patrol."

She thought about it for a minute and I started to tire. I already knew that the level of power I had expended on this trip was going to leave me with a massive headache. Finally Niko nodded and smiled at me. "That could work. I think the longer the soldiers stay stimmed up the more careless they're going to be on patrols." She stopped and looked at me with a sad frown. "I wish that you had time to teach me more. Maybe I could have gotten out of here by now."

I shook my head at her. "There was simply too much. There are things I'm only just now learning that I can do and some of those things are extremely draining." The evidence of my words washed over me while I stood right in front of Niko.

"You're fading!"

"I'm sorry, Niko, but I used too much energy and I have to go back now. All I can say for you is to be ready this coming evening."

She held a hand out in my direction, then dropped it again. Niko's eyes were shiny with tears when she finally spoke. "You should run far away from this place, Jules. You should run and never let them catch you again. I can't bear it if something happens to you because of me. Go north and make a life elsewhere."

I felt another tug pulling me toward my body and gave her a sad smile. "Oh you stupid BEN, don't you know that I've already made a life and it's standing right here in this room?"

"Julia..."

I nodded. "Without you, there is no place in the world I could go and be happy. Without you, I may as well be dead." I moved back to the door. "Until tomorrow. Don't give up faith in me, and be ready." Then I was gone, speeding the morning away to my body.

Chapter Fifteen

Waiting for Chaos

PAIN LANCED THROUGH my skull when I returned my mind to that dark room below ground. I grabbed my head reflexively and curled inward willing it to stop. I could feel blood trickling from my nose and I knew that I'd overextended myself again on the last walk. I had to get better at reading the signs of my exhaustion or I would run the risk of doing permanent damage to myself. I fumbled for the pack of analgesic tabs on the stand next to the bed and successfully grabbed three to shove under my tongue. It took seconds for the pain to come down to a tolerable level and tears streamed from my eyes in relief. Not for the first time in recent days, my face was a mess of salt and blood. But rather than get up to clean it off I grabbed the water canister and tried to collect my thoughts. I glanced at my wrist comp and took heart in the fact that it was late morning, which left plenty of time to rest, refuel, and plan for the evening to come.

After downing the entire container and eating a protein bar, I pulled myself from the surprisingly comfortable bed and made my way into the living area. I felt as rough as the black Walkers looked on my last visit, and I knew that I had put the next part of my mission in jeopardy. Rather than attempting to contact Souza right away, I opted for a meal that was high in protein and carbs. I drank two more canisters of water and spent a good amount of time showering in the facility just trying to feel human again. It would be better if I got everything ready to go before heading into some solid REM sleep so I started inspecting all my gear. The bolt guns that Souza had given me were tactical issues and highly illegal in the hands of a private cit. The gas canisters were a special mix that made for higher bolt speed out of the barrel, and the tips of the bolts were hardened to a razor point that would penetrate even the best BEN armor.

I loaded the panier of my bike with tech goodies I found around the bunker, which included a few more small weapons. There were knives, Tasers, and more ammunition, although not of the armor piercing type. I also made sure my comp tablet was secured and added all Souza's program chips but the main one. A person never knew when they'd need some of the stuff that Souza could come up with. The important chip drive went into a secret pocket in my solar suit, one that was easily accessed but not necessarily easily found. The other panier had a spare synth suit, dry rations, and a few other things I thought I may need once I left the bunker behind. After making sure everything was ready I filled the water pack that could be worn below my suit and refilled the syringe of my belt mounted adrenaline pump. When all my preparations were complete, I opened the secret wall and pushed my bike into the escape tunnel. The only thing left to do was call my favorite hacker and see if he had come up with a better plan. He answered the comp call right away.

"You look like shit, Jules." Souza was never one to mince words.

I shrugged at him. "What can I say? It's been a rough couple days."

"I had concerns that the BENs were going to find you. My entry alarms tripped in the tunnels but when I checked from my end it appeared as though the soldiers went in the opposite direction from your bunker. Based on their current search patterns you've probably got another twenty-four hours of safety but that's it."

I nodded my head at him with a grim look pulling my lips into a frown. "I already know about the tunnel breach. But luckily I only need about ten of those hours then I'm out of here."

"So you're for sure going in to get her?"

"Yes. Tell me you've thought of something that will help me to get inside the compound."

Souza slowly nodded yes but there was no confidence to the motion. "I may have a way in, but there are details I can't seem to work out. Half a dozen supply drones a day come into the compound from the production plants. The Network always gets the first shipment and the rest of the lab food gets shipped out on cargo ships and maglev trains to be distributed and sold throughout the region. I think it would be fairly easy to stow away in the large transport drone but the soldiers always check incoming cargo before allowing a porter to unload it. I don't know how to keep the BEN or the unloader from reporting you once you land. "

I thought about his plan. "Doesn't the transport have sensors onboard that will tell the BENs if there is a stowaway?"

He gave me a serious look through the vid screen. "Ah, but that's where I come in. Not only can I unlock the transport and get you in, but I can make it seem like all that's inside is the normal cargo from the production facility. I can't hack someone's eyes though so I don't think it will work."

I smiled and felt hope starting to blossom in my chest. "You can't hack people but I can. If you can get me into the compound, I can make sure no one sees me on that transport. The agent who checks the cargo will see exactly what they expect."

Souza didn't ask any questions. He merely took me at my word. "And the porter?"

I shook my head. "I'll take care of the porter too. Now tell me about the produce transports. Are they ground based or flight like the fire drones?"

"They're flight based with VTOL, exactly like the drones. With four engines they can lift both you and Niko easily. They're used to much heavier cargo."

My head raced with ideas about what I could do and what I would need. "What about bikes? Are they large enough to hold a couple of cycles and still lift?"

He nodded. "Absolutely. As I said, they're made to handle large crates of cargo."

"When can you have one ready for me? When are deliveries usually made?"

"Well despite the fact that it was going to be a suicide mission I had a feeling you'd choose the drone route so I already broke the security on one and it will be ready when they start making deliveries around 2300 hours. As you already know, factories aren't allowed to ship until the midnight shift because of noise and daytime commuters. The transport drones are auto loaded so I also made sure that one would stay empty but read as full. I can land it just outside the production warehouse for you to load yourself and your kit then I'll send it to the compound. The digital log won't record the brief stop."

"That sounds good. Push me the map of where you'll have it land and I'll be there on time."

He brought his wrist comp into view of the monitor and punched in the directions and a few seconds later my own vibrated. When he was finished he looked back up at me. "What are you going to do now?"

"I should probably get some sleep."

"You should get some sleep."

We both spoke at the same time and I had to laugh at the coincidence of it. "Yes, rest is definitely needed if I want to successfully navigate the next twenty-four hours." I scrubbed a hand over my stubbly scalp. "I don't even know what to do if this actually works and we get away. I don't know where to go that is safe."

"Come to Toronto." I looked at him curiously and he elaborated. "There was a lot I wasn't aware of until I hit town a few days ago. The Network isn't as strong here. They've become a sanctuary city of sorts. It's not at all like living in the capital beneath the General's thumb. I'll have work for both of you if you need it. But trust me when I say that Toronto is safe in a way that Chicago never was."

I mulled over the possibilities in my head and finally nodded at him. "If we make it out we'll head your way."

His smile was very bright on his dark face. "I'll be expecting you then. I have the utmost faith in your abilities."

His belief in me was empowering and something I desperately needed. "I can never thank you enough for your help with this."

Souza shook his head. "After what you've done for me in the past? There will never be thanks necessary. I am forever in your debt." And that was the crux of it. Even though we had become acquaintances over the years, and even friends on some level, Souza owed me a debt. There was no greater currency than one that dealt in coin of the soul. I couldn't help the sigh as the quote came unbidden to my mind. I missed having Niko near me to answer the author to my quotes, or give one in return. I missed Niko. Souza disconnected after that, we had nothing more to say. Only time would tell if I'd see him again, or if I'd be buried in the city of my dreams. Despite years of doctors and testing, despite being on the run for a third of my life, Chicago had always been my home. It was the place that my family had lived and died and the very place my heart had been brought to life. The thought of leaving it filled me with a sorrow that was hard to bear. But the thought of spending another day without Niko by my side was unimaginable. We would move on together or we would die in a glorious attempt at freedom.

My REM sleep was strange and disconcerting again. I had never been to the city that used to fly the pre-war flag of Canada. In the years after the droughts and global disasters hit, it had easily grown as large as Chicago. It was situated on one of the Great Lakes and had access to the shipping routes just as much as the capital. However, Chicago had always been a hub from the old days of North American travel. Traditional railways had been converted to maglev lines decades ago and the airport flew travelers all over the world. Of course, it was just as hard to get visas to leave as it was to come into the country. But while Toronto was a large populous city, it wasn't the center of trade, travel, and power that capital city was.

In my dream I lived in an apartment with Niko. It looked a lot like my courier housing. Most large companies took over apartment high-rises to house their employees. In the dream our Toronto apartment overlooked the lake, very similar to my Chicago residence, and it gave me a sense of familiarity. I wasn't sure why I would have such a vision. The two of us flew high into the sky as our Dream Walker selves, our spirits soaring together with freedom and joy. The sky was blue and clear. The lake was the same. It was as if the world of our past had never existed. Sparkling green showed far below and I smiled at the image of seeing so many trees in one place. Then I looked over at Niko where she flew beside me and I smiled even more. We took a long time just enjoying the world around our building and eventually came to rest again in our own bodies. Niko whispered words of wonder to me at the same time she grabbed my wrist to pull me closer. My heart felt light and I playfully refused to come toward her. My stomach sank when she frowned and pulled again harder. That was the moment that I woke to the vibration of my wrist comp.

My voice was nothing more than a hoarse whisper in the dark room. "No." It seemed cruel to me that when I was nearest to my possible demise I should be dreaming of all that I loved and would surely lose. My sleep had been full of beauty that had either died long ago or would never come to pass. I rubbed my chest over my aching heart, as though it were producing physical pain. It seemed so real. In all actuality I was shocked that I needed the wrist comp to wake me. Despite how fast time went in my dream, I never anticipated actually needing the alarm. I set it for later than I would normally sleep and ended up utilizing the entire time. It was obvious that I sorely needed the rest, and I still had plenty of time to take care of my physical needs before making my way to the pickup point. The real challenge would be getting to the place where the food hauler would pick me up, undetected by the heightened BEN patrols.

After eating and using the facility I finished prepping to leave. Following the map on the comp, the escape tunnel took me just south of the loop and ended with a ramp that led up into the new blue line tunnel. Rather than run above ground like the original track, the city planners decided to move as much shipping as possible underground when Chicago became the capital city. I suspected that Souza's escape route must have originally been used for service purposes decades before. I checked the time and cross-checked that with the transport train schedules. I had about a twenty minute window to head west and cross under the river before the first midnight train came along. It was not a comfortable ride. The tunnel was narrow enough that I had to ride over partially buried magline supports and my teeth rattled inside my helmet. Just when I thought I could take no more abuse I arrived at the Clinton platform. The bike handled the steps up with as much grace as could be expected, but I was able to power through it. I damaged the lock on the large gate in order to get my bike out of the station, but it was purely mechanical and nothing that would set off an alarm to the local patrols.

Making sure the coast was clear, I rode out of the station and immediately turned into a dark alley behind one of the nearby buildings. I needed time to see what patrols were in the area. Unlike the past scouting I had done as a courier, I didn't need to find a place to hide for a handful of minutes. I was able to sit on my bike and fly out of my body within a few seconds, the gyro sufficient to keep me from falling. I made a fast circuit around a three-block area and over the tops of the buildings. My meeting point was still seven blocks away and I had to be sure I would arrive unseen and stay unseen once I got there. After investigating my immediate location I flew toward the grower facility where Souza had said he'd set down the transport. The architecture of the building had multiple alcoves built in. All were in full shadow. I glanced at my wrist comp again and saw that I had fifteen minutes to pick up.

I knew that the time was right to go so I returned to my body and raced through the streets as fast as I could. Weaving back and forth through the city blocks it didn't take long to reach my new hiding place at such a reckless speed. I had to alter my route once when my heat sensor picked up a group of de-gens exiting a building, but after that it was clear. A short time later I backed into an alcove and readied myself to wait for the remaining ten minutes.

In all the years that I had known Souza, he had never let me down. That said a lot about a person, especially about someone who operated outside the laws dictated by the militarized government of North America. He may have been a criminal, but he still had honor. I heard the hum of its engines before the drone came into view. As soon as it touched down the back cargo hatch opened and I raced out of the alcove into the safety of the transport. Though I supposed that safety was a relative word considering I was headed into the center of my greatest hell. I quickly worked to secure the bike to the floor so that it wouldn't be jostled or tipped. The transport was large enough to fit half a dozen bikes in the cargo area. I was relieved to see that even though it was remotely programmed, it could be switched to manual operation if the need arose. Many of the old delivery crafts had been converted into auto piloted drones years before because it was cheaper than buying all new carriers. The ground transports weren't as expensive to buy but anything capable of flight, especially something that could do the vertical takeoff and landing, was a lot more expensive. Souza had chosen well. The drone was barely up in the air before I felt it start to drop altitude again as it approached the compound. My palms began to sweat and I did one last check of the bolt pistols on my waist as well as the one slung over my back. I stood off to the side and closed my eyes. I searched and quickly found the single BEN in full armor that stood waiting for the back hatch to open. I dipped into his mind just enough to project an image of a full transport as soon as the hatched cycled open. He used his helmet to scan for heat signature and I made him see what I wanted rather than the hot white image of a lone person sanding inside.

"This one is clear!" He called out the okay to the other soldiers and walked away. There were no floodlights where the supply transports had landed. I waited for the rest of the BENs to complete their drone checks before readying myself to leave the relative safety of the cargo area. When I peeked my head out, I saw that my drone had landed closest to the side of the enormous building. A large cargo door opened in the side of the main facility and a single enclosed fork truck came rumbling out. The porter pulled up to the back of the transport I was in and I projected the thought that he had already unloaded the drone. He shook his head. He then sent the code to the transport telling it to head back to its home and frowned inside the clear plas-enclosed machine. The lights from his inside display screen lit his features and I silently thanked Souza for all his hard work. If the machine malfunctioned, they would have to wait until someone from the production facility could come retrieve it manually, or until they sent someone to repair the drone. Neither would happen during the midnight shift, which meant the drone would be stuck there for the night.

After he moved on to the next drone in line, I slipped out the back of the carrier and closed the hatch. Four hauler bots had followed the man out. I watched from the shadows to see how the process worked. The bots were programmed to return back to the service cargo area as they were filled by the porter. I waited for one to fill and trundle away then leaped aboard and nestled down between large sealed black bags of algae paste. The bolt rifle made it impossible to get down far enough so I placed that on top and hoped it wouldn't be seen. Once inside I found another area to hide out of the way. Along with the map to the pickup location, Souza had also sent me an old schematic of the complex. Luck was with me again when I saw that there was a stairwell that led up to the Walker wing, not very far from my location. Unfortunately, I knew from previous trips that there were security cameras in every stairwell and elevator within the complex. I had to do something about the guards in the security room.

I shut my eyes to float my psyche free and did a quick search of the receiving area to be sure no one would find my body while I was walking. I remembered the location of the security room from my previous visits and made my way there. It wasn't like I would come across any other Dream Walkers on the first floor so I didn't have to worry about anyone giving warning of my presence. The inside of the room was full of monitors. There were five comp stations and a guard to monitor each. I found the ones that covered the stairwell and the fourth floor. Luckily they were on the same bank of monitors and it was one guard that watched them all. That guard needed to take a break and I was going to facilitate that urge. It was difficult but I pushed my way into his mind. Rob Simmons hated being stimmed because some damn Walker was hell-bent on fucking with their lives. He hadn't eaten in about six hours and he was thinking about how hungry he was. All the shifts were short-handed so Rob had to start his shift two hours early and he was not a happy man. I put thoughts of a steaming lab beef meal with hydro vegetables on the side. I smiled when his stomach gave a massive growl. It was a benefit that the guard sitting at the next comp station heard it.

"Holy shit, Rob! Did you skip dinner tonight or what?"

Rob flipped the woman off. "I had to start two hours early because Sheila got moved to first and I haven't had a chance to eat tonight."

One of the other guards called out to him. "Jesus man, go get something to eat! We've got this." He waved his hand toward the door. "Go on, we'll cover for you. If Captain Dain comes in we'll tell him you went to take a piss."

I felt my guard relax and settle into the idea of going to get food. "Thanks guys, I'll be back in thirty." He stood and made his way to the door. I left his mind and stayed in the room to see what the other guards would do. I didn't have long to wait. The woman at the station next to Rob's spoke to the other three.

"Should I jump over and cover his station?"

The other guard that had suggested Rob go grab some dinner just shook his head at her. "He just finished his two hour check and yours is due to start so just get your stuff done. It's only thirty minutes, it should be fine." That was exactly what I wanted to hear.

I quickly returned to my body and made ready to take off. I scouted my route on the way back to the receiving area so I knew there were no guards between my position and the stairwell. Without overthinking it I was immediately in motion. I ran down the hallway and up the stairs to the fourth floor, and when I got to the top I spirit walked just a ways out into the hallway to see if there were people around. I knew the Walkers were awake but most likely in their own wing. They probably wouldn't be allowed to walk around at such a late hour. While I was in the stairwell I also scouted around the now locked lab and found an alternate route into the secured hallway where Niko was being kept. There were two guards outside the room as I slipped inside. Niko was clearly still being stimmed and I was glad to see that she remained free from the paralysis drug. She didn't see me when I first came in because she was intently focused on her exercise. I was caught frozen as I watched her count out pushups on the floor about three meters from the door. Even with the generic synth suit I could make out the flexing muscles in her back and arms. Shaking myself from fascinated stupor, I called out to her. "Niko."

In a single move she collapsed to the floor and rolled to the side so she could sit up. "Julia! Are you here this time, in the facility?"

I smiled at her. "I'm in the stairwell not far from here. I need help though. I can get through one guard by clouding his mind, but I can't manipulate two at the same time. Do you have a suggestion?"

"Are you armed?"

"I have my stun batons, two pistols, and an auto-fire rifle."

She thought for a second and nodded her head. "That's good. Can you make one leave?"

I thought about the two guards outside the door and knew that Niko would be the highest priority. Something told me that they wouldn't be able to leave on break like the security officer. "I don't think one will leave easily and I don't want to make one do something that will make either of them panic and call an alarm."

Niko was one of the few people I'd ever met that I truly enjoyed just watching her think. Her blue eyes grew unfocused and darted back and forth with her racing thoughts. "What if—" She paused to finalize her thought then looked up at me and finished her idea. "You drew one's attention in a nonthreatening way? If someone walked by in the hall that wasn't supposed to be there? Or if one got a com call?"

I smiled at her. "Well without any other option it's worth a try. I can skim both of their thoughts and see what might work best. Are you all right? Will you be okay to keep up? I mean, you've been stimmed for days now and you're going to crash as soon as you start coming down."

She grimaced. "I'll be fine until we both get out of here. And Julia..." I looked up to meet those amazingly sincere eyes. "We will get out of here. Let's take this one step at a time."

"One step at a time." I would make those words work for me. "One way or another, I'll be back. I'm going to go see what I can do."

Outside in the hall both guards projected feelings of anxious exhaustion. The one guard, Sam Donovan, was especially irritated to be brought inside for special guard duty. His thoughts were like a fast current and I really had to focus to understand his stream of consciousness. The Walker for Sam's team had been taken off duty so they scattered the team throughout the complex to help bolster security inside. And he was stuck on midnight shift guarding a high profile prisoner. It was a thankless job standing in the hall all night and he hated it. His Walker teammate was currently on the fourth floor in the Walker wing, probably doing nothing but sitting on her ass like the rest of the dream freaks. That was enough information to help me out. I focused and made him see the image of his Walker wander by the end of the hall. The other guard was watching the other direction so would not know that Sam hadn't really seen anything.

"What the hell is she doing down at this end?"

The other guard spun his gaze in Sam's direction. "Who?"

Sam's face was a study of irritation and puzzlement. "My team's Walker just wandered down the hall. They're not supposed to be out of their wing at all let alone on midnight shift." He made a face. "But then Davis has always played it fast and loose with the rules. I'm just going to run down there and send her ass back to her room."

The first guard, Stephen, looked unsure. "I don't know. Is that a good idea?" He was a slim man, just a little larger than me, and had a nervous look about him.

Sam was bigger and I read from his thoughts that he was a little bit of a bully. "Relax, it will literally take me five seconds. Be right back." He didn't even wait for Stephen to acknowledge his statement before he was off jogging down the hall and around the corner toward my stairwell. In his mind, he saw the Walker push through the door of the stairwell so he followed and called out to her. I was back in my body in an instant and used both stun batons on him at max power as he pushed into the stairwell. He didn't see me because I was in his head and didn't let him. The door to the stairwell closed right before his bulky body dropped liked a stone. I tucked his bolt pistol into my belt and secured his wrists to the railing with a set of flex cuffs that I found on his belt. He had his gloves tucked into his belt too so I used one to stuff his mouth as full as I could and hoped that would keep him quiet when he finally woke. He would be obvious to anyone using the stairs, but I was at least trying to keep him from getting away or yelling for help. The last thing I grabbed was his RFD key for Niko's room. I checked my wrist comp and saw that seventeen of my initial thirty minutes had elapsed. After that I left him behind and rounded the corner into the secured hall where Stephen waited. He saw his fellow guard returning, not an insurgent walker with stun batons ready.

"Did she say why she was out of her wing?" Of course I didn't answer him verbally. I projected a response into his mind, one that matched Sam's voice and tone.

"She said that she was meeting a lover down on the second floor. I told her if she didn't immediately return to her room that I was going to file a report. Nobody else should have any fun while I'm stuck here!" I felt Stephen relax when he got the response he expected. The moment he let down his guard I hit him with the stun batons. I caught him as he dropped and used the key card to unlock Niko's room then removed my helmet. I pushed through the heavy security door and found myself caught up in a hug that was much too tight and absolutely perfect.

Her voice was a whisper in my ear. "I've missed you."

I shuddered and forced myself not to burrow into her embrace the way I had been longing to do for days. I pulled back and looked into those strange blue eyes and the kiss that followed seemed natural. "I've missed you too." I gestured to the guard with his government-issue solar suit. "Will that fit you? Or do you know where they stowed your kit?" I put my helmet back on but kept the face shield clear so she could see me better.

Niko nodded. "I actually do know where it's at as long as they didn't move it again. I was awake when I arrived at the lab. They stripped me then and locked all my gear in a cabinet."

We slid the guard inside Niko's room and decided to come back and strip his gear only if hers was no longer in the storage cabinet. I looked at my wrist comp. "We need to hurry. We only have about eight minutes before the guy downstairs that's monitoring this floor comes back on duty." She nodded and we used the guard's key card to scan our way into the lab where Niko's kit was located. She went in search of her gear and I went to the nearest comp and removed my helmet then pulled out Souza's chip. The computers were already online, though they were password protected. I assumed that Souza knew that would be the case so I simply plugged the chip into the load port. A light came on and the vid screen started flickering at a rapid pace, doing whatever he had programmed it to do.

"What is that?"

I watched as Niko finished fastening her black suit and donned her gloves. Her boots were already on. I loved her in that suit. I nodded toward the comp screen. "It's a little gift that Souza made. I'm hoping it will crash the system sooner rather than later. He said it would create enough chaos that it should facilitate our escape."

Keen eyes gazed at the flickering screen then around the lab that was lit by security lights. "What's our time table?"

I glanced at my wrist comp. "Three minutes until the security guard returns to monitor this section. The only ones who have seen me so far are the two guards outside your room. One is flex-cuffed to the railing in the stairwell with a glove stuffed in his mouth." Before I could forget, I handed his bolt pistol to her as well as the auto-fire rifle I carried on my back. I reveled in the appreciation and respect that came from Niko.

For not being a soldier, you have sure performed like a professional so far.

Her voice in my head was a soothing balm to help heal all the days I'd been without her. I smiled as I stood from the comp desk and stepped in close. Our lips met and I pushed every emotion I had been feeling toward her and held tight when she sucked in a desperate breath. My own mental response was a pledge from my heart to hers. *No matter what, I will never leave you again.*

"Julia—"

I cut her off and stepped away to re-don my helmet. "No, don't ask me to make any more promises. We make it out together or not at all!"

She nodded. "Fair enough." While Niko's face looked upset by my declaration, the emotions battering away at my mind screamed *don't leave me,* and my choice was made.

I glanced back at the screen, which still showed signs of scrolling code and flickering scrambled image. "What do we do now?"

Niko laughed quietly and put on her own helmet. "I thought you had a plan?"

"I had a plan to get in and get you free and a plan to get us out of the compound, but the place between the two was a little sketchy. And our time is now up on the guard so if we leave this room we'll be seen for sure. I was counting on you for this part. This is your territory after all."

She glanced at the screen then back at me. "Then I guess we stay in this room and wait."

It wouldn't have been hard for her to read the concern on my face or coming from my mind. "Wait for what, to get caught?"

Niko grinned and it seemed nearly feral behind the cleared faceplate and in the low light of the room. "We wait for the chaos to begin." As if on cue with her words, the alarm sounded and lights started flashing above the doorways. They might not have known where I was, but they knew I was here.

Chapter Sixteen

The Greatest Betrayal

"FUCK." I HAD never felt an exclamation so fiercely or so thoroughly than the one that fell from my lips in that moment. "This is the first place they'll check. We'll be trapped in here!"

"Let me think for a minute."

As impatient as I was, I just nodded and Niko closed her eyes. She was the soldier and I had confidence that she would know what to do. Plus she knew the layout of the massive complex much better than I ever could have by studying Souza's old schematic. A change in flickering patterns on the comp screen drew my attention. I wondered what else the virus was supposed to do besides release data and crash the system. My wrist comp vibrated and I checked the incoming message. "He really did it!"

Niko looked up at me. "Who did what?"

I lifted my wrist slightly. "Souza said data packets are transferring and said we have about five minutes before the virus starts killing the Network. His words, not mine."

"That's good, really goo—"

"I knew you would come."

We both spun toward the voice that emanated from the darkened corner near the farthest entrance into the lab. I recognized the voice, although it had been decades since I'd heard her in person. I dipped into her thoughts and grew wary at what I discovered. Her mind was like a dark cloud but I knew she had something dangerous in her hand, I just didn't know what. Her lab coat had typical large pockets so I just assumed it was a bolt pistol. "You bitch!" Niko stepped toward her mother, but I grabbed her arm to hold her back.

"Don't, she's armed."

Olivia Morgan peered back at me curiously in the dim light of the lab. "Now how would you know that?"

I shrugged, not wanting to give too much away. "You wouldn't come here alone to face intruders if you were unarmed. You are many things, Dr. Morgan, but you're not stupid."

She laughed. "No, I'm not stupid and that is how I know that you're not telling me the whole truth, are you, Julia?" I watched her face change expression as she tried a different tack. "You can join me you know. There is still plenty to learn, plenty we need to explore. There is a lifetime of science within your grasp! Think of the possibilities. And you, Niko, you could be by my side for the entire journey!"

I looked askance at Niko and she answered my unasked question. "I had three degrees by the time I was fifteen, one was in genetic coding." She looked back at her mother, the woman who had lied to her for a decade. The very same woman who had tortured her for days all in the name of science. "I would rather be dead than work with you!"

I sensed something from Dr. Morgan and called a warning. "Niko..." She tore her gaze from her mother and brought it back to me. *I'm pretty sure she has a bolt pistol aimed at one of us right now. I didn't get a thorough read but I know that she'll shoot if she has to. Right now she's stalling, I can feel it.*

Niko's face became a mask of anger and it was directed at the woman who held us hostage. "She's stalling for the General! How long ago did you call him?"

Olivia Morgan smiled at us. "Right before I came in here." She pulled the gun out fully and kept it aimed at me. Her left hand remained in her pocket. Something still didn't sit right in her thoughts so I probed deeper and gasped aloud at what I found.

My words felt hollow as they entered the alarm filled room. "You're a monster!"

"Julia?" I continued to stare at Dr. Morgan and Niko tried again. *What's going on?*

I glanced back at Niko and had to know. "Turn around."

Confusion washed over her face. "Why?"

Fear and impatience ate at me because minutes were wasting with each breath. "Turn around, Niko!" She turned and my fears were confirmed. There was a small incision on the back of her neck. I spun my head back to Niko's mother. "Are you out of your mind? How could you do something like that to your own daughter?"

I felt a tide of anger rising from Niko just before she spoke. "What are you talking about? What did you see?" She reached back and her face registered surprise as she felt the puckered flesh of the incision. Her mother once again bore her wrath. "What did you do to me?"

Dr. Morgan slowly pulled a small box from her opposite pocket. It had a single diode light and one button. "I took out a little insurance to make sure you stayed on your best behavior.

You didn't think I'd let you off the Neuromuscular block without taking precautions, did you?"

"What precautions?"

I spoke to Niko without taking my eyes off the older woman. "She put a chip in your neck between the C4 and C5 vertebrae. If she presses the button, the box will send a signal that will cause a cauterizing plasma burn to the spinal cord in that spot, rendering you permanently paralyzed."

"Now that is a little more than simply guessing that I'm armed. What were you doing at the computer when I came in, Julia? I had no idea you'd turned into such a little hacker!"

I was tired of hiding. I was tired of letting Dr. Morgan instill fear in me. "Do you really want to know what I'm doing? I'm bringing down the Network, piece by piece!" I started slowly walking toward her. "You may be smart, Doctor, but you've been wrong for decades. You have no idea what you're dealing with when it comes to Dream Walkers."

Surprise washed through her mind and she cocked her head to the side. "What do you mean? We've made great strides with the research!"

I laughed, a broken horrible sound. "Oh, I know all about your research. But see, you've been running under a base assumption for decades. You have just assumed that Dream Walkers were limited to their dreams. But the truth is—" I glanced at Niko and she looked sadly back.

Do what you have to do, Jules. I understand.

"The truth is we're not Walkers at all."

My heart skipped a beat when Olivia Morgan's hand convulsed on the control box. "What?"

"It's simple really. The sleeping mind is more malleable, is weaker and slower than the waking mind. What you've failed to discover all this time is that Dream Walkers are nothing more than psychics communicating within a separate plane of awareness." It was as if time slowed down in preparation for my next words. Maybe it did. "And we don't need to be asleep to make ourselves heard." Then to make my revenge that much sweeter, I spoke directly into her mind. *Olivia Morgan, you have been found guilty of crimes against Dream Walkers and crimes against children. And worst of all, you've betrayed your daughter's trust. Your work here is done!* I sensed her panic a second before she intended to stab her finger on the button but I didn't need that second to act. I was already inside. I envisioned a great beast ripping its way through her psyche. The box flew into the air as she brought her hands up to her skull and shrieked with agony. Even as I died with her own mother, Niko moved in a blur of speed next to me. Faster than I'd ever seen anyone fire, Niko had drawn the bolt pistol and destroyed the box before it could hit the ground. As soon as I realized she was safe I fell to my knees, body washed out by pain and exhaustion.

"Julia!" She rushed over to me and knelt on the floor. "Dammit!" I held still while she wrenched off my helmet and gently brought both thumbs to wipe the blood that trickled sluggishly from my nose.

I tried to push her hand away. "Don't worry about me. I'm fine."

"You're bleeding!"

I shook my head at her. "It's normal. Come on, we have to go now."

Niko helped me stand and despite having the clear plate of her helmet between us, the concern wasn't hard to read on her face. "It may be normal but it's definitely not good. How long have you been able to do that?"

Fumbling for the zipper that held my stim tabs gave me a small amount of time to think about her question. I popped two stims under my tongue and once they were dissolved, I went back for two analgesic tabs to combat the throbbing that had begun behind my eyes. "I've been able to shred minds while walking for a few days, but I'd never done anything like this in person." There was no way I was going to admit to her how much worse it was in person than it was while walking. I held out a shaking hand for my helmet and she gave it back. I felt safer with it on, more in control. I took one last glance of the woman lying on the floor and shivered at how much she looked like Niko from the back. "I'm sorry about your mother."

Niko shook her head back and forth and I knew she was saying goodbye in her mind. "I never knew my mother. That woman on the floor was nothing more than an opportunistic stranger. I would have killed her if you hadn't. I owe her nothing."

Her words rang somewhat false to me, and it wasn't because I could see inside her head or that my power had grown tremendously in a short period of time. It was because I knew Niko better than anyone on the planet. She may have been blocking the pain but I knew that deep inside she still grieved. When everything was done, if we could make our escape, I would help her in any way I could. Despite the fact that we both knew the risks and circumstances and that she gave me permission, I also knew there was very little that would ever alleviate the guilt I felt from killing her mother. I shook my head and pushed the conversation away. "Have you thought of something to get us out of here?"

Niko frowned. "Not really. This level is pretty secure. The only bright spot is that the General's quarters are on the opposite side of the structure so it will take time for him to get here. I don't know why he hasn't sent soldiers ahead of him. It makes no sense."

"I can walk and scout around the floor..."

She cut me off. "No! You're hurt and I don't think that would be a good idea right now."

"Niko, I'm fine! Besides, you can't do it while you're stimmed. It has to be me."

She tried again. "But you're stimmed too."

The sigh slipped out unbidden. There was so much she had missed in a short amount of time. I wanted to share it all with her. I wanted to show her everything we could both do together. But there simply was no time. "That doesn't matter for me anymore." I looked into those wounded eyes and knew she agreed with me. There were no chairs near us so I stepped close to her. "Hold me up. This will only take a minute." The feel of her arms wrapping around me in such a solid embrace brought me comfort that the situation should have never allowed.

I flew from my body quickly and her eyes watched me go. I made a quick circuit down the nearby hallways and even farther off toward the Walker wing. The farther I went, the more baffled I became at the lack of soldiers. Then I started checking the stairwells. BENs in full armor lined up above and below our floor, waiting for some signal perhaps to come through the door. Traveling even farther, I noticed the elevator on the far side of the Walker wing was in motion. Numbers ticked down as I watched, nineteen, eighteen, seventeen — and I made a split second decision. I regretted that I couldn't tell Niko about it ahead of time. I flew up into the descending elevator and saw in person the man who had caused me so much pain over the years. Niko was right, General Rennet was an old man. He wore a military uniform but you could see that he was tired and I could read that his mind was tired as well. I had never tried to actually control someone, I wasn't sure if it was even possible. I watched as the number above the door stopped at four and knew my time had run out.

I pushed into his head and found it soft, almost like a sleeper. I went deeper than I'd ever gone before until I could start to feel the rasping breaths in my lungs and the pain that throbbed in my joints. I'd had both knees replaced, and a shoulder, but nothing seemed to slow the steady progression of age, nor the inevitability of death. I lifted a hand and the four other guards looked at me. "I need them both alive, no matter what!" I was convinced that the two Walkers held the key to getting out of this body and they were of utmost importance to me. And I had known Captain Morgan since she was just a girl. I trusted her with my life. As the door opened I silently crept out of his deepest thoughts and returned back to my body. Pain met me on my return but I ignored it as best as I was able.

"What did you see?"

I shook my head to fully separate who I had been as Rennet and who I was standing in front of Niko. "Soldiers lined up in every stairwell. General Rennet has just entered the floor from the elevator and is making his way here with four personal guards." I looked into her eyes. "He doesn't want to hurt us and he trusts you above all others."

She gave me a puzzled look. "That makes no sense. He should want my head!"

"He trusts you now. And when the time comes, you will prove that trust. I can't control him if he tries to fight me, but I can fabricate an opportunity for you to solidify the thoughts I already put into his head. I'll warn you if I can but be ready." She nodded and I smiled at her, a grim slash of lips on what I knew to be a face washed pale with pain and exhaustion. "Let's go meet the General."

We went through the door that Dr. Olivia Morgan had used not long before. Unfortunately it required us to step over her body. I felt a brief flash of pain from Niko but her expression behind the faceplate of the helmet never changed. We entered into another hall and about ten meters away, the General turned the corner with his guards. Despite the fact that we were obviously armed, he continued to approach slowly with the guards flanking his sides and back. "Hello Captain, who's your friend?"

He eventually stopped a little over three meters from us so I answered his question. "My name is Jules Page."

"Ah yes, Jules Page, secure tech courier for Vanguard. But that's not really who you are is it? You've been gone a long time, Julia Thiel." He smiled at us, looking more like someone's kindly grandfather than the despotic general that he was. It was an act that he used time and time again. A master manipulator, General Rennet could be whomever you wanted him to be if it got him close enough to strike. "You've come a long way since that little girl I met more than twenty years ago."

I shrugged. "Well you know what they say, we all grow up sometime." It was time to get serious because I knew the longer the standoff went on the less likely we'd get out. I hadn't seen any other effects from Souza's virus and I feared we would be stuck. "We'd like to leave, General. I have intel you need and I'm willing to work out a deal with you."

His true self slipped a little then. "Deal? It doesn't look like you're in any position to make a deal right now. What could you possibly have to offer?"

When they brought Niko in, they didn't actually have any proof that she was a Walker. They only knew that a fellow soldier reported her and she ran. Because of who she was, it made the chase and search that much more intense. And she'd been kept stimmed since arriving at the complex so they had no actual verification of her Walker status. I nodded toward her. "Niko wasn't the Walker you had hiding in your division. She was set up. But I know who the real Walker is—I've seen him." Three of the four guards surrounding General Rennet were men, and they all looked startled at each other. I could see in their minds they wondered who was the Walker in their midst.

That meant it was my time to act again. I pushed into the mind of the guard that was to the left of the General. He had suspicions about another in their group, Denevel. The name came from his lips and I encouraged him to eliminate the threat. Unfortunately the soldier he suspected was on the other side of General Rennet and when he raised his bolt gun to fire the rest of them went into action, thinking he was aiming at Rennet.

As if Niko had been privy to my plan from the beginning, she played along perfectly. "General, get down!" She sighted and fired before the rest of the soldiers could react. The soldier's head snapped back and his helmet exploded in a spray of blood and gore. Rennet had been shoved aside and the remaining three guards went into action, aiming their pistols at us.

"Hold! That is an order!" Rennet's voice boomed through the hallway, belying a man of his years. He turned to Niko. "You could have killed me, instead you saved me. Why?"

Niko's answer was all her own. "I don't like betrayal." She was certainly playing her part perfectly.

It was my turn again. I called out slowly, fearfully. "General, it wasn't him." Realization washed over his face at the same time another soldier swung his pistol toward me. That was when the General drew his own bolt gun and shot the guard. Two down, two to go.

The woman on the other side of the second dead man frantically wiped the blood splatter from her face. "Shit! We've worked with him for years!"

"It's funny how you can think you know someone and end up on the wrong end of betrayal." Niko's voice was low but easily heard by the other four of us in the hallway.

I didn't know the reason for her guarded emotion so I asked. *What's wrong?*

She shook her head and nodded slightly toward the woman who had just spoke. *She of all people should know what it feels like to be betrayed.*

Pushing a little way into the soldier's head, I saw exactly what Niko was talking about. The woman was her previous lover, the one who turned her in. Anger caused the throbbing in my head to intensify and I struggled to maintain control. She was the one who betrayed someone so noble, so honest, and loyal. I hated her, but on the other hand, I was grateful. Had she not set Niko on her current path, we would have never met and I would still be sleeping my way through life. I had to continue the charade just a little longer. "I'm sorry, General, I only knew of the one. I had no idea the other guard was a collaborator. I don't know who else may have been working with him. My dream walking is strong, but even I have limits." I felt it then, that subtle twist inside Rennet's mind and knew he had made the decision that we were the ones to trust over all others. He often feared infiltrators. He feared insurrection and the tableau in the hallway only fed into those fears. In a time of betrayal and suspicion, Niko and I had just sealed his trust in us.

Before I could say anything more there was a commotion coming down another hallway. Men and women wearing white synth suits and sporting buzzed hair on their heads came toward us with intent. They were the Walkers that Dr. Morgan and the other scientists had been experimenting on and I wondered if Souza's program had unlocked the doors in the facility. One man called out and I could feel the anger pouring from him. "Where is Dr. Morgan?" As a mass, their minds had joined together with mob mentality. They had been tortured for years, kept alive to fuel her many experiments and tests. And together they wanted retribution. They stopped once they saw General Rennet, confused and frightened once again. I didn't want that. It didn't help my plan. I spoke directly into the mind of the man at the front of the group. *He was the one who gave Dr. Morgan her orders.*

Shock rippled through him and awareness followed. His words were quiet but the entire group still heard. "He gave her orders. He is the one responsible!"

Sensing imminent danger from nearly thirty hostile men and women armed with everything from makeshift clubs to syringes filled with who knows what, Niko made a choice. "General, we need to get you out of here!" In my head she said something different. *He is our ticket out of here. We need a hostage and he is perfect for the job.*

He nodded and I slipped inside again to help guide his thoughts. He turned to the remaining two soldiers. "You two are rear guards, don't let them by you!" The woman started to protest and he cut her off. "Do you have a problem with that, soldier? You do as I say!" The soldiers looked angry, but they assumed a rear guard position in the hall.

Chapter Seventeen

You've Misjudged Us All

WE MOVED UP and began ushering General Rennet back the way he had come from, toward the elevator. "Sir, is the personal transport on the roof?" He nodded, a little in shock at the turn of events. "Let's get you out of here then."

The elevator was in sight when the power abruptly cut off. Emergency lights came on but nothing else would be operational. I glanced at Niko and felt a tendril of happiness escape from me to her. *Souza!*

She nodded and led the General to the nearby stairwell, one that was blissfully empty of BENs. They had all taken over the opposite side of the fourth floor. "We'll have to take the stairs, General."

He pulled up short and I could tell he warred with himself over admitting weakness. "I can't walk all the way up there!"

Niko thought for a second and acknowledged him with a chin tilt. "We'll go down then. I can take a transport to get you out of here and we can get you someplace more secure. Perhaps the BEN facility in Detroit. Is that acceptable?"

My admiration grew with leaps and bounds. She was good, there was no mistaking it. Niko subtly guided him but allowed the General to make the final call. That played into retaining his trust and got us closer to our own goal. He had become a hostage and didn't even know it. When we made it to the bottom, the first floor near our stairs was eerily empty. I was the one who saw smoke first then we turned a corner and saw the flames blocking our way to the front entrance. "Shit!"

The General started to cough. "Why isn't the alarm kicking on? What the hell is happening here?"

Niko's voice responded loudly through the helm speaker. "I suspect sabotage sir. We need to find a suit for you and get you out of here."

He stopped then and looked at us both suspiciously. His own thoughts were starting to push through my implanted ones. He glared at me. "You were the one who broke into the facility. How do I know it's not all your doing?"

I shook my head. "I came to rescue Niko because I knew she

was innocent. But on my way here there was a crowd of de-gens starting to gather near the west entrance." I reinforced the idea straight into his mind again. The smoke thickened and coughing spasms wracked his body.

"Sir, we have to go!"

Niko, we need to go back out the cargo entrance. That is where the unlocked food transport is located. All the BEN machines will be offline. Their comps and guidance systems are all tied in with the system Souza crashed.

She glanced at me as we made our way to the opposite side of the first floor. *Do you know where my cycle is?*

I kept walking but gently sifted back through the Generals thoughts again. Her bike had been repaired and sent into general holding for eventual use as a compensation gift for one of his council cronies. It was a beautiful bike and worth at least a few votes. I passed on the information to her. I didn't know where the general holding area was. *Someplace called general holding, and it's been repaired.*

She grinned at me and the lurid red security lights filtered through the clear faceplate and gave her the countenance of a demon. *General holding is right next to the cargo entrance.*

It took about ten minutes to make it through the maze of halls and security doors but we eventually arrived at the holding area. I was amazed when the doors opened and I saw the sheer amount of confiscated stuff inside. We found a suit that would fit Rennet and he dressed while Niko went in search of her bike. Her voice came through my helmet com as the General pulled on the borrowed helmet. "Found it!" When she came around the corner, Rennet turned his helmet toward her.

"What are you doing?"

She stopped nearby and pulled the auto-shot bolt gun from her back. "You're going to need cover if we're going to get you to safety."

Even as she spoke, five BENs came through the door we had just used. "There they are!"

Thinking quickly, Niko called out to the General, playing up to his paranoia. "They're infiltrators!" The two soldiers reacted immediately to the perceived threat. Niko brought her bolt rifle up at the same time Rennet brought his pistol to bear. Before I could even draw one of the pistols from my holster they had all five on the ground. Niko moved her bike forward a bit and used it to usher Rennet toward the door that led outside. While she paced him across the floor of the storage area, I leaned onto a nearby crate and left my body behind. When I exited the building I could see the food transport I had arrived in. It was sitting about thirty meters away from our current location. All the other transports had been sent back to the grower facilities. Once again I thanked Souza for his foresight. If he hadn't disabled the auto-flight function of the drone we would have been left stranded. I flew even farther away and saw that my words had been prophetic in a way. Soldiers around the corner were in a firefight with what appeared to be a large group of de-gens. I couldn't help but wonder if the leak of government data to all the comps and coms across the nation had anything to do with the riot. There really was an insurrection and I had started it. I also realized another thing. The war that the Network had been waging against Walkers for decades wasn't really about the Walkers. It was about control. The people in the highest ranks of the government wanted it, and we were nothing more than pawns. With the data breach, the de-gens recognized their opportunity to take some of that control back.

Movement and concern drew me back to my body much too fast. I thought perhaps Niko had returned for me but froze in fear to see that the hands that had grabbed me belonged to a BEN. It wasn't just any BEN either, it was her ex-lover. "I see I've caught quite the prize with you. Where is General Rennet and what have you done to him?"

I shook my head. "I haven't done anything."

"Liar! You've done something to him and to Niko!" Just saying her name, I felt a query from where they were near the exit.

Despite her betrayal and months of separation, Janis Solken still vibrated with jealousy. I probed into her mind even as she held a bolt pistol to my helmet. Just her surface thoughts told me all I needed to know. Her jealousy flared greatest when she thought about her lack of power and prestige. She wanted to be Captain but Niko got the promotion years ahead of her. I also saw that even if Niko hadn't been a Walker, her lover would have still betrayed her in the end. My discovery that First Lieutenant Solken was also a vain soldier and had left a string of broken hearts in her past sealed my decision for me. I spoke to answer her question in the most infuriating way possible. "The only thing I've done to Niko is love her like none other before."

"You bitch!"

Two things happened at once. I felt First Lieutenant Solken's mind in my grasp slip with imminent action, and second Niko rounded the corner. She must have recognized the look on my captor's face because she cried out in alarm. "Janis, no!"

I couldn't let her shoot me, and I didn't. There was no time to consider the consequences to my already taxed system. I simply acted. Her mind came apart easily within my mental grasp and her scream of agony was more than physical. Her mental shriek brought me to my knees as she landed in a heap beside me. It was too much, certainly more than I was used to doing and I knew I'd overextended myself. Hands on my helmet, I couldn't even think to find the analgesic tabs that would counteract the pain of dying with someone the second time in an hour. I started to shake and a disparate part of me realized that I might be going into shock. A voice pierced the darkness around me.

"Julia!"

I felt Niko's panic beating against my mind, hammering with blows that perfectly matched the slow rhythm of my pulse. Pain flared with each beat of my heart and nausea rose within my belly. At least I learned something new. Killing someone with my mind was the worst when in physical contact. There was a feedback involved that made it a lot more dangerous when done without walls. But I didn't know how to do anything with them in place. Niko pulled my helmet from my head and frantically tried to wipe the blood from my face. I glanced over at the dead woman at my side. *I'm sorry, self-preservation is all I know...*

Her hands shook. "Stop it and just talk to me!"

All I could see was the First Lieutenant's empty dead eyes and my words were a whisper. "I'm so sorry. First your mother, then your lover—I've taken everything from you." I shivered and felt weakness wash through me again. I felt like I was fading. It was a very similar feeling to that which drew me back to my body when I'd been walking too long, only I was in my body and I had no place left to go.

With a cry she moved her hands from my face. Niko grabbed the body next to mine and physically lifted it and threw it away from us. Then she was right back at my side again. "You took nothing from me! Nothing, Julia."

I shook my head. "I'm tired..." Everything was fading.

No, just stay with me. Please, you gave me everything!

Sleep or more pulled at me. *Please, just let me go.*

Niko grabbed me by the shoulders and physically shook me. "No, you promised you'd never leave me again!"

Before I could protest that some promises couldn't be kept, I felt a wave of love and strength flow into me from her. Just as she had done in that locked room, she bolstered me with her own energy. I knew that her actions were instinct alone. Something within me had called to that part of her that I touched so often. But no matter the reason why or how of it, she had just saved my life. I gasped and the pain that had been fading with my mind came back in full. I grabbed my head and only managed to get out one word. "Tabs."

She got three more from my suit pocket and quickly placed them under my tongue. The relief hit almost immediately. She met my eyes when I was able to see clearly again. "If you can move now, we really need to go." I nodded and she helped me stand and gave me back my helmet. I still felt dizzy when we started walking but it passed as my blood began moving through my limbs again.

"What took you so long? The fighting has gotten closer outside the door!"

Niko glared at the impatient man. "Yes sir, but you don't have to worry. I'll handle anyone that tries to stop us." She mounted the bike again and unslung the bolt rifle from her back. With one hand on the handlebars and the other on the gun, she was as ready as she could be. She turned to me at the last second. "Just get him to the transport and I'll be there as soon as I make sure you both have a clear path."

Got it.

There was nobody right by the door when she flew through it on the cycle but fighting was nearby and getting closer with each second. If she didn't head them off we'd never make it to the transport. She began shooting as soon as she cleared the steps that lead down to the ground. Meanwhile I pulled both pistols and used them to cover our mad scramble to the food hauler. Rennet didn't move as fast as I would have liked but if Niko thought we needed him, then I was going to get him safely to the transport. She rode ahead and bolted as many as possible on her way. She was amazing, like poetry in motion the way she weaved in and out of the fighters that came ever closer. When she ran out of ammo she drew the pistol I had given her from the guard. When she couldn't take them down with a bolt, she would incapacitate both BENs and de-gens alike with a well-placed kick as she rode by. I pushed the entry code for the hauler as we arrived at the back hatch and pushed the General inside before it was all the way open. I called out to her over the com. "We're in!"

She responded slightly out of breath. "Spool up the engines and move Rennet out of the way. I'm coming in hot." I quickly moved our guest toward the front and hit the power switch on the console. The engines began spooling and I could just make out the shape of Niko's bike approaching out of the darkened complex courtyard. BENs in full armor were rapidly approaching and I hit the switch to shut the hatch as soon as she was inside. *Cue the external mic at its max so they can hear me through their helmets. Their coms will be down from the virus.* I didn't say anything, just hit the switch she was asking for at the same time General Rennet's patience snapped.

"What is the meaning of this?" I could hear General Rennet's voice loudly sound outside the carrier. There was no way the soldiers outside didn't hear him.

Niko cleared her faceplate so he could look her in the eye. Her words echoed outside, following Rennet's. "The meaning of this is insurance, nothing more. And right now all the soldiers outside this carrier know you're on board and that you're my hostage." Before he could react beyond immediate surprise, she stripped him of his weapon.

Through the clear plas windows, I could see that all the BENs had stopped their advance. Niko quickly sat down in the pilot seat and finished the rest of the flight prep while I covered Rennet with my own pistol. The men and women outside were fairly powerless. Souza's attack on the Network's systems had crippled anything that had a comp tied to their mainframe. That meant they had no transports, flight or otherwise, no HUD in their suits, and no way to communicate with the agents still inside the main facility. I directed the General to sit on a fold down bench as Niko lifted us from the ground. Keeping one eye on him, I grabbed a cargo tie and quickly secured Niko's bike next to my own. When I was done I grabbed another cable and wrapped it around my waist. I felt so weak I could barely keep myself upright, let alone withstand the buffeting winds of the carrier hatch being opened. I sensed that we had finally stopped rising so I called out to Niko. "How high are we?"

I felt the tendril of her mind brush across my own and couldn't prevent the smile that came with such a familiar touch. I knew then she could see what was in my head, my thoughts and my ultimate goal. She answered me with a wash of love and relief. "High enough."

"High enough for what?" Despite my bolt gun aimed squarely at his heart, he stood in defiance. I felt his fear, but I also felt his determination. I wasn't the only one that held a core of self-preservation. I hit the button to open the back hatch and the wind came straight out of the blackness to lick at our suits. "If you think I'll willingly step off this transport you've clearly misjudged me!"

My voice thundered through his head. *No, Malcom Rennet, you've misjudged us all!* I had no strength of mind left to back up my words nor did I have the strength of body that it would take to force him out the back. But I didn't need either because I had Niko. I watched her flip the switch to hover in place and in an instant she was out of the pilot's chair and grabbing the General by his suit. The General was old and with one powerful heave, she sent him flying out the back into the caustic night air. My last image of him was of his arms and legs flailing around as he disappeared into the blackness below. His mind screamed all the way down. Niko held onto the strap near the secured bikes and watched him fall with me then she hit the button to close the hatch again and immediately took me into her arms.

"It's done and we made it. Are you okay?"

Niko's words brought a sense of freedom that I had never in my life experienced. With the demise of the Network, we were all free. Tears stung my eyes and my answer whispered out, amplified by my helm mic. "Yes." I wanted to rip both our helmets off and pull her to me. I wanted to crawl inside the safety of Niko's arms and the warmth of her mind. But I couldn't have any of those things. The transport wasn't filtered so we were stuck in our suits for the entirety of the trip.

She looked at me with those startling blue eyes. Despite the darkness of the transport, her HUD was turned up inside her helmet and it gave her face an almost eerie glow. "Where to now? You mentioned more plans once we got away."

I smiled and sent her every bit of joy within my head. "Toronto. We have a job waiting for us with Souza if we want it. It will be nice not to hide anymore."

She smiled back and I felt the tenderness of her caress someplace deep inside me. With one last squeeze, she stepped away and searched until she found a fabric cargo cover. She mounded it up into a bed of sorts and called me over. "With the auto-flight disabled, I'll have to fly us manually all the way there using my HUD as guidance. Why don't you try to get some sleep?"

Concern caused me to lift my hand toward her. "You've been stimmed for days. Shouldn't you sleep first?"

Niko led me over to the mound. "I can handle a few more hours. You nearly died, Julia. I—I can't lose you so please just get some rest. I'll wake you when we get there." Still I hesitated. "Just this once. After tonight I promise you'll never sleep alone again."

Her words meant everything and they left my heart hammering in my chest. "Promise?"

"Always." I smiled as the last words slipped from her lips. "While wars of wickedness rage outside my head, you and you alone remain steady within my heart."

I smiled at her. "That's yours." I knew her, my Niko, and I knew her heart. She smiled back, telling with its tenderness. I had no energy left to fight the pull of sleep after that so I curled up on the bed she had made for me. And without another thought, I slipped into the same strange dreams of before. All I knew was that I had Niko and we were safe.

Chapter Eighteen

The Life That Wasn't

PANIC GRIPPED ME as I bolted upright in bed. My mind was lost in the vivid imagery of my dreams and for nearly sixty seconds I had no idea where I was. I could feel Niko still asleep beside me in our bed and the gentle hum of the air conditioner as it fought to combat the heat wave that had gripped Chicago for the past week. I ran a shaking hand over my shorn hair, still not quite used to the feel of it. The treatments had left not enough to even mess with so I buzzed it all off before it got any worse. My wife just shrugged and cut all her long hair off with me. For better or worse—she had certainly gotten the poorer deal out of the two of us. No matter how long I sat there, the panic refused to go away. I had conquered my fears nearly a year ago when I agreed to the first operation. It had been two months since my remission diagnosis and I was only just starting to feel like myself again. I tried taking deep breaths but the fear continued to rise.

As if she could feel me through the gentle caress of sleep, Niko stirred. "Babe, what's wrong? Did you have a nightmare again?"

We could just make out each other's faces in the dim room. I preferred the natural light that came through the uncovered windows of our condo, and I loved the view we had of the lake. And at night the lights of the city made a twinkling blanket far below. It soothed me. I shook my head because it wasn't a nightmare. It was real. My voice was a whisper that followed the thought. "It was real."

It must have been the tone of my voice but Niko sat up and gathered me into her arms. She pulled us back against the headboard and spoke quietly. "Talk to me, what was real?"

I sighed. "Everything. Us, the Network, General Rennet, a man named Souza—it was all real."

"Julia, look at me." I turned my head and was struck by the clean lines of Niko's face and the sheer handsome beauty of her. I found myself trapped by the angle of her jaw and the fine arch of those light brown brows. But most of all, I was drawn to her curious blue eyes. They held a weight of sincerity as she spoke again. "It was a dream, nothing more."

My head moved before I thought, shaking back and forth to deny the words that fell from her sweet lips. The longer I sat there awake, the more convinced I was that something was wrong. My wife, my best friend, Nikolette Morgan Jones, just waited for me to explain. When we first met she was the most infuriating, impatient person I'd ever come across. Ten years ago, when my parents were killed in a random mugging, she had been the detective assigned to the case. Four years later we were married and living in our dream home on Lake Michigan. It was strange how things worked out. A small amount of regret rippled through me as I thought about how her fire seemed to dim when I was diagnosed with a non-malignant brain tumor. My glorious detective, former marine, and love of my life had grown — softer. Each day when I wanted nothing more than to give in, her patience and strength bolstered me. I struggled to find the words to explain. "I can't tell you why I'm afraid right now. I don't even have my thoughts organized enough to make you see the reality that just was. I'm not sure I know how. It was too much, too fantastical to be real, but it was!"

Niko still had her arm around my shoulders and she pulled me just a little closer. "You're the best selling writer, love. If anyone can paint the picture for me, it would be you."

I gazed at Niko's tired face and felt guilty for taking away her sleep. She had been working overtime on a case all week and I could tell it was getting to her. I gently rubbed the dark smudge below her left eye. "Sleep is a gentle mistress, fickle when we need her most yet she is the only lover to leave us rested at the end of a tryst."

Niko smiled and played the game with me. It took mere seconds for her to come up with the author. "Janis Solken, The Insomnia of Twilight."

Why I picked that particular quote, I had no idea. But it didn't escape my notice that the author had the same name as Niko's ex-lover in my dream. Perhaps I had stolen her after all and the thought left me more confused than ever. I did the best I could after that. I spoke for an hour, intimately aware of each minute that passed, knowing she had to be up early for her shift at the station. When my voice grew hoarse, she left the warmth of our bed to get a bottle of water from the fridge. I finally took a break when I got to the point where I met her. She had her cheek pressed against the side of my head so I couldn't see the expression on her face. But she was much too quiet. "What are you thinking?"

Awe colored her words and made her quiet in the space beside me. "You lived an entire life and you were so alone!"

I pulled back so I could see her face then and the tears tracking down her cheeks were unmistakable. "Hey, don't cry. Tough cops don't cry." She laughed and I knew I had to cheer her up. "I haven't even gotten to the good part yet."

"What is that?"

I smiled and snuggled further into her arms. "The part where I met you." I went on and on, speaking for another hour and a half to get the rest of the story out. There was so much to tell, so many things that I had discovered in those days before we escaped to Toronto. There were things that I wanted her to know, to feel. I wished that I could just speak into her mind as I had done in that other life. When I completed the tale I stopped and the room seemed so quiet wrapped in our mutual silence. Niko broke it first.

"So we made it?"

I turned my head at the emotion of her words and her lips were right there. The weight of her gaze pulled me in and we met in a gentle exploration that was less about passion and more about connecting on some deep level. When we both came up for air, I reached out my palm to cup her cheek. The tears had dried leaving an opaque white trail of salt. I nodded at her, belatedly answering her question. "We made it. I fell asleep as you were flying us away and I—woke here."

Niko's face lit up. "Karen is going to freak when you send this to her. Tell me you're going to write it. You are going to write it, yes?"

I got lost for a moment, thinking that Karen was my boss at Vanguard and forgetting that she was my publisher. A publisher that had made me very rich and successful. My thoughts wandered down that track but I quickly pulled them back again. Niko still didn't get it, she didn't understand that it was all real. I started to reiterate that fact again, my voice laced with frustration. "No!" I pulled up short at the look on Niko's face. Sleep had faded long ago but the fear still clung to me like a thick odor or memory of a time purposely forgotten. I felt an almost desperate need for her to understand me. "It was real, Niko. Please believe me." Niko's face had always been an open book to me and it was no different after my pleading. She struggled to find an answer at the same time that she was feeling the pain of my distress.

"I believe that you believe it was real. But remember what

your doctor said, that tumor was pushing on your pineal gland. When they took it out he told us it left a hole of sorts that the gland itself may grow to fill. This dream of yours was probably just a side effect of the surgery. If you remember, the only reason we realized you had something wrong was when your sleep patterns went all haywire. You started having strange waking dreams until I got you to go in for testing."

I tried to protest the overwhelming evidence she had behind her words. "But—"

She caught my hands within her own. "Babe, it was just a dream, albeit an amazing one, but still nothing more than your brain making a movie for you while you were asleep."

That movie continued to play through my head, as vivid or more than my own memories of growing up. I closed my eyes as the first tear fell and whispered to her, willing her to understand. "It was real."

Niko tried again and I knew that she would. "I think you're just under a lot of stress right now. We both are. Maybe this is all just a delayed reaction to the election and all the terrible things we've watched the administration do to the environment and the people. With the 2020 election just four months away, we have a chance to make it right."

I turned to look at her. "But don't you see? That's how it all started, that's how all of it started to go bad. We are at a turning point right now and it took just one man to fuck it all up! That was part of my future!"

"Babe, it is part of everyone's future. But you said your dream took place nearly a hundred years from now. Neither one of us would be alive." I shook my head, stubborn, defiant to her words. All the frustration that she had been holding for over a year suddenly broke over her in a flood. She turned me within her arms and just—shook me, the way you'd shake an obstinate person who refused to see truth. "It wasn't real, Julia! Please, please, I'm already worried all the time that it will come back. I'm worried that I'll lose you! This is madness and what if it's a symptom of something worse?"

I was struck then by the amount of pain and fear in her eyes. How much had she been keeping in? How much did she carry on her shoulders each day? As if her job weren't hard enough, my sickness had only made it worse. But I couldn't help what was in my head or in my heart. The fear was too real, too heavy. "I'm sorry. I'm just so scared right now. That whole life was me. It was everything. You were everything. I don't know how to explain the reason I know it's true. I just know."

Niko sighed then glanced over at the clock on her side of the bed. The numbers were a lurid red in the city-lit room. Four in the morning meant that she'd have to get up in a few hours and run all day on little to no sleep. In my fear I had been selfish. My internal chastisement was interrupted by her defeated voice. "I'm going to go make coffee. I forgot to set the timer last night."

I rested my hand on her wrist before she could escape the nest of our bed. "I'm sorry."

She shook her head. "It is madness that follows the easiest path into oblivion while sanity claws its way back out."

"Graham Bishop. Are you trying to tell me something?"

She shrugged and gave me that grin I had come to love so very much. "Just that you're making me crazy and it's going to take some effort to pull us both out again."

I smiled back at her, feeling mischievous despite my continuing fear. "I thought you liked me crazy?" Niko laughed quietly and slipped on a pajama shirt and pants. I mourned the loss of that glorious body to my sight. I sighed and she smirked over her shoulder at me as she left the room. To combat the chill I pulled on my t-shirt that I had left in a cloth puddle on the floor. I relished the feel of soft cotton against my skin and waited for it to warm with my body heat. I lifted the edge around my neck to smell the fabric softener we used. It wasn't that I loved the scent, it was because I loved the smell of it against Niko's skin. I was no longer tired. The images of my other life made me feel like I'd been asleep forever. Since I was waiting for edits of my last manuscript I decided to check my email. The tablet was charging next to the bed and it only took seconds for me to grab it and swipe in my password. I quickly brought up the browser then stopped at the headline on my news feed. Cold dread twisted my stomach and all the fears that Niko had been trying to convince me were baseless, suddenly came to life. The tablet fell quietly to the comforter as shaking nerveless fingers covered my lips. My voice was soft as if I too had not quite believed until that moment. "Oh my God." I shook my head and felt dazed at what was on the screen. "Oh my God, oh my God—" Images of what I'd seen of my other life superimposed over my current one. The history I had learned as a child in my dream collided with the present and details assailed me, spinning my mind just out of reach. Even as my thoughts spread out, pain lanced through my head with the surety of a hammer blow. I grabbed my shorn scalp as the throbbing sharp pain continued, timed with the beating of my heart. I could no more stop the agony of it than I could stifle the scream that followed. "Niko!"

I was vaguely aware of a crash and running footsteps before she just appeared in the room like magic. "I'm here, what's wrong? Baby, tell me what's wrong! Does your head hurt?"

Her voice, normally one I loved to hear, assailed me with its loudness. I clawed at my head, willing the pain to stop, whimpering as she grabbed my hands to keep me from hurting myself more. "Make it stop—please make it stop!" Wetness trickling from my nose took me by surprise and I opened my eyes just in time to see it drip onto the clean whiteness of my shirt. The red droplet hit the fabric and spread out, seeking to infect more of the plain expanse with its wasted life.

"I'm calling an ambulance!"

I couldn't have that. I needed to make her see and understand that it was all real, that the proof was lost in mounds of soft covers, that I wasn't crazy. I stilled her hand as she reached for my cell phone. "No, just pills." She hesitated and I pushed. "Please?"

Even though I had shut my eyes again I could hear Niko rustle in the nightstand on my side of the bed and the rattle of the pill bottle she pulled it out. I listened as she unscrewed the lid and shook two into her hand then I registered the distinctive crinkle of the plastic water bottle crushing in her fingers as she struggled to get the cap off. Her hands were shaking and I knew my brave Niko was terrified. "Here." Her voice had quieted with barely controlled panic as she opened my fingers and placed the pills in the palm of my hand. I shoved them between my lips and blindly reached for the water bottle. As I waited for the strong medication to kick in, Niko got into bed behind me and pulled us together, offering her silent strength. Her fear was palpable in the room and the guilt of being the cause ate at me. I tried to control my breathing, to slow it down. Eventually, the pills took effect.

I patted her hand and took my first deep breath since the pain began. "It feels better. I'm okay now."

Niko wrapped her arms around me and hugged me tighter. "It's not okay nor is it normal. We need to get you back to your doctor today!" Her words jogged my memory and I struggled to sit forward from her embrace. When I turned my head I caught a fleeting look of hurt on her expressive face but it faded almost immediately to one of shock. "You're bleeding!" Niko brought her fingers up to gently wipe the blood that had trickled from my nostrils. "That's it, Julia, I'm calling your doctor now."

She made to get up and I turned within Niko's embrace and grabbed her wrists to stop her. "No!" She grew confused and I held her hands tighter. "It was real! It was all real!" The look in her eyes made me want to hang my head and weep. They spoke more surely than any words that she didn't believe me. The one person who had kept me sane over the past year had given up. Just like that. I tried one last time. "In my other life, one of the moments in history that I studied in school was the meltdown of the Fukushima reactor in Japan."

Niko shook her head. "Babe, that's already happened."

I sighed. "No, a second one. In the summer of 2020 there is a great earthquake off the coast of Japan that sends the reactor into a meltdown that is never stopped. The resulting disaster causes irreversible damage to the area around Japan and to the Pacific Ocean. Not only that, but the earthquake is so strong it creates a tsunami that strikes the Pacific Northwest coast just nine hours later."

Niko knew me and she knew I wouldn't be telling her the details unless I had a point to make. "And?"

I reached over for the forgotten tablet and placed it into her hands. "Read the headline."

"Japan is under a state of emergency as the Pacific Northwest scrambles to evacuate ahead of a predicted fifty foot wall of water." She paused then continued reading the article. "The tsunami is expected to hit the coast around five-thirty in the morning, Pacific Standard Time and officials say the logistics of getting everyone evacuated in the middle of the night are a nightmare. The governors of both Washington and Oregon have already declared states of emergency while the national guards of neighboring states are already mobilizing in preparation of the unprecedented modern disaster..." She trailed off and looked up at me then, her eyes awash with confusion. "But how?"

I had to know if she was going to be my rock, or if I would be set adrift when everything was going to change. "Do you believe me now?"

Our eyes met and held. Her breathtaking blue ones did nothing to hide the intelligence inside as she worked her way through the information and the problems ahead. Focus came back quickly and she nodded. "I believe you. I don't understand it and I don't know how, but God help us all, I believe you."

All the pressure and pain of my dream—my life that was both before and after, came crashing down and the first sob escaped my lips. I collapsed on top of her, my solidity and heart, my reason for living each day. I could do anything with her. We could get through anything. Niko had slid down on the bed and held me to her chest as I cried myself out. The steady beat of her heart calmed me. I couldn't speak again until the beat of my own matched it. "What do we do?"

Before she could answer I sat up again, needing action and space to think. Niko sighed and ran a hand through hair that had grown out just enough to flop delightfully over one eye. "I need to call my captain and ask if I can take a personal day." She held up a hand to forestall the protest she knew would come. "We're on a holding pattern until lab results come back so I'd probably just be cooling my heels at the station most of the day. And at this point I'd most likely fall asleep at my desk."

"And after that?"

Her eyes were like blue fire and I knew she had gone into that mode she had, the one that solved problems, solved cases, and kept us all safe. She told me once that she tested as a high genius when she was a kid but that having her mother abandon her at the age of fifteen to pursue her career in science had left a bad taste in her mouth. Niko was raised by her father's parents for the next few years, which was how she ended up in America. She graduated with a degree in criminal psychology and went into the marines. After serving her initial stint she returned to Chicago and joined the police force, following in her paternal grandfather's footsteps. Olivia Jones may have been at the top of her field in genetics, but she had never been a mother. And to think that people had always said that Canadians were so nice. "We're going to sit down and make a list of everything you can remember. I'll write down every single name, date and event from your dream, or vision, or whatever it was. Then we'll have some decisions to make. Okay?" I nodded and that soft look returned to her eyes. "Why don't you go grab a shower and clean up, and I'll whip up some breakfast. They say people think better on a full stomach."

The thought of food did anything but appetize me. "I'm not hungry."

"Julia..." The tone of her voice drew my eyes off the strong hands she had been using to emphasis her point. I loved her hands but I dutifully raised my eyes to hers. "You're weight is still down. Will you eat something for me?"

For her I'd do anything. "Yes." I did feel better after a long hot shower, and when I caught my first whiff of bacon my stomach growled.

Niko grinned at me from the breakfast bar where she was busy pouring coffee for both of us. "I like the sound of that."

"What, bodily functions reacting to the olfaction of a scent I've always enjoyed in the past?"

She shook her head. "No, your appetite." I couldn't say anything to that. Instead I sat on the bar stool and tucked into my food. Bacon, scrambled eggs, and toast were nothing fancy but they were comforting. I think she sensed that we both needed a little comfort for what was to come. Niko refused to let me turn on the news until we'd finished eating, insisting that there was no point in ruining a good meal. I concurred but as soon as the dishes had been cleared away I grabbed the remote and put on our regular news network. Images of Japan were already showing, as well as the horrifying video of the wave as it approached our country. The ticker at the bottom of the page said that the tsunami was around seventy-five feet and still had about three and a half hours before it hit. The estimates of fifty feet when it reached the mainland were still in place.

I grabbed my laptop from the coffee table and she pulled hers out of the carrying case by the door to the condo. Once we were both booted she brought up a new document to make notes. It didn't take long to recount the details that she wanted from me. I was only reciting facts from my memory, not telling the entire story yet again. I pointed at her computer screen. "So what do you think?"

Niko looked at the data she'd compiled with a critical eye. It listed historical events, the state of the world, governments, climate, cities, and environment. The writing was on the wall, so to speak, and she shook her head in dismay. "Everything changes. It's all affected in one way or another and nothing will be safe. No place."

"What if—" she looked at me expectantly and I shoved the thought all the way out. "What if we go north? Maybe to Canada?" At her incredulous look I pointed out the obvious. "We can go anywhere, Niko. And you hold dual citizenship so it's not like it would be a stretch."

She blew out a frustrated breath and ran a hand through hair that had already been mussed a thousand times. "You can go anywhere, but my career is here! I can't just pick up and leave, Jules. What would I do there if we moved?"

I wanted to say that she didn't need to work at all. Truthfully my career kept us very well, but I didn't dare turn those words free. Through intelligence, hard work, and perseverance, Niko had earned the gold badge that she wore. And she was proud of her accomplishments, both in the military and as a detective. I would never think to tell her that none of it was necessary, that her contributions meant nothing when it came to our life together. At an impasse, I stood and stretched my tired body. Grabbing my coffee cup, I offered a truce of sorts. "I'm going for a refill, want some?"

She nodded. "Sure. I'm going to check my email and see if the captain responded to the message I sent earlier."

The breakfast bar was only feet from where the coffee maker sat on the counter so refilling our mugs and adding the correct amount of cream and sugar took barely any time at all. But it was just long enough. I felt something change in the room and spun my head around in time to see Niko sit up straight on her stool. "What is it?"

Words that were not an answer to my question slipped from her lips. "Holy fuck." Coffee forgotten, I rushed to her side to see what she had read.

"Did Captain Bennet write you back?"

She turned her head to look at me, shock still filling the air around us. "No, it's my old marine buddy, Cam. He says that he and his husband have started a security consultation firm and asked if I'd ever consider coming on board."

I knew exactly who she was talking about. I'd met Cam on a few occasions over the years but it had been a few since we'd last seen him. "Is he still in Chicago? And why didn't he tell us that he and John got married?"

Niko shrugged. "No, they moved. And the email doesn't say anything about the wedding so I'm guessing it was fairly recent. But that's not what has me so shocked I guess. I never knew John's last name."

Curiosity had me more alert than coffee ever would. "And?"

Niko's eyes got me every single time. I stared into them and swore I could feel her shock and fear. I didn't know how, and I didn't know why, but it was there deep inside me. Niko was there. Her words only sealed my certainty of our future. "Souza. His last name is Souza. And they live in Toronto now. They're offering me nearly double my current salary and they already have contracts lined up with the Canadian government. This is real, Jules."

I nodded. "This is real."

Niko abruptly got up from her stool and walked across the living room to stand in front of the wall of windows. The city was waking up below as the sky lightened with the approaching sun. Unlike Niko, Chicago had always been my home. I lived, breathed, and loved the city of my youth. And Niko had made her home here too, with me. She stood silent and alone ten feet from me as she watched the fleeing night. Sunrise would be any minute, bringing with it a sense of anticipation. I knew Niko better than anyone and her thoughts would be racing with everything we'd learned over the past few hours. In the quiet of the room we had life altering choices to make. I had friends that lived in the Northwest. Some were authors, and others I'd just known for what seemed like forever. I wished more than anything to call the ones I felt closest to one last time. But I knew it would be impossible with the impending disaster. The future I saw, that I lived, was built on the back of more than just one disaster or a series of natural catastrophes. That future formed from a rash of bad decisions and failed resistance.

I left the space by the kitchenette and walked over to Niko. I would not let her stand alone with thoughts so dark. Without saying a word she drew me in front of her to watch the rising sun, safe in her strong embrace. She spoke as the first brilliant rays broke the city skyline off to the east. "I hear Toronto is beautiful in the fall."

I waited until the sun was up then turned in the circle of her arms. "While wars of wickedness rage outside my head, you and you alone remain steady within my heart."

Niko looked at me curiously, her mind spinning as she tried to pin down what was obviously a quote. Finally she sighed, always hating defeat. "I give up, who said it?"

"You did."

She smiled back at me then, delighted that her dream self could perfectly speak her feelings of love. It seemed fitting that our lips would meet with such love in our hearts and heads. I clung to her desperately as the kiss grew deeper, both of us wanting to never let go. And it felt natural to aim my deepest thoughts at the person I loved most in the world. *You are everything to me.*

Niko stiffened in my arms and pulled her head back. Her mind blazed with shock and realization. "I heard you."

I nodded. "Good." Then I kissed her again.

About the Author

Born and raised in Michigan, Kelly is a latecomer to the writing scene. She works in the automotive industry coding in Visual basic and Excel. Her avid reading and writing provide a nice balance to the daily order of data, allowing her to juggle passion and responsibility. Her writing style is as varied as her reading taste and it shows as she tackles each new genre with glee. But beneath it all, no matter the subject or setting, Kelly carries a core belief that good should triumph. She's not afraid of pain or adversity, but loves a happy ending. She's been pouring words into novels since 2015 and probably won't run out of things to say any time soon.

Other K. Aten titles to look for:

The Fletcher

Kyri is a fletcher, following in the footsteps of her father, and his father before him. However, fate is a fickle mistress, and six years after the death of her mother, she's faced with the fact that her father is dying as well. Forced to leave her sheltered little homestead in the woods, Kyri discovers that there is more to life than just hunting and making master quality arrows. During her journey to find a new home and happiness, she struggles with the path that seems to take her away from the quiet life of a fletcher. She learns that sometimes the hardest part of growing up is reconciling who we were, with who we will become.

ISBN: 978-1-61929-356-4
eISBN: 978-1-61929-357-1

The Archer

Kyri was raised a fletcher but after finding a new home and family with the Telequire Amazons, she discovers a desire to take on more responsibility within the tribe. She has skills they desperately need and she is called to action to protect those around her. But Kyri's path is ever-changing even as she finds herself altered by love, loyalty, and grief. Far away from home, the new Amazon is forced to decide what to sacrifice and who to become in order to get back to all that she has left behind. And she wonders what is worse, losing everyone she's ever loved or having those people lose her?

ISBN: 978-1-61929-370-0
eISBN: 978-1-61929-371-7

Rules of the Road

Jamie is an engineer who keeps humor close to her heart and people at arm's length. Kelsey is a dental assistant who deals with everything from the hilarious to the disgusting on a daily basis. What happens when a driving app brings them together as friends? The nerd car and the rainbow car both know a thing or two about hazard avoidance. When a flat tire brings them together in person, Jamie immediately realizes that Kelsey isn't just another woman on her radar. Both of them have struggled to break free from stereotypes while they navigate the road of life. As their friendship deepens they realize that sometimes you have to break the rules to get where you need to go.

ISBN: 978-1-61929-366-3
eISBN: 978-1-61929-367-0

OTHER REGAL CREST PUBLICATIONS

Brenda Adcock	Pipeline	978-1-932300-64-2
Brenda Adcock	Redress of Grievances	978-1-932300-86-4
Brenda Adcock	The Chameleon	978-1-61929-102-7
Brenda Adcock	Tunnel Vision	978-1-935053-19-4
Brenda Adcock	Unresolved Conflicts	978-1-61929-374-8
Brenda Adcock	Gift of the Redeemer	978-1-61929-360-1
Carole Avalaon	Lauren's Manifesto	978-1-61929-346-5
Reba Birmingham	Floodlight	978-1-61929-344-1
Sharon G. Clark	Into the Mist	978-1-935053-34-7
Moondancer Drake	Natural Order	978-1-61929-246-8
Moondancer Drake	Ancestral Magic	978-1-61929-264-2
Moondancer Drake	Shadow Magic	978-1-61929-276-5
Jane DiLucchio	Teaching Can Be Murder	978-1-61929-262-8
Jane DiLucchio	Going Coastal	978-1-61929-268-0
Jane DiLucchio	Vacations Can Be Murder	978-1-61929-256-7
Dakota Hudson	White Roses Calling	978-1-61929-234-5
Dakota Hudson	Collateral Damage	978-1-61929-270-3
Heather Jane	Potential	978-1-61929-364-9
Kate McLachlan	Hearts, Dead and Alive	978-1-61929-017-4
Kate McLachlan	Murder and the Hurdy Gurdy Girl	978-1-61929-126-3
Kate McLachlan	Rip Van Dyke	978-1-935053-29-3
Kate McLachlan	Rescue At Inspiration Point	978-1-61929-005-1
Kate McLachlan	Return of An Impetuous Pilot	978-1-61929-152-2
Kate McLachlan	Ten Little Lesbians	978-1-61929-236-9
Kate McLachlan	Alias Mrs. Jones	978-1-61929-282-6
Paula Offutt	To Sleep	978-1-61929-128-7
Paula Offutt	To Dream	978-1-61929-208-6
Kelly Sinclair	Getting Back	978-1-61929-242-0
Kelly Sinclair	Accidental Rebels	978-1-61929-260-4
Nita Round	Knight's Sacrifice	978-1-61929-314-4
Nita Round	The Ghost of Emily Tapper	978-1-61929-328-1
Nita Round	A Touch of Truth Book One: Raven, Fire and Ice	
		978-1-61929-372-4
Barbara Valletto	Pulse Points	978-1-61929-254-3
Barbara Valletto	Everlong	978-1-61929-266-6
Barbara Valletto	Limbo	978-1-61929-358-8

Be sure to check out our other imprints,
Blue Beacon Books, Quest Books, Silver Dragon Books,
Troubadour Books, Yellow Rose Books, and Young Adult Books.